CORE OF DECEPTION

A KNOWLEDGE WELL SERIES BOOK

CHRIS HAUGHT

ISBN: 978-1-7352900-6-5

Cover Design by 100 Covers

Visit the author's website at https://www.chrishaughtauthor.com

1

AFTERMATH

Liam personally oversaw the complete demolition of Brill's underground facility, making sure he took every piece of equipment he could find. If there were any clues left of Brill's research, he was confident his team would decipher them. They would soon find the computers which were left had a little surprise that would show itself in due time. The demolition took several days, as Liam wanted to seal every tunnel leading into the lake and then completely collapse the chamber over the lake. By the time they were done, the pile of rubble looked like a mini-mountain and covered the distance of several football fields.

Liam was reviewing the conversations between Brill and Sirum from computer remnants his team had found in that pile of rubble. He was puzzled at the discussion. Brill and Sirum were talking about using dark matter in some chair that would take him to some special place. Liam was certain this had something to do with Brill's secret research. With Sirum still around, Liam would catch an opportunity to pull that info out of his head. Filing this away for the future, he set his sights on the task at hand, getting results from Brill's former team. Liam's superiors were getting impatient at the amount of money he was pouring into this effort and he knew they would soon have demands. Liam was not one to fail, so he would make sure they succeeded, at all costs.

WITH A HEAVY HEART, Sirum placed Brill into the chair and closed the canopy. He took Liora by the hand and pulled her to the stairs, while both stumbled their way back to the surface where she finally collapsed into tears. Sirum left her where she lay, scanning the surroundings till he spotted his target, a row of bushes disguising a hidden access point. He rummaged through the pile of rubble that had been carefully placed over a door leading down to a different underground chamber. With the door opened, he grabbed Liora's hand, urging her to come with him. Having made their way back down, the air was much cooler with the sun and heat of the day far above them. Sirum fumbled through a cabinet nestled against the wall, letting out a shriek of joy as he landed on his prize. Liora looked up at him, momentarily recovering from her grief.

"What have you found?"

"Power!"

"What?"

"Brill was always planning. He gave me special instructions to follow if some catastrophe ever happened to where the chair lost power when someone was using it. This..." gesturing to the contents he was holding, "is a power pack. One part is for the computer, and the other is for the chair. Brill said the person in the chair may appear dead, but as long as the chair had power, it would keep them alive for years if need be. So, I am going to follow his instructions and go connect these."

"Let me help you. Please."

"Liora, you are in no condition..."

"You either let me help, or I'll break your arm."

"I...doubt you would do that, but if it makes you feel better, I could use the help."

They shouldered the power packs and headed up and then back

down the other set of stairs that led to Brill. The trip down was as treacherous as the previous trip down, especially with Liam bombarding the original lab. The tremors were shaking rocks loose with every step as they descended. The wet stones added another layer of difficulty to the downward trek. The weight of the packs making the trip even slower. Reaching the bottom, they were exhausted. Sirum immediately connected the first set of packs to the computer. If Brill was in there, the quantum computer absolutely could not lose power or he may never find the signposts marking the way back to reality. He opened the canopy and, with a trembling hand, injected Brill with a bright fluorescent solution. Then he hooked up an IV to his arm and some electrodes to Brill's chest over his heart. Closing the canopy, he powered up the chair after attaching the backup power pack, and then connected the reservoir of fluorescent solution to Brill's IV. Even with the dim light from their flashlights, the bag had a glow to it. Powering up, they could see the canopy fog over as the humidity in the cave condensed on the now very cold surface. Again, Sirum had to pull Liora away, as she didn't want to leave him ever again.

"Liora, Brill said the chair would keep him alive for up to five years if it had enough power. See how cold it's getting? That will help to preserve his mind until his heart can start pumping oxygenated blood again."

"What was that glowing solution stuff you injected him with?"

"That is how he will breathe. It is a special fluorocarbon oxygenated solution that will displace the gas in his lungs, allowing him to breath. The electrodes will force his heart to beat ten times per minute. That will keep his blood flowing and his brain alive."

"How long can he stay in there and how do we know he is alive?"

"Brill said up to five years, though I am not sure on either question. These were his instructions. Remember the twins? They were trapped for days in the computer."

"I can't leave him here."

"We have too. If we don't, we may never get him back."

With that, they left. Their hearts heavy with sadness. Back in the second underground chamber, Sirum uncovered the entrance that led down to a lower cavern. Before they descended down to the deeper cavern, Sirum pulled from a hidden locker a set of LED headlamps and shoulder lamps, throwing a set to Liora. She followed his lead in placing them on her body which illuminated them both. They began to descend again, going for what seemed forever. As they went down, Sirum described where they were headed. "A few years ago, Brill and I found these dried up underground riverbeds. They snake all throughout this country. We found one set that went up into the mountains about a hundred miles to the North, and that's where we are going."

They continued on for a while until coming to a set of train tracks. Sirum continued, "These..." motioning to the tracks, "were just completed a few weeks ago. Brill put in two sets of monorail tracks, both leading to an old mine shaft in Reno." They stopped at a small monorail car. Sirum connected a power-pack, that until now, Liora hadn't noticed he was carrying. Once aboard, he powered up the car and began their long trip North.

"Sirum, how long will the power last on Brill's chair?"

"The power from those will last for more years than Brill said he could stay in the chair. The IV's though will likely never need replenishing. As long as there's power, the IV's will automatically change out and the empty ones will refill, as there is about 200 gallons of that stuff in the chair. The excrement from Bill will be shunted to the lake from that drain hose I connected. With his heart beating only ten times per minute, that solution will last well beyond five years. Another contingency he planned out."

After that exchange, they travelled in silence for the remainder of the trip. The destination was an old mine shaft several stories below the surface. Sirum and Brill had mapped all the underground channels out from the lake several years ago, using drones equipped with ground penetrating radar so they could track their location. There were numerous old underground riverbeds that flowed south from the mountains, but only one that was intact the whole way and wide enough to accommodate a rail car. The cars had been equipped with oxygen generators due to the thin air, being so far underground and the endpoint was a very old mine that had been decommissioned a hundred years earlier. The riverbed exited into the side of the shaft, continuing deep underground. Realizing that anything he did outside of his normal activities would be monitored by Liam, Brill got creative in disguising his real objective of building an access point to his underground lab. He had a good friend of his purchase the land and build a tourist site over the mine, while Brill fronted the money for his friend. This kept his name off the books and he hoped off of Liam's radar. Since the building of that tourist site required rail tracks, it was an easy distraction siphoning off the tracks needed for his monorail and hiding the entrance to it. Old mines in this area were common tourist destinations, so one more would not raise any eyebrows.

When they reached the endpoint, it took them a while to locate the crawl ladder to the surface. In order to discourage any curious workers from finding the tracks, Brill had put in one of those ladders bolted into the rock with a protective cage around it. Given it was a four story drop to the bottom, one would have to be very curious to climb down, especially since it was pitch black and not well ventilated. The upper end of the ladder was a sealed door exiting in the service closet. One had to know the code to unlock it from either side, as an added layer of protection.

Each step up the ladder was an effort for both of them, taking about forty-five minutes to make that climb. At the top, they sat exhausted in the service closet for several minutes before resealing the entrance to hide its existence.

This tourist site was teeming with people, so Sirum and Liora would be of little notice. Brill had stashed cash in several cabinets, along with multiple fake identities, as a just in case, if he ever needed a quick getaway. There were also service worker uniforms, along with working credentials that would allow them to enter any building they chose. This location worked well for their food and beverage needs, but two weeks were all they could take of this. They were starting to go stir crazy. Having made the decision to let Liam find them, they would make it appear as if they had resurfaced from underground.

Sirum removed enough cash to get them out of this mess. There were several car keys in the storage boxes, each imprinted with the coordinates of the vehicle it would start. Brill had hidden several cars throughout the city, in case he ever needed unmarked transportation, as these were old cars from the late sixties, ones before any electronic means could track their whereabouts. Paying cash for gas and food would enable them to make their trip without Liam suspecting they were up here.

Brill had also setup the fake identities with memberships at several gyms throughout the city. Each location had a locker full of fresh clothes and a heat dampening gel for their bodies. They exited the service closet and quickly hopped in the back of a service truck that would be making stops throughout the city. Their goal was to get to the gym with the attached parking garage. They made their way to one of those gyms, where both he and Liora were able to shower and refresh themselves. After their showers, they completely covered themselves in the heat dampening gel as an added layer of security to keep from being seen by infrared detection from satellites and drones. They put on hats and made their way to the parking garage connected to the gym.

Sirum chose this particular gym because of the covered garage and the ready supply of homeless people outside of the gym. They made their way on foot to the exit of the structure, as the homeless would beg folks who left it. Sirum found his mark. As a homeless guy made eye contact with him, the guy thought he had a taker for giving up some money. Little did he know it would be so much more, as Sirum motioned him to enter the structure.

"Come closer, out of the way of that camera."

"I don't know man. Show me what you have."

Waving a wad of cash, Sirum motioned for him to follow. "It's all yours if you follow me." The guy was hesitant, but hunger overtook him and he reluctantly made his way to the car. "Dude I'm here, what do you have for me?"

"This cash, probably five thousand dollars' worth, but we need you to drive us up into the mountains and then forget you ever saw us."

"Are you guys in trouble with the law?"

"Even worse, but they don't know we are here. If you drive us to where we need to go, you can also have the car, no questions asked. Plus, there is a suitcase full of clothes in the trunk and you can have this gym membership and fake ID."

"Okay, but I need to get something to eat first."

"No. Those cameras in the drive through will spot us. You can wait till you drop us off. We have a bit to eat and some water you can have."

With that, they made their way up into the mountains. Once they arrived, they gave their car to the homeless man. They instructed him head in the opposite direction from where they were dropped off. From there, Sirum and Liora, covered with the heat dampening gel, would not be tracked as they hiked up the mountain to a place where they knew an underground stream emerged from the mountainside.

They waited at the edge of the stream till dark. They chose to jump in at the point where the stream exits from its underground source and swam down as deep as they could, since the heat dampening gel would dissolve off. That way, when their heat signature showed up on the satellite mapping of that region, their story would be validated, as their heat signature would be highly visible at night and the slow dissolution of the gel would make it look like they were rising up from underground from their two-week disappearance. After cresting the surface that exited from underground, they waited another ten minutes to be sure the heat dampening gel was gone, and then they inflated their flotation devices and began the long journey down to lake Mead. With the snow melts heavy this time of year, the water flow was in their favor for a swift journey.

~

LIAM WAS eager to see Brill's work ripped down to its core and then rebuilt by his team. He had the top minds in the world working under him at Area 51. After 6 months since stealing them away from Brill, the lack of progress had Liam frustrated. These folks were supposed to be the best of the best. They were able to identify the genetic changes Brill had placed into the primates but couldn't figure out the combination he used in the savants. They firmly believed there was some unknown variable that Brill had used and they were unable to identify it. The savants were increasing daily in their cognitive abilities and social abilities. Liam's team identified that not all genetic changes were introduced into the savants, in fact each one had different elements of what was in the primates. There was no pattern to the changes, just the random DNA here and there which made no sense to Liam's team.

Frustrated at every turn, the Swazi twins constantly complained, "Colonel Rhett, every avenue leads to a dead end. Each member of Brill's research team had a single function. Even knowing those functions, we can't see how to put them together."

"Please. We have the most sophisticated deep learning artificial intelligence machines in the world, and you're telling me that you can't figure it out?"

"The AI can't find the right algorithm, even knowing the end product in the savants. Nothing makes sense."

"Then try everything that seems preposterous. Try the unexpected."

"Colonel Rhett, we have the most advanced science in the world, even with the alien science, but we still can't make headway in his research."

"I don't buy it, the tech from the Roswell grays is so sophisticated. Just sounds like you are giving up. You have two weeks or you will be reassigned." With that, Liam turned around and exited.

The Swazi twins were Liam's hope for success. They had both mentioned some psychic connection via the apparatus Brill had used, a connected chair, the one item that was destroyed by Brill before he left the underground lab. They didn't know about the dark matter, but everything else fit with the conversation Liam had found between Brill and Sirum. Liam's team was unable to reconstruct them and were unsure even what they were supposed to do. His team began random psychic experiments on the twins to see if they could initiate any of the amended genes. Without the chairs though, their psychic connection could not be focused, keeping them out of sync with one another. Since these were women, they lacked the crucial Y-chromosome that was so critical to Brill's experiments of focused intellect without the chair. When Liam's team found some of the thirteen and fifteen chromosomes which activated in response to psychic stimuli, they thought they hit pay dirt. It was the confirmation that Liam needed that Brill was actually doing genetic modifications.

He thought these must be important, since they showed up in most of the primates and some of the savants. These genetic modifications, however, were fixes to a mutation that cropped up in small segments of the population. Before Brill implemented any genetic modifications, he would fix all identified mutations. It was one of the main purposes of the primate work which allowed for a clean slate when he pushed the desired modifications. Brill used the primates to be sure the updates would not negatively impact any of the bodily functions, as sometimes mutations become a dependent feature of the body and taking it away could cause severe harm. This seemed to be enough to keep Liam's team occupied for the foreseeable future and kept Liam happy with their progress.

As RIGHT AS RAIN, their heat signatures had been registered by the monitoring systems in this region the moment the heat dampening gel wore off, plus they knew Liam would be looking for any trace of them.

About a mile before they entered the lake, a military boat intercepted them. They had prepared for this over the last few days, making sure every inch of their story matched. Any discrepancy would immediately alert Liam to deception. Once aboard the boat, they were cuffed, and a bag placed over their faces. At some location they could not determine, they were loaded aboard a helicopter and flown to who knows where and then injected with something that knocked them out.

With groggy awareness, Sirum looked around the room. He was cuffed to a table in some type of interrogation room. A voice from behind startled him as it bellowed out, "Dr. Lars, nice of you to join us."

Not being able to see who he was talking to was a bit disturbing, but he answered anyway. "I don't recall having a choice."

The military officer made his way to the other side of the table and sat across from Sirum, placing a plate of food and cup of water just out of reach. As the officer began to eat and drink in front of him, Sirum recognized the mind games this guy was trying to play, especially given his dire thirst and hunger. "Smells good, doesn't it? Boy this water really refreshes one's thirst."

"I know what you're doing, and it won't work."

"Not sure I follow, Dr. Lars."

"You must not realize who you are dealing with. I have incredible will power. A little hunger and thirst won't allow you to bend my will to yours."

"I'm just here having dinner and a drink. Not sure why you are making a mountain out of a mole hill."

"Then where is my food and drink?"

"All in due time Dr. Lars."

Sirum tired of this nonsense, "What is it you want me to tell you? I have nothing to hide and everything to gain."

"Everyone has something to hide. You should be asking yourself this question; Is it worth hiding it?"

"First, I have to know if what you're asking is something that's not worth answering?"

"Touché Dr. Lars. Tell me how you showed up in a river in the middle of nowhere when you were last seen in downtown Las Vegas over two weeks ago?"

"That implies you were looking for me, to know my whereabouts at all times."

"Everyone has a digital trace Dr. Lars. You, of all people, would know this better than I."

"If what you are implying is true, then you would also expect me to disguise my digital signals, but I doubt I could hide them from your surveillance."

"Yet, you disappeared for two weeks and then just showed up in the northern Nevada mountains. How long would you like to play this game Dr. Lars?"

"I didn't realize this was a game. You still have not introduced yourself to me."

"My identity is unimportant to your situation. Please enlighten me with some useful information."

"I am tired of talking to you. Send in Colonel Rhett."

"Colonel Rhett? What makes you think I know him, and why would you think him to be here?"

Sirum immediately realized his mistake. If he revealed how he knew Liam was here, then he would have to give away his observations of Liam at Brill's hidden lab.

"Colonel Rhett always seems to be at odds with me and my friends, so you can see my natural inclination to make the assumption that he is here."

"You assume we are at odds with each other? Dr. Lars, you are here because you were trespassing on military property."

"If that is the case, then you got me. Yes, I was looking for UFO's and Area 51."

When the conversation continued on for several hours staying at a stalemate, they injected Sirum with something. He assumed it was some type of truth serum and wasn't sure he could hold out very long with that taking down his barriers. The man got up and left, leaving Sirum to the silence.

When he came back, they picked up where they left off. "Dr. Lars, we have already established I know of your last know whereabouts, so let's not take this useless tactic. What were you doing these last few weeks while you were off the grid?"

Sirum tried to dodge this question by asking a question of his own. "I lost track of time. What days and what do you mean off the grid?"

The interrogator knew his stuff, and Sirum's tactic was a clear tell that he was trying to evade answering. "Dr. Lars lets try this again, tell me about the chair."

Several hours later, Liam entered the room and started the questioning all over.

"Dr. Lars, tell me what you were doing with Brill?"

The truth chemicals had finally overcome any of Sirum's mental blocks, and he began to tell all he knew. Sirum was hoping they wouldn't probe too deeply into the chair's function, as he was sure he could not hold back.

Unable to not tell, Sirum let out a stream of information, but he and Brill had prepared for most interrogations that they may have to undergo at some point. The information that flowed from his lips was a preconditioned response, triggered by the release of inhibitions. One thing Brill knew well was how mind chemistry works. He lived by the saying, "In vino veritas" which is Latin for, "in wine lies the truth." That old idiom underlaid the core of the truth serums, as they merely loosen the brain's ability to form the complex thought associated with lying. Knowing that the so-called truth serums merely inhibit the complexity of lying and allow for the underlying knowledge to seep through as a reflexive response, Brill used memory techniques to bury the lie within Sirum's long-term memories. That way, it would flow out as the 'truth' because Sirum had time to often think of it and keep telling himself over and over that information. After a while, his brain would accept it as the truth without any inhibitions or needed complexities.

"I was helping Brill to build chairs which bridge the psychic links between two people's minds."

Liam asked, "Oh, one other thing, tell me about dark matter, Dr. Everly's special place, and how it relates to these chairs?"

The color drained from Sirum's face. They had not prepared for questioning on the dark matter topic. With those chemicals wearing him down, Sirum was certain he could not resist answering, so he tried the question with a question tactic. "What special place? You mean his desert lab?"

Liam was unfazed by Sirum's reticence, "Dr. Lars, why connect two minds, what purpose would that serve?"

"When two minds are focused on a problem, they can work in tandem to fill in the unknowns and solve it much faster than one mind ever could."

"How does dark matter fit into this?"

Sirum could not resist telling the truth, but this topic had so many truths, it gave him the opportunity to choose which truth would cause the least damage to Brill's secret research. "Dark matter is something we view as a lensing material that helps to bridge the thoughts. I was lucky to create a small amount one time but have never been able to recreate it."

Liam paused to ponder on this for a while before he continued the questioning. "Why all the primate research and genetic modifications?"

"All I know is what Brill mentioned. He said people had to be genetically similar to bridge the mental gap between them in the absence of dark matter, as those twins are genetically similar. Even they needed minor genetic modification to be the same."

"Where do the savants fit into all this?"

"Savants have unique mental abilities to start. Brill thought if he could make them genetically similar, he could greatly amplify their mental abilities, though we were never able to be successful with them."

Liam stared for a long while at Sirum and then got up and left without saying another word. Sirum sat alone in silence waiting for what would come next. A few hours later, Sirum was uncuffed and escorted to a room containing a table with food on it and a bed. He was left to himself without any instructions, and the door was not locked. Seeing that he was not a prisoner, or at least with the illusion of not being one, he returned to the table, ate, and then fell sound asleep.

~

WHEN LIORA AWOKE, she was lying in a bed not very comfortable by her standards. She nearly passed out as she rose, very disoriented to her surroundings. After a few minutes, she realized where she was. It was a military base, one that looked familiar to her. The familiarity hit home, it was her old room, even some of her old belongings were here. They were in North Carolina, or at least the belongings were from her room there. She knew right away that Liam was behind this, but why? Why separate her from Sirum and leave her with her old stuff? She thought. Possibly ease what was to come next? She figured it was Liam's way of making the questioning easier. Food was left on the table, so she indulged herself and waited.

It was not long before Liam entered. "Glad to see you are awake."

"I would have been much sooner if your men had not drugged us."

"All necessary precautions, as you well know."

"Yes, yes, I knew it would happen."

"What happened Liora? Why did you turn on me?"

"Not sure why you would think that?"

"Come now. You helped Brill break into and back out of the hospital to get into his office, and for what? Why hide for two months?"

"I was helping him to gain his trust, as you had ordered. We were hiding, we were trying to find a way out of the underground, after you destroyed our access points."

"That may be so. However, you then helped him out in the desert and turned on my team. Why?"

"It was needed to gain his..." she stammered as Liam cut her off.

"Dammit, Liora. Stop lying to me, as we both know you had ulterior motives. You have long since had his trust. Don't even try to play me."

The words, "He needed my..." were stopped as Liam raised his voice, something she had rarely heard in her time growing up with him.

"Stop this shit Liora. Your helping him cost me the knowledge of what he was ultimately trying to achieve, and now he is gone."

"No thanks to you."

"You left me no choice."

"You know, he was going to leave me there as he fled, but he came back for me.

Tears were streaming down her face, "I...love him and didn't realize it until that moment when he came back."

"You were not placed in this assignment to develop feelings. Had I known, I would have pulled you a long time ago."

Sobbing now, "You...you...killed him. Why?"

"How did I kill him? He is the one who fled under the mountains that were caving in, along with you and Dr. Lars."

"They were only caving in because you were blowing them up. Damn you, Liam! Now I have lost him forever."

"Liora, that is for the better. In time, you will thank me for that."

"If you weren't my uncle, I would beat the shit out of you."

"It's only because you are my niece that you are not arrested for insubordination."

"Hardly, Liam. You forget that I work for the Mossad, not the US military."

A smile crossed his face, "You seem to forget, they loaned you to me permanently."

"Tell me, my young niece, why did you stay underground for two weeks? You had to have planned for that in order to have enough food and heat."

"When you started invading, Brill came back for me and pulled me into a boat. From there, he navigated to some underground cave way downstream. Brill had placed himself in some chair, not sure what it did, and then injected himself with the vial we took from his lab. When the chair lost power, Brill died."

"Are you sure he died?"

"Of course, he did...I think. I held him in my arms with his cold lifeless body pressed against mine."

"That explains where you were, but not how you escaped."

"I'm getting there. As Sirum and I sat in the dark with Brill, the roof of the cave gave way, and we retreated back to the water. It was still caving in when we jumped in and let the current take us where it would. We were in the water for a very long time before we found a way to rise up as the water made its way into a fast-moving stream. We jumped in and almost froze to death.

From there, we found a cave that Brill had equipped with enough food and water for months. It took us two weeks to figure out that none of the tunnels lead upward. Eventually, we found a stream that flowed into the rocks. Once we got into that hole, we found that it was a cavern leading to the surface. We were able to get in there and climb our way up. At the top, a stream flowed out of the top of the cavern and branched, one going down the way we came up, and another exiting the mountain. Had it not been daylight, we would have never seen its exit point, so we jumped in and hoped for the best. Not long after that, we burst forth from underground to see the sun rising. Still having our flotation devices, we kept in the river, as it got warmer and warmer. We were hoping to make it to Lake Mead and then back home."

"It all fits too well Liora. Way to perfect. I'm sure there is more to the story and you will tell me in due time. For now, let's call a truce. I must be getting sentimental in my old age."

"I assume you got what you need from Brill's research?"

"Time will tell."

A bit after Liam left, Sirum was escorted to Liora's room. They spent time catching up on their experiences before they were shuttled to an aircraft and then back to Vegas. She wasn't sure if Liam would talk to her ever again. She knew she had crossed a line with him that would take a long time to repair, unless he got what he needed from Brill's research. Then all would be forgiven, as it was always about his ability to achieve the goal he had set his sights upon. She would take her leave and wait things out. When they got back to the city, she and Sirum wished each other well and parted ways for a few weeks. It took that long for Liora to get back into the routine of life. She poured herself into her work with a few new patients that all had difficult but interesting problems. She also took up rock climbing with Sirum to pass the time.

2

LIORA'S LIFE

few weeks After Brill's Death

A Being released by Liam was a blessing and a curse. She knew her loyalty would always be with him, he was family. The loss of Brill hit her hard. Feelings were a new experience for her and she was not sure how to properly express them. She had learned from the best at controlling every situation around her, yet she had zero control of the events that unfolded with Brill, and this had her frustrated. The avalanche of emotions was almost more than she could take.

The woes of her patients enabled her to forget about her feelings for a time. She worked long hours and began to use the sessions with her patients as a catharsis for herself. All was fine and good till she had to go home in the evenings. Sleep just brought about the "what ifs" from the past several months. She knew dealing with those was needed before she could move on to a better place, her own council rang true for her feelings. She was on the verge of a breakdown when she got a call from Sirum.

"Hi Liora. How are you this fine evening?"

"What's up?" The sadness in her voice painted her mood.

"Are you okay? You don't sound so good."

"Just one of those days."

"Have you ever been rock climbing?"

"Some. What did you have in mind?" Not wanting to give away too much of her past, she hedged her answer, as she had trained in rock climbing in her spy training days.

"I've just started back, as it seems to be a good stress release for me, and I thought you might want to come along, if for nothing else other than to get out of your office."

Without hesitation she replied, "Would love to, when did you want to go?"

"Was planning on Red Rock Canyon this weekend, heading up there Friday night and camping out till Sunday."

Her perky response said it all. "I'm in, just tell me what time you'll pick me up."

～

ONLY A 20 MINUTE drive out of Vegas, they were able to get to the canyon early enough in the evening to get a few one pitch climbs in before sunset. They had their packs on them during these easy climbs, as Sirum had planned to camp in the Calico Basin. It was an easy climb and nice hike to the basin where they settled in for the night. Sun rises early in the desert, and they were up at first light, trying to hit the trails before the morning heat set up for the day. They made their way up several class 5.0 climbs to get their legs under them and then increased in gradual difficulty, with the target of Mount Wilson in their sites. They spent the better part of Saturday on the moderate climbs and then finished the day on the Resolution Arete section, one of the moderate difficulty climbs. Sirum was concerned of Liora's skill level, so he didn't push her into the more difficult climbs, as he wanted her to do more climbing with him.

Liora now had the climbing bug since there was little else in her life, and she was in desperate need of an emotional outlet. She joined one of the indoor climbing gyms and spent most nights learning to climb more and more difficult surfaces. After two months of training,

Sirum could no longer keep up. Now Liora was scheduling the climbs and enticing Sirum to join her. The trip she had planned for the weekend required travel to Colorado. They spent the better part of the week with a professional climber teaching them the ropes on the most difficult terrain. One face in Clear Creek had Sirum terrified, as they were free climbing and needed to climb under a long edge of an outcrop and then back over to the topside. Sirum had to bolt in at this point, as he was not confident in his skill level. While he was clipping in, she zipped right past him to the topside, grabbing his line as she went, so she could bolt it in up top. A bit embarrassed, he took what help he could get and nearly slipped several times as he made his way under and then over the edge to the top side. Liora's skill at climbing soon surpassed that of even the most skilled guides, which gave her a false sense of surety on those difficult climbs.

She was constantly pushing the boundaries and kept telling herself it was an escape, but deep down she knew there was little in the way of earthly ties to make her afraid of dying. That lack of fear of death was always a primer for making mistakes and on her last climb one of those mistakes finally caught up with her.

They were camping in the Lake Tahoe region one weekend when Liora spotted a climb like no other, the unknown chimney in Eagle Lake Cliff. She and Sirum were making their way up the face of the cliff when Liora hammered in a clip. She started to reach for the overhang with her left hand while trying to clip in the rope with her right hand. Just as she made that reach with her right hand, the wall under her right foot gave way. With her body weight now off balance, she started to fade back into a sideways fall as the ground beneath her fully gave way. The ground opened up the entrance in a long-hidden cave. Liora's body followed the rocks in the hundred-foot fall into the shallow water covering the floor of the cave. Her body hit the water with the impact of a cement truck, as she didn't have time to adjust her position during the fall. If she had been in a swimsuit, this would have made a great belly buster. Her body being perpendicular to the surface, absorbed the impact of the fall and knocked her unconscious. Liora was fortunate to have grabbed a tree branch while grasping at the rock wall during her fall. That tree was now keeping her head afloat and preventing her from drowning.

Sirum watched the horrific accident from afar, being way down the cliff wall and not close enough to help her. He scrambled as fast as he could up to where she fell and tried to see if he could reach her. His headlamp did not illuminate anything below and the echo of his yells told him it was a big cavern. He knew time was of the essence for Liora. If he could not get to her soon, she may die. In his mind, he ran down the list of options. He had a rope back in the truck, but it was about two hours there and another two back. He doubted she could wait that long. They always carried an emergency aid pack, which would allow him to patch small wounds and create a stint if needed. First though, he had to find her. She could be under a pile of rubble, or worse, impaled by some spire of rock. He decided he could not wait any longer and went over the edge, fumbling for a foothold in the dark cavern. He was pleased when his foot found purchase. The climb down wore on his nerves, being in complete darkness the deeper he went. Being unsure of how far it went, every downward move brought his nerves a bit under control. It took him the better part of an hour to reach what he felt was the floor of the cavern, though his headlamp did little to convince him of that. Once he hit the water's edge, he was fairly certain he was on level ground and began to set about searching at a more rapid rate. He called out many times with no answer.

Exhausted, Sirum sat on a large rock to gather both his thoughts and strength. Realizing he had been running on adrenalin and not using his noggin in his search, he sat for a minute to clear his thoughts and use the tools at hand. He rummaged through his backpack to find anything that would help in his search. His headlamp landed on the LED flashlight tucked away in the inner pocket, something that came with the pack he never realized was there. This was a beauty of a flashlight, since it had a multi-mode color spectrum. In the other pockets he found a clear plastic bowl, a knife, some epoxy glue, and food. Without giving it a second thought, he downed the food and water and then set to create a spotlight out of the flashlight, really trying to widen the field of vision the beam would make. His engineering came in handy as he utilized the bowl and epoxy. He cut a hole in the bowl to allow for the flashlight beam to shine through it. Then he fixed the hole right over the lens and glued it down. Once the seal was tight enough, he then added epoxy to the bowl, covering about an inch in the bottom of the bowl. He turned the flashlight on and positioned it upright in ultraviolet mode so that the UV light from the LED would catalyze the drying of the epoxy. He guessed it would take about ten minutes to completely harden. Not wanting to sit and wait, he explored the shoreline to see if he could spot her.

Daylight was waning, reducing the light that was filtering through the passage in the cave ceiling where she fell through. He used this time to also study the hole and estimate where a body of Liora's size and shape would have landed, extrapolating from the light shining directly through at this point. That gave him the best indication of where to start. With that direction in sight, he grabbed the modified flashlight and let it shine. The beam now casted a wide field of illumination, about twenty feet across. With the better vision, he raced as best as the terrain would let him. The spot where he suspected Liora to be was over the edge of a hill that he was now running up. As he crested the hill, he almost plunged headfirst into the water, since the other side of the hill was a steep slope right into the water. Catching himself and directing his momentum to the side where he was able to slow to a stop. Seeing the water was the exact spot where he suspected Liora hit, he was both relieved and terrified. Relieved from the standpoint that she wasn't under a pile of rubble, but terrified that she may have drowned. He scanned the beam of light across the surface of the water. Something caught his eye. It seemed to be a branch that was floating, yet it wasn't staying still. He observed it moving deeper into the cavern, indicating to him that the lake had a current. He had no measure of distance here and was unable to guess the speed of the current. He followed it until the shoreline ended. To go any further, he would have to get in the water and float with the current. Not wanting to jump in without looking for some floatation, he scanned the floor of the cave for anything that would help, finally coming across a dried-up tree, likely from some prior cave-in he thought. It was big, but light enough for him to have hope that it would float.

With a hefty heave, he was able to get the tree to the water. To his surprise and hope, the log floated. Not wanting it to get away from him, he flung his pack on top and wrapped his arm around it as the current took hold. Once inside the cavern, he shined the light everywhere. The water soon turned into an underground river and picked up speed. He was now fully committed to this course of action and hoped his search would turn up Liora. Time no longer had meaning here, and he was uncertain how long he floated until the river slowed and dumped into a much larger body of water. The current stopped, or at least, it was too deep to feel the movement. He guessed the place was huge based on the echo of his yells.

LIORA FLOATED for some time before she regained consciousness. The pain in her side told her she had broken ribs. How many she didn't know, but the pain helped her to focus her thoughts on staying alive. Her survival training instinctually kicked in, helping her to flip on her back and allowing her to float without drowning. She finally came to rest against a rock ledge. The water seemed to wedge her into a cleft in the rock, bracing her on each side with her bottom coming to rest on an underwater ledge. Feeling too weak to pull herself out of the water, she fell into unconsciousness as the tiredness on her body pulled her deep into a sleep state.

'This is an odd dream she thought.' Drip, drip, drip, this damn water is a nuisance.' This thought kept echoing through her semi-conscious mind. Each drip hitting her nose almost choking her made this dream seem too real. After several minutes of this, her mind realized this was no dream, but a condition putting her in peril. This caused her to bolt upright, along with all the pain that action brought. Now the dripping was hitting the top of her head, and in her semi-lucid state she let out a string of profanities. Sitting upright and more awake now, she took stock of her surroundings. She was shivering uncontrollably now, probably from being submerged in frigid mountain water for several hours. She moved to the left and an intense pain burst from her side up through her ear. Slowly moving back to center, she tried the right side. The pain was less, just sharp enough to help her focus her thoughts. She rolled to the right, almost clearing the ledge to dry land. One more push she told herself. The pain was almost too much to handle as she pulled her feet up under herself and bolted up out of the water. "Made it," she kept saying to herself as she lay face down on the slimy rock.

The taste of moss and dirt was a welcome distraction from the cold. Liora lay there for an hour or two or more, time seemed to float away as she drifted in and out of sleep. Hunger pulled her out of her dream state. She managed to get her feet far enough under herself to position her body upright into a sitting position. At this point, she slowly untangled her arms from her backpack. The left arm was of no use, since the pain of lifting anything was too intense. With her right arm, she brought the pack around to inspect it. Remembering she had on a headlamp, she flipped it on. Her eyes now accustomed to the darkness of the cave, squinted in pain at the light, as it was one of those high intensity LED's. A few minutes later, her eyes adapted to the light and she fumbled through the pack, mainly looking for food and water.

The first things she pulled out were a flashlight and med kit, which she knew would come in handy later. The energy bar was a welcome sight. Before she could eat that, water was a necessity as her mouth was parched. Sipping the water down caused her to tremble with the use of those muscles inducing immense pain. With the energy bar, pain pills, and water now in their proper place, her stomach, she continued to unload the contents of her pack. Fortunately, she had planned on camping when they reached the summit, so she had a full change of clothes and flint for fire. Sirum had argued with her about camping up there and was expecting to return to their base camp. She had planned otherwise, and it now worked in her favor.

Getting out of the wet clothes and into the dry ones proved to be more difficult than anticipated. Removing wet pants and undergarments was like peeling the skin off a catfish. The right leg, though painful, came off with relative ease. Once she started on the left leg, everything was going as good as could be expected until she got the pants down past her knee. The pants had been tight enough to put pressure on the femur that she had fractured in the fall. Once removed, the nerves in her thigh let her know of her predicament, causing her to fall back in pain. The stars appearing before her eyes also told her that she was going to be unconscious for a while. She came back to after a bit, guessing the pain killers must have kicked in and were now allowing her to at least tolerate the throbbing pain in her left side while get fully dressed in dry clothes. With the ordeal of changing clothes now behind her, she wrapped herself in the Mylar sheet she had found folded up in her pack. It took about ten minutes before her body heat began to lessen the chill.

She worked herself into a standing position, teetering from side to side as she regained her footing. Using the extremely bright flashlight, at least to her eyes, she searched around for wood. It didn't take too long to collect enough for a fire. The flint helped in the task of getting it going, and before long, she had a roaring fire going. Feeding the fire enough large pieces of wood to last a long while, she cuddled up next to the pack, using it as a pillow, wrapped the Mylar sheet around herself, and fell off into a fitful sleep.

SIRUM'S SEARCH was soon made easier, as he spotted a bright light way down the cavern. As he got closer, he realized it was a fire. This caused him to increase his speed with his legs kicking frantically behind him. Getting out of the water was much easier for him than it was for Liora, and he was relieved to see Liora huddled up next to the fire. Seeing she was asleep and not wanting to wake her, he quietly pulled up to enjoy the heat of the fire. Soon, he decided to create a clothesline out of a spool of wire he had packed. He hung up their wet clothes and threw a few more logs on the fire. He wrapped himself up in his Mylar blanket and fell fast asleep. He was startled awake by a scream from Liora. His eyes acclimated to the light of the fire, and he could see it was a yell of pain, rather than one of danger. Seeing she was also awake, he offered her some words of comfort.

"Great to see you Liora. I'm glad you're alive."

Between the cries of pain, she stammered out, "Me too. What happened?"

"When we were climbing, a part of the wall collapsed and you fell through."

"Explains the pain I feel now. Where are we?"

Gesturing around, Sirum responded, "This place is some type of underground cavern, and the water must feed the lake down below the mountain."

"Any idea how we get out of here?"

"Not a clue. My main goal was to find you. I figured we would work out that last part later."

"Well, now is as good a time as any."

"Can you walk?"

"Some, but I expect it to be painful."

"Let me have a look at it." He inspected her leg for any obvious signs of breakage. "Do you want the good or bad news first?"

"Let me have both."

"Your leg is not broken, but your hip is dislocated."

"Can you reset it?"

"I can try, but it's going to hurt like hell."

"Do it."

Handing her a small cloth, "Bite this, and I need you put as much pressure as you can on that hip joint as I lift up your knee."

Even with the cloth in her mouth, Liora let out such an ear-piercing scream that the bats on the cave ceiling took flight. Her breathing was shallow for several minutes until the pain subsided. Gingerly sitting upright, she tested her weight on the leg. The pain seemed manageable enough to her to push on further into the cavern. Sirum offered the suggestion of going back the way they came. The look she gave him could have cut through a diamond.

Realizing his mistake, he quickly packed up everything and looked about to make a torch. There were several pieces of wood laying near the water's edge. He grabbed the only one large enough to make a torch and dabbed it heavily in the bat droppings piled up near the cave wall. He ripped one of their wash towels in half and doused it in water, then tied it around the middle of the piece of wood. He was hoping to soak the lower part of the wood in water to slow the torch from burning down too fast. His trick worked, but he figured it would only last a few hours. The heat from it was a welcome feeling on their faces as they walked deeper and deeper into the damp cavern. He gave the modified flashlight to Liora, who shined it on the right, and he carried the torch with which he kept to the left of them to illuminate the surroundings. Both were enough to give a wide field of vision for any signs of an exit.

They continued on till the cavern narrowed to a point where only the stream made headway. Seeing their torch come to the end of its useful life, they decided to make camp and get some much-needed rest. They had brought enough wood to make a roaring fire and found a few other pieces of debris they could use as kindling as the fire died down. As soon their heads hit their makeshift pillows, their backpacks, their eyes shut almost on command. They were both exhausted, so the sleep, though much needed, was less than refreshing. Several hours later, they both woke within minutes of each other, stiff and sore from the previous day's adventure and laying on the hard cave floor. They looked at each other and nodded, knowing the only way forward was to plunge in the cold water and see where it takes them.

There were enough pieces of wood debris for Sirum to make a float for them both to hold onto when they decide to embark. Sirum had some twine, not much, but enough to tie together several pieces of wood. As he plunked it in the water and positioned a torch on each end of it, they took each other's hand and plunged into the ice-cold water. The chill of the water brought some clarity to their aching bodies and gave them a sense of hurriedness. The current of the river was too slow for their liking, so Sirum used a makeshift paddle to gain some momentum while both of them were laying prostrate on the top of it. They were soon moving at a rapid clip, going through the narrow opening in the cave wall.

There was a head's height of clearance as the raft they were laying on zipped through the opening. They barely got their heads low enough to prevent them from scraping on the ceiling. Sirum was quick enough to grab one torch and Liora followed his lead with the one in the back, barely keeping the flame low enough to keep burning but high enough to stay out of the water. They were both starting to get a bit claustrophobic, as the sides and top of the water tunnel narrowed to the point that they started scraping the top of their heads and backs. Liora kept a count in her head to get a feel for how long this was taking, and when they finally emerged into a large open cavern, it had been an hour traveling like that. Their speed picked up on its own, and they soon realized why. The unmistakable sound of a waterfall told them that they needed to get to a bank or to some rock formation where they could approach the fall with caution. Nothing presented itself until they were almost upon the falls. The dim light of morning peeking through the upper cavern helped them to spot a landing, enabling them to get out of the water. They paddled with all their might, fighting against the current and were able to make the landing.

Both of them collapsed on the shoreline after hauling their packs out of the water. Sleep hit them hard as neither had the strength to do anything else. The daylight finally stretched across Liora's face, easing her out of her slumber. As she started to rise, her eyes were drawn to the wall of the cavern. Sirum was still sleeping, so she began to explore on her own. Out of the corner of her eye a sparkle on the wall caught her gaze. Focusing in on that area, she noticed some faint paintings on the wall. It was cave art from some long forgotten people. "Could have been the Native Americans of this region," was her first thought. The familiarity of the paintings had her entranced for some time before she heard Sirum calling her name.

"Over here, Sirum. You have got to see this."

Hobbling over to her, "What is it?"

"Look at the wall, way up there," pointing to the upper part of the wall that the sun was illuminating.

"Looks like cave art. Maybe by the Native Americans that used to roam these mountains."

"Most likely. It is very similar to art in New Zealand that Brill and I uncovered. I wonder if these Native Americans are related the Maori progenitors."

The images depicted a group of people sitting around something, probably a fire, but the rock there had long ago erased its treasure by falling to the cave floor. They continued further into the cavern, trying to see what else was painted there. The next scene was a similar group in the process of building structures out of trees, though it resembled pyramids beneath the image of an illuminated whirlpool. Brill had thought these were the ancient builders of all the great wonders of the world, but Liora had her doubts. Unlike the images she and Brill observed, this one showed a different scene. From the wood pyramids there was the painting of a road or water-way, she wasn't sure. She and Sirum had to climb through and over several mounds of grassy bat droppings, not the most pleasant experi-ence, as they followed the paintings on the wall. This 'road' continued for some ways along the wall, circling around what appeared to be a planet. It kept going, circling several more planets, even one with a ring around it, stopping at a blood red one. She was so used to reading from left to right and had to caution herself to question if this was the end or the beginning of the journey of those long dead people. It also occurred to her that this could be the middle, especially if other parts of the wall had crumbled.

When they reached this spot, they noticed a path leading up to the sunlight. The bear droppings made it clear why there was a trail. Once they spotted the droppings, they froze in their tracks. Looking from side to side, they didn't spot any bears and then picked up the pace, as fast a Liora could hobble along. The climb up took its toll on her. The hip, though back in its socket, still smarted. It was an agonizing trek for her, even on the well-worn bear path. Their eyes, having grown accustomed to the low lighting, winced in pain as the sun was in its full glory at mid-day. Regaining their day sight, they pushed on to get as far away from the cave as possible, hoping to avoid any of the bears.

They left the trail and headed toward the river, as it should be the one feeding Eagle Lake. The sounds of rushing water kept them going, and they were soon rewarded with the sights and sounds of civilization. No sooner than seeing the river, they spotted the lake and the resorts lining it. Help was slow in arriving. They finally got the attention of a few fishermen who were able to call in some help for them. For Liora, waiting on the ambulance only intensified the pain that she had mentally blocked when survival was the forethought. Both of them spent several days in the hospital recovering from dehydration, and Liora had surgery on her hip and her broken ribs were set.

∼

One Month *Since Brill's Death*

A month after the cave adventure, Liora now had a deeper appreciation of her work. One of her new patients consumed most of her time and thoughts. This individual was a male who served in the Army as a combat medic. He served three tours of duty in the war-torn region of Jammu and Kashmir. The USA had been drawn into this international dispute to stem the flow of drugs and weapons from Russia to the Middle East. The Army had suffered heavy losses, and this medic had treated several hundred severely injured soldiers. Liora took on the treatment of this man when all others had abandoned their efforts, as she could sympathize with his history. Notes from the previous psychiatrists all read the same, paranoid schizophrenic with severe delusions, hallucinations, and fits of rage and terror.

"Hi Major Thomas. I am Dr. Abrams."

His mumbling was inaudible at first and soon became enraged as he put his hands to his ears. "MAKE THEM GO AWAY. MAKE

THEM STOP." Over and over, he emphatically repeated this, eventually falling to the floor and hugging himself in his tremors.

She reached out a hand to touch his. He gently took it.

"I know your pain." Her voice was almost a whisper.

His words stopped in mid-sentence and looked up at her. "How?" The anger in his voice stabbed like a knife.

"I served in Asia for several years. I've lost those close to me and had to take lives as well. I don't know your exact circumstances, but I would like to find out, if you would let me."

He jerked his hand to himself uttering, "You are like all the rest. Just give me my meds and leave me alone."

"Do you know who you are right now?"

"What the fuck do you think?"

"I introduced myself, but I have yet to hear your name."

"Get away from me you fucking bitch."

"I'll make you a deal. You play nice and I won't have you medicated."

"Now you are going to torture me? I need that fucking medication, or the voices will drive me crazy?"

His mood soured after that and she had him taken to his room. Keeping her word, she did not prescribe any mood-altering drugs, just placebos. She knew how strong the power of thought was and giving him a placebo pill would at least convince him that he was getting what he needed.

The next few visits were equally contentious. Every visit helped her learn more and more of his story. His memory seemed to be limited to the past two years. Something blocked his memory beyond that point. This was the nexus point she was looking to find. The hypnosis techniques she used inched her closer and closer to the event that forever changed his life. Every session from that point on helped to frame the story for her until she finally had a breakthrough with him.

"Tell me Major, what was your unit doing in the Kashmir mountains that day?"

Under hypnosis, he stammered. "The rain started and never

seemed to stop. That day the fog prevented us from seeing our hands in front of our faces. Explosions everywhere. Jack was bleeding out the side of his head. I ran over to him to put pressure on the wound and then another flash, and another, and another. Jack died that day with my hand in his head, at least that's what they told me. I thought it odd as I remember talking with Jack as those flashes were going on around us. It was bright everywhere, almost blinding. I distinctly remember walking Jack to a boat and seeing him leave. There is no way he died." He faded off for a bit, seemingly lost in thought.

"What happened next?"

"Then I felt heat in the back of my head. Something very hot, causing pain. Oh, the pain. It hurt so bad. I was wiping the tears from my eyes when I heard the voice. Some dude with the weird name, I couldn't quite understand his name. Over and over he kept asking questions. I kept saying I had no idea what he wanted to know. Something about nanobots. Then the other voices started, almost like they were answering him. I couldn't understand a word they were saying. A bunch of gibberish. I kept shouting, "I don't know. I don't know," but he didn't listen. Just kept asking questions."

"Then what happened?"

"Next thing I recall is waking up in the med tent barely able to see. There was a bandage all around my head. Jason, the acting medic, told me a large piece of shrapnel and some metal from the soil buried themselves in my head. They couldn't risk removing them, or I might die. They were treating the infection that had formed. They said the voices were likely due to the infection, but the voices only got louder and more persistent. They still bother me today."

Liora didn't know what to make of his story. Did he exhibit some psychotic illusion in a near death state? She wasn't yet sure. One thing was certain, and that was his imagining these voices. This was a common symptom of schizophrenia. Could be his escape to a fantasy world and the pain is a manifestation of his guilt of the loss of people he couldn't save, blaming himself for their deaths. Something to explore more with the next session.

As Major Thomas was brought out of the hypnosis, his demeanor immediately changed. He looked angry and muttered several profanities before she picked up on a few.

"What the fuck you looking at?"

"Major Thomas, we were just getting to know each other. No need to be so mean."

"I don't give a rat's ass what you want. Just give me my fucking meds and let me be."

"In a minute. I have a few more questions now that you are awake."

"What the hell are you talking about? I was not asleep."

Ignoring his animosity, "Would you tell me about your friend Jack?"

"How...you have no right to ask."

"I know that must have been difficult for you to see him die. Tell me how you grieved."

"What...Jack is dead?"

"I'm sorry, I thought you knew."

He started sobbing. "It can't be. I just talked to him yesterday."

"Okay. I would like to talk more with you tomorrow. Would that be okay?"

He put his hands to his head in what was perceived to be pain. "The voices. Make them stop. Please!"

"Can you tell me what the voices are saying?"

"No, No, No, Stop! I don't understand what they are asking. There are hundreds of them screaming at me, and I don't know what they are saying." He started screaming and thrashing. The orderlies had to subdue him.

"Take him back to his room and give him some sedatives."

The back and forth of this scene played out over and over for the next few months. She was starting to make progress when she got a call from Liam.

3

OBLIVION

uring & After the Destruction – Stuck Underground
Brill was learning about the nanobots in the Knowledge Well when he felt a sudden and immediate disconnect from what he was. That living part of him, his body, had ceased to exist as it died. The Well drew him in deeper. This part of him became more aware of this place and what it was and could do. He seemed to watch parts of himself scatter throughout the Well, since he hadn't yet learned how to remain whole here. He was still a living thing, odd he thought or felt, as he wasn't sure if what he was in here was a thought or an extension of what his mind was. All the parts of himself that were scattered throughout the Well seemed to be connected, yet each piece of his consciousness could act independently of the other parts. Time had no meaning here, as did none of the bodily needs that existed in what he used to be.

The main part of himself had been pulled into the light near its center, something was drawing him close to the core of this place, which he perceived to be a very old place. This part of him was being drawn further and further in, away from all that he was and is and further away from the rest of his consciousness that were splintered across the upper parts of the Well. Those pieces seemed to be more like thoughts or whispers of who he was. In that upper part of the Well, identity no longer had meaning, self was an abstract concept in this place. He had some emotion here, but most of him was pure thought and intellect. He could 'see' by his consciousness translating the knowledge of this place into images like his mind used to do. The part of him being pulled closer to the core was fading into the background, but all the questions he had ever thought of were flooding forward and some were now being solved right in front of...not eyes but whatever part of himself was seeing or sensing these solutions.

He thought for a moment about self and who he was. He had an identity, a name, what was it...Brill, yes, that was it. That name, as it took form in his consciousness, was like a line of light heading away from the center and back to the outer regions of the Well, back to the rest of himself, away from all those answers and whatever was pulling him down to the core. This line of light grew stronger and stronger as the part of him in the upper regions was beginning to take hold and prevent him from being lost in the core. The knowledge he was 'seeing' was now minimally connected back to who he was, due to the nanobots still coursing throughout his earthly body, and that part of him was trying to pull together all parts of his consciousness that had splintered apart in here. That part of him knew that he should not be, what was the term, alive? That part of him helped to bring awareness to this place. Now he could 'see' it for so much more. The question that came from the part of him that was barely alive fed down to his consciousness at the core and asked, what is this place? The solutions to that question were many and vast. They appeared as buckets of answers right in front of him. His consciousness reached out to the largest bucket of solutions, as he grabbed it, it unraveled, and so did something else.

Something was here...Brill experienced his first sense of emotion in this place and that was deep fear. Everything that was still part of his being screamed to escape...but how? He was being pulled further down to the core by his deep desire to learn and know, and by something that was living here. Not finding a means of escape, Brill overcame his fear and dove deeper into the darkness. Soon after crossing the threshold of the darkness in the core, they latched onto him. Brill was not seeing them close in on him. When he realized they already had him, he was desperate to find an escape. Everything was closing in around him, then a lifeline to his splintered parts became a clear path to Brill as a way out. Like a fishing line in dark water, Brill was whisked out of his predicament toward the rest of himself. Clearing the imminent danger, but not too far out of the center of the core, the most ancient of all knowledge of the universe that was buried in this part of the Well began to present itself.

The questions of life itself was always on his mind when he was alive, and now the answers from the Well were providing enlightenment to the very essence of life. This place could be the mythical fountain of youth that appeared in the mythos of many alien and human societies. Another possible answer was that this was Galunlati, the Cherokee legend of creation that his Grandma used to tell him about when he was young. Then another suggestion that this place was the Elysian Fields of Greek mythology came to him. Odd, thought Brill. These were all myths, yet the true answer never landed in his sights. Then Brill perceived a wisp of an answer, but it was evading his attempts to reach it. Brill's conscious followed this wisp and gained on it with an increase in effort of his will, not realizing where it was taking him. When Brill's conscious finally grabbed that answer and started to unfold it, he soon realized his peril. It had taken him deeper into the core than he had ever ventured before. Once he opened that answer, he was frozen to the core. It said one word, hell.

Regaining his strength of will, Brill explored a bit further. If he was truly trapped in hell, he figured he might as well learn as much as possible. The information he began to unravel made little sense to him. The first looked to be a history of some alien species, as did every answer he unraveled in that place. The common theme Brill noticed was that the histories of each of these species all ended in catastrophic failure, usually by some hubris of that race. The hundredth he opened shook him hard. Either the species he was seeing was Earth's or one eerily similar as he saw their destruction as well, some cataclysmic explosion where the Earth or the Earth "look alike" was completely annihilated. Brill tried to dive deeper into this history to understand its details, but just as he was opening up individual timelines, the sense of the enemy approaching made Brill flee in terror.

On his way out of the core, he caught the trail of thought that led to something even more ancient, something before all life began, yet foreign to this universe. If he had a neck here, the hair on the back of it would have been standing up, along with the sense of deep terror this line of thought brought. Brill felt pulled deeper into this line of thought, following it deeper into what appeared to be a safer place in the core, yet perception is many times shrouded by deception and this place was no different, this core of deception. His curiosity was stronger than his fear. The stronger this line of thought became, the less Brill could detach himself from it. Every fiber of this part of his being in this place revolted at moving forward, yet he was trapped and could not divert himself. The thought of this place was filling in with bits of consciousness and was very alien to Brill. It became one forceful thought that yelled, "AWARENESS."

The things that were trapped here were different than those he had previously encountered, and they began to grow in awareness of Brill's presence. They almost found him when a blinding light hit him right as those things were homing in on him. This line of light was pushing/pulling him out of the core and back into the periphery of this place. "What was that?" A question that echoed through his being on his way out. Regaining his sense of self, Brill couldn't help but ponder what had just happened. An answer that floated out of these old regions of the Knowledge Well was one of two phrases, "Invaders of light," or "Ancient Enemies." Brill wasn't sure if one or both applied. He felt there was something or things in that place where he had been drawn to go. Those dark places seemed to have many different beings, and he perceived that they had been there a long time. The little bit he learned from the core showed this place to be the aftermath of an invasion that led to the formation of many universes, not just Brill's. He couldn't understand what that meant.

Who or what was invading, and how were they stopped, or were they? Too much to learn with very little understanding on how to learn it had Brill trying to latch on to something that would give him answers.

ABLE TO FINALLY SLOW DOWN, he moved on to another 'bucket of answers/solutions' nearby which showed this place to be a knowledge bridge which was very different from what he saw at the core. The next one he grabbed showed it to be something like what he used to know as a computer chip. The next one showed him the details of that computer chip analogy as he grabbed it. He was certain that this place was a connection to threads of consciousness spread across all of time and space, but not all minds, only those with the genetic ability to connect to this place. He didn't understand why minds would be connected to wherever here was. A lot of ideas and solutions to those, but he was not sure which ones were right. He could see those consciousnesses spread across time were real and connected to a sliver of their bodies, allowing them to essentially share the problem-solving power of millions of minds spread across all time and space. Every time he came across this answer, he kept asking himself, "Why? Why would minds be connected?" It didn't make sense to him. He was certain these minds were here and connected from the points in time they were alive, but how and why?

Taking a step back and looking at the whole of this place, he perceived what appeared to be mountains of bright spots followed by valleys of nothingness, all on the periphery of this place. Something told him those were the connections to minds at different times in the history of Earth, or other Earth-like planets, which were similar to the inside of the quantum computer just on a much more massive scale. The minds connected to it act similar to logic codes that computer chips use to translate a problem into a solution. Here the active logic from those minds allowed for infinite problem solving.

He kept asking 'Why' on these solutions, but never got an answer back from the Well.

Irrespective of the underlying core of this place, it was full of answers, and Brill had many questions. He was starting to get the hang of finding answers to his long unanswered questions while learning the pitfalls of this place. Since his body had almost completely stopped, all that was buried in his mind was now part of who he was here, and he had an infinite number of questions. Those questions followed with infinite answers when asked in here. The answers jumped at him at a furious pace. If Brill could have been startled here, the awe of what he perceived left him 'staring' in a longing to escape this place and be part of that great sight, but much of it was too massive and complex for even all these minds here to wrap an understanding around.

The complexity of that information centered around the beginning...of everything. He headed back down to the core, as the lure of that knowledge was too great. This ancient part of the Well provided a unique answer to life before life began. The answer started at a point before what scientists thought of as the "Big Bang." It showed him there were billions of Earth-like planets that existed outside of a semi-fluid medium connected to it by rivers of light. Then he saw it, an unknown number of things/beings flooded into those stems of light, *must be the invasion the core mentioned,* he thought. Something called X-points were popping up, almost as if to stop those things, which were colliding with everything. The X-points were mostly at those 'stems of light' that exited the semi-fluid substance, but many landed in the center of some of those planets. This released massive amounts of energy, pushing those planets away from this place, out across the expanse that became his existence. For those where the X-points landed in the planet, they sank to its core and now provide the heat that keeps the core of those planets molten.

Then he watched as if in slow motion, the history of how time began. Those things now trapped at the core burst through the X-points that seemed to be placed in their path and they hurled themselves into the planets. All of those planets were teaming with life.

What they did there was not revealed to Brill. Next, the Knowledge Well seemed to emerge in an instant from the semi-fluid substance to contain the plague infecting the beauty of what was. Those X-points caused so much destruction to the beauty, the sadness of that event spread throughout Brill's existence. The invaders seemed to cause the planets to explode out across the expanse of the void in what we call the "Big Bang." What remained of them were then sucked into the core when the Knowledge Well was created as it emerged out of that semi-fluid substance, preventing any more of them from invading. The questions he now had about who or what these things were, and why would they invade, were effusive ones that kept circling upon themselves without a definitive answer. Having a sense of frustration, he gave up for now. Then he was forcibly rejoined to some, but not all of his consciousness as the nanobots were pulling him back into his mind.

4

RISE UP

ine Months After the Destruction of Avalon
Coming around with a sensation of immense pain returning to all his appendages, the canopy opened up, and the IV was automatically removed from his arm. Groggy, partly due to exhaustion from near death and the rest from the missing parts of his consciousness still trapped in the Well, he tried to exit the chair with great difficulty. His muscles grudgingly responded. He was barely able to get his legs over the edge where he promptly plopped on the ground the moment his feet hit the floor. They just didn't have the strength to support his body weight. He stayed in that spot for several hours just staring at the ground, unable to lift his head. He tried several more times to right himself, and each time, he found himself in a worse position. Finally laying prostrate on the ground, he was able to roll over on his back and fall into a deep slumber.

When he awoke, there was a bit more strength in his body. This time he was able to prop himself up long enough to search around the chair for the hidden compartments. He could not see a thing due to the minimal amount of light coming from the glow of the quantum computer. His hand roamed the bottom side of the chair to find his prize, a slot that opened up into a compartment that was stocked with freeze-dried food and several bottles of water. Another compartment yielded a flashlight, and another had clothes. Brill had planned for all contingencies and was now glad he had done so. The food and water were a welcome reprieve from his thirst and hunger. The nanobots had kept his mind alive, but his body was slowly withering away since the IV was only able to provide basic nutrients, making the nanobots low on energy as they needed neural sugars to keep powered. This prevented them from fully repairing Brill's injured body, at least until he got some proper food in him and his mind became fully active.

With his hunger abated, Brill inspected his surroundings. The power had been cut, and the darkness of this underground cavern ate up all the light from his flashlight. He found the stairwell and began the long climb upward. Halfway up he met the devastation Liam had unleashed on this mountain. The stairwell had collapsed from this point on up. Debris was everywhere, and he dared not pull lose any rocks lest the rest of debris decide to make its way on down and possibly take him with it. He carefully backed down and made his way to the chair and quantum computer. The light screen he and Sirum had put in place to block the light from this cavern was still up. Brill removed this and stumbled towards the lake in the quasi darkness. Walking down the trail, he feared it might be destroyed as well. Much to his surprise and delight, the path was clear all the way to the water with the water still flowing. Seeing this as a positive, Brill hatched a last-ditch plan, one he had contemplated long ago but never thought he would need. The plan was to get the chair and quantum computer into the lake and make his way as far as the water would take him. The computer was encased in a flotation device since that is how they got it there in the first place. Similarly, the chair floated, but it also had propellers built into it. It could be driven if need be, though he never thought he would need to do it a second time, as the first time was how they got the chair here so long ago.

Brill explored the chair and its power. Sirum had brought down a backup battery giving it extra life if needed. He estimated he was in the Well for about nine months, which allowed the primary power source to still be near capacity.

What he felt he needed to do now was to go back into the Knowledge Well, a gnawing feeling that he was missing a piece of himself, something seemed off. He felt like he had a sense of loss, possibly significant. He decided to jump back into the chair to go back into the Well one more time to see what he may have lost, just in case he never got the chance again. Lying down to insert the IV into himself, his hesitation overcame him, but something in his mind said do it now, almost forcibly pulling him into the chair. Not understanding what that meant, he was about to abandon this journey when it was more unavoidable this time, and his body felt like it was pushed into unconsciousness as he inserted the IV.

Entering the Well, he met parts of himself that were splintered off when the nanobots pulled him out earlier, just before his body died. Those parts were not able to reconnect when the bots pulled him back to his mind. This time his exploration was different, as his mind was extrapolating the interpretation of his surroundings and pulling in the information his consciousness was learning, allowing him to see and sense far more than he was previously able to do, mostly with the help of the quantum computer's calculation speed. He now saw/felt the source of his fear, that evil trapped in the core. Yet he knew they were able to reach out and grab him anywhere in this place, if they so desired. Those splintered parts of his consciousness that had been left here began to rejoin him and fill him up with even more information.

Exploring around and through this place, caution was key. He came across many minds that were linked into this place. Though he could not sense them, he suspected they could not sense him either. Starting to poke through the reasoning on that, the answers that returned were minds in different points in time spanning across all of history. These minds were somehow immune from the beings at the core, or the beings at the core were using them somehow. Their access here was independent of time. Their minds were always here and accessible to other minds throughout history, adding to the brilliance of their time in history. Looking deeper into the answers that returned to this line of questions, he saw that those in his present reality could form a quasi-connection to him and he likewise to them, but only those within the realm of time that his body was still living. He looked for stronger consciousnesses to see the types of questions they were trying to answer. Most had simplistic questioning, the basic math or music sorts, nothing spectacular nor very insightful. He finally found one that was posing interesting questions. Some ranging from quantum mechanics to building ships for interstellar travel.

He got a bit too close to the consciousness that was asking about interstellar travel and became acutely aware of its thoughts. Brill was certain this being was aware of him, after Brill's consciousness collided with his. He was very curious if this was someone from Earth at some point during his lifetime.

The language at first was garbled, but then the Well provided the means to translate, as his mind interpreted the stranger's words. "Greetings," it said after the translation.

Brill's reply was hinged in a bit of trepidation, especially after his encounter with whatever existed at the core. "Who are you?"

"Like you, I am seeking answers."

"What answers do you seek?"

Before the stranger could answer, the Well provided an answer. Brill reached out to grab more of the information when the stranger tried to use his will to intervene, briefly stopping Brill from learning that critical knowledge. Being connected back to his organic mind allowed his consciousness to be stronger here than before, and he was able to start unraveling that tidbit of information. As he did so, he was opened up to the existence of this evil, an alien race called, "Nurizzi." He was shown the location of that planet in relation to Earth, which at light speed was about five years away.

The more he saw, the greater his fear. These were the remnants of the beings trapped at the core, essentially their children. The images shown to Brill took him back to the moments before the Well came into existence. In that instance, the beings at the core tore through the place where the semi-fluid substance existed. That substance seemed to go on forever, and from it rose rivers of light like stalks of a flower. Every river of light had a planet at its terminal point. This very much reminded Brill of a flower. Focusing in on the planets, Brill could sense they were teeming with life. He couldn't count the number of them, billions, trillions, or more he didn't know. Those invading beings interrupted whatever that river of light was that flowed out of the semi-fluid substance. The resulting scene showed a hideous tear due to the X-points emerging at each point where a planet was attached to the end of the river of light. The X-point was how those beings were trying to infiltrate those planets. Such destruction in the beauty of what was. The semi-fluid substance holding the planets and rivers of light tightened up, pulling away from the planets and leaving only the X-points connected to the planets. In the next instant, the whirlpool of light he knew as the Knowledge Well formed from the rivers of light and encased these beings, trapping them into that core region like a fly in honey, but pieces of them splintered off through the X-points down to the planets before being caught by the Well. They only made it to one planet out of all of them. The image he now saw was more vivid than before. It showed him that these Nurizzi were formed when the largest piece of the beings at the core had broken themselves apart to enter the planets. The only planet they made it to contained the Nurizzi. This being that called himself a Nurizzi was looking for his purpose and a path to the core in order to find his ancestors. Brill's sense of fear grew to uncontrollable levels as those beings at the core had shaken the very foundations of his consciousness.

BRILL WAS TRYING to unwrap what the Nurizzi were doing on Earth when he got a sense of something coming for him. He didn't have eyes in here, but he 'saw' images through what his consciousness translated, as that is how he was taught to learn in here. The image he perceived was that of a deep dark shadow entangling him. What made up his consciousness pulled and pushed against the darkness. He was being pulled back into the core. Not knowing how to navigate this place, he reached with his consciousness to grasp anything he could find. The Nurizzi was also fleeing just out of his grasp and trying to head into that thing. His mind/body perceived his peril and gave his consciousness just enough boost to grab a sliver of the Nurizzi...with Brill in tow. The Nurizzi realized this and turn out of the core into the peripheral regions. It was barely enough for him to clear that suction into the core from whatever was in there trying to pull him down. Back to the periphery, Brill began to frantically search for an exit. Still being pulled by the Nurizzi, he perceived more of this alien's thought and found it to be the same creature as the Roswell Grays that had visited Earth so many years ago. They had been to Earth over the last several hundreds of years and were there now. This he glimpsed in snippets of images with no reason behind it.

Brill lost his grip on the Nurizzi and drifted on the outskirts of the Well, desperately searching for a way out so to get back to his body. There was a pressing need to understand the X-points. Those were beginning to become clearer when a way out was revealed to him. These X-points were rips in the very fabric of space which were created by those first beings at the core, in their effort to invade this universe. Since then, many other aliens followed their lead and also tried to invade Brill's universe. The X-points now created a means for them to influence the Nurizzi, as they were part of those 'core' beings. The first ones to invade seeded themselves on the Nurizzi's world and created their race out of the native beings there. Now the X-point above the Nurizzi planet was actively transmitting thoughts from the beings at the core down to their children on the Nurizzi home world. Until Brill arrived here, those beings at the core were not aware of Earth. Now they knew Earth had advanced far enough to enter the Well.

The image of X-points near and in the core of nearly every inhabited world in the universe gave Brill the avenue he needed to escape. He desperately wanted to know how to wield the power of the X-points. Even with the knowledge at his disposal here, using the X-points as a portal to travel to and from the Well, or even from planet to planet, was not information that was readily available. Those creatures at the core had been searching for such information since before time began. Brill was not aware of their failures, and in his hubris, he set out to utilize the X-points in any way he could. He was a willing participant in any bad decisions he knew he was bound to make.

Brill began to figure out that an X-point seemed to be some type of outlet for energy from his universe. The more Brill studied the X-points from inside the Well, the more he figured out, and everything Brill learned, so did the beings at the core. It seemed to him that X-points released energy from one part of the universe into another. Brill suspected each star contained a large X-point at its heart. He guessed that planets with molten cores like Earth also contained an X-point deep in its center and that may be what causes the Earth's core to be so hot. The energy that fed the stars and the core of planets was the outlet for the universe to balance energy that builds up in one place and needs to be released to somewhere else. These X-points were those release spots. Having rejoined with the rest of his splintered consciousness, he now had a connection to his corporeal body. This connection kept growing stronger and stronger, the more and more his consciousness became whole, enabling him to see how to exit this place and get back into his body.

ONCE BACK IN HIS BODY, the nanobots, with the aid of the quantum computer, began processing the massive calculations needed to solve this problem of using the X-points as transfer portals. The nanobots, directed by the quantum computer, created a quantum bridge between the dark matter and the X-point, but only for a fraction of a fraction of a nanosecond. Brill went back into the chair and tried to enter this X-point from the Well. That fraction of a nanosecond was just enough for Brill to reach for the closest X-point to Earth that he could see. His consciousness entered that X-point from the Well, and Brill was instantly splintered into pieces, as every part of his consciousness was now pulled into all the adjoining X-points in planets and stars. Brill could not 'see' that this spot in the Well was a nexus of X-points; all of them actively pushing and pulling energy into and out of the Well. Brill began to split into billions of pieces when something like a bolt of lightning struck him, giving him more strength of consciousness, causing his being in here to reform. He knew what it was in that moment, the lifeline to his body.

The nanobots had found the path from his body to the X-point in the Well and activated it, connecting both sides of his consciousness, the part connected to his body and the parts that were splintered across the Well's X-points. Brill utilized the Knowledge Well to gain a minuscule piece knowledge. Just what he needed to exit the X-point and return to his body without the enemy following him, so he thought.

Before all of Brill's consciousness was pulled back into his mind, he was able to devise a plan on getting the chair and computer out of the cavern and to a new location. His mind had every detail of the underground river, with its speeds and depth, along with the knowledge of every exit point and all the tools he had available to him down there. That information poured into him as he returned to his body.

Rising up out of the chair, he thought a bit on what his consciousness had just perceived and whether there would even be a need any longer to rescue the chair and computer from the cavern. The solutions that the Well provided had showed him how to motorize the computer and chair along the river and find his exit point, as well as how to potentially enter back into the Well without the need of the chair and computer.

IN HIS BODY NOW, he worked on getting the quantum computer into the river, something that weighed several thousand pounds. This was accomplished by taking the battery core out of one of the spent batteries and melting it with a propane torch that was left in the cavern. The battery core was made out of Promethium and Praseodymium, both of which when melted and kept at one hundred degrees centigrade would create a super thin layer that would not compress, essentially allowing anything on top of it to float. A nice bit of knowledge the Well helped him learn. Brill melted the battery core and spread it over the underside of the quantum computer. He was fortunate to have a hoist that was built into the cavern when he and Sirum had moved it here. That is how they were able to get it to its current place and was now the means he used to lift it off the ground. Once it was in place, he used the propane torch to get it to the temp he needed, as the surface of the computer was a conductive metal and resonated the heat nicely back into the metals. At one hundred centigrade that thin layer of metals spread out beautifully on the computer, allowing him to easily move it to the water. It levitated there for a short while till the water cooled it below its critical temperature. With that in place, the chair required much less effort to get into the water with its built-in wheels. Brill connected the quantum computer to the chair with a tow cable. Using the chair's built in propeller system, he began the long trek to his exit point. Before he began his trip, he loaded up the several thousand-foot tension cables, hyper strong compression springs, petroleum jelly, and thermite powder; items that Sirum had left behind for one reason or another.

The trek down the river was slow going, as the chair did not have much in the way of propulsion with its battery powered propeller now pushing thousands of pounds of quantum computer. Brill's sense of time was lost in this place with only the light of his head-lamp giving his eyes any respite from the darkness. It took upwards of eight hours for him to arrive at his destination, a landing where the river turned in a sharp bend.

The chair rolled right up on the landing, but the computer proved more challenging and remained in the stream. Getting the computer out of the water and onto the landing was the most challenging part, requiring engineering he had yet to learn. Without the help of the Well, Brill was sure he was unable to solve this problem. Even with the danger of those creatures in the Well, Brill decided to go back. With the chair safely out of the water, Brill climbed in and drifted into that nether world to figure out the engineering of getting the computer out and over to the mineshaft. When his conscious coalesced to the edge of that center light, he stayed in this spot and began to query the Well with his problem. While watching those solutions appear, he managed to muster one of the disguises he had learned on his way out last time which helped to prevent him from being found by those beings at the core. Knowing a bit more about the X-points, he located the one that would pull him back to his body. He seized that opportunity once he found it along with the much needed answers, not wanting to give those creatures any opportunity to find him. Little did Brill know those creatures were watching and analyzing everything he did in the Well each time he appeared, including how he could come and go at will.

Adding his list of supplies at hand to the query, different solutions started to appear. He combed through them one after one, looking for the solution that would meet his time demands and limited supplies. Having gone through dozens of potential solutions, he opened one that looked better than the rest. This exercise showed him that not everything he learned from the Well was always applicable, as there were many theoretical solutions with few that could be played out in reality. Simulations seemed to be a lacking quality of this place, or at least he had yet to figure out how to make it run through the solutions to see how they would actually work. He absorbed the best solution and returned to his body through that X-point.

The time stamp in the chair showed him to be gone only a fraction of a second, yet it seemed to him he was there for hours, must be something to do with relativity and how time was not expressed on that quantum scale. Returning to his conscious state, Brill put his solution into action.

The first step was to mix the thermite and petroleum jelly

together and then coat the coil springs with that mixture. The next step required attaching those coils to the bottom of the computer. Using the high-tension cable, Brill was able to attach the coils to the legs of the computer while it was still floating in the stream. Brill scoured the cavern overhead and spotted a point on one of the rock spires that would serve his purpose. This particular spire had a groove around the top, perfect to utilize as a pulley. Coating the steel wire with petroleum jelly gave it the reduction in friction he needed. With the additional high-tension cable, Brill was able to create a lever.

Levers are only as good as the number of pulleys you have to differ the force. This makeshift lever was only good enough to raise it up, but he needed to get it onto the landing. Pulling with all his might, Brill was able get it high enough to start it swinging. He knew this was going to hurt like hell, but he would have to push it with one hand and hold the cable in the other. Then he would let it go when it was far enough onto the landing during the seesawing back and forth. When it hit the apex of its swing, Brill let go of the cable he was holding tightly in his right hand. The cable moved in the direction of the opposing force, which was his hand. Brill let out a scream of intense pain as it rapidly pulled away from his hand, slicing deeply into his palm. Blood was gushing everywhere, almost causing him to lose consciousness. He fumbled for the remaining thermite powder. In this light-headed state, Brill threw a pile of the powder down on the ground. With his left hand, he pinched the cut as closed as he could while trying to embed enough of the powder into the wound to achieve the desired effect when he set it on fire. Crawling to the chair with the use of only his left hand, he found the lighter and managed to get a flame going. Sitting with his back against the chair, he braced for what was going to come next. With that flame, he set the thermite powder on fire to try to cauterize the wound. After a long stream of profanities, the pain finally caused him to lose consciousness.

"Water. I need water." Brill kept mumbling to himself when he came to. As best he could, he made his way to the stream and slid over the edge. His body was now raging with fever and the cool mountain stream helped to take the edge off. The nanobots were hard at work repairing the damage to his hand, but they were not programmed to take care of microbial invaders such as those coursing abruptly through his system. Once he hit the stream, with his back against the edge of the landing and water up to his chin, he passed out for what amounted to several hours. The level of the river must have risen a few inches, as it was now lapping into his mouth and bringing him to as he coughed the water out of his lungs.

Brill came to his senses long enough to realize that he was in dire need of medical attention. Surveying his surroundings, he decided that his best bet would be to get into the chair. It took every ounce of energy that he could obtain to get himself out of the water and into the chair. Once there, he managed to hook up the IV and close the canopy before he passed out, a move that proved to be his saving grace as the IV was loaded with antibiotics and electrolytes. Between the IV and the nanobots, Brill had a chance. After three weeks in the chair hooked to an IV, Brill's fever started to subside, allowing his body returned to some semblance of normalcy. His eyes opened. It took several minutes to focus on what had transpired. The first reaction was to look at his right hand which was now almost as good as new, minus the excessive scarring. Even with the nanobots fully powered from his neural fluids, they could only do so much. Macro repairs were beyond their abilities.

The canopy opened, and the stale cave air shocked his lungs. But it was refreshing because he knew he was lucky to be alive. Rummaging through the stash of food in the chair, he found a few energy bars and gobbled those up. With his hunger abated, he was now able to focus on getting the computer over to the mining elevator shaft that had long ago been abandoned. The plan, which he had set out to accomplish, was to utilize the kinetic energy trapped in those coil springs. That was the purpose of coating them with petroleum jelly embedded with thermite. While in the Knowledge Well, he had calculated the exact length of fuse he would need to get the springs to all light simultaneously. When all fuses are lit, the flame should arrive on all four springs at the exact same moment. When the thermite on the coil springs ignited, it would heat the springs all at once, causing them to expand simultaneously. That should have the effect of causing the springs to bounce, which will allow movement in any direction if the computer has a force applied to it. Brill used this little bit of physics and chemistry to essentially push the computer with very little effort over to the elevator shaft. Once there, he had to steady it for several minutes until the heat dissipated from the springs and it settled into place. Getting it to the surface was a matter he would deal with later. For now, he just needed to get himself to the surface.

STANDING beneath the long unused elevator shaft, he looked up and saw nothing but darkness. By his estimates from survey reports from this area, the shaft was likely a mile beneath the surface. There were no guarantees that it had not collapsed at some mid-level, but he had no other choice than to try. If he kept going in this underground river, he was not sure if it would be completely submerged or still have caverns, so he determined he had to stop here and push upward. The rock was a granite blend which made climbing easier than a sandstone would have. He was able to find purchase for each hand and foot going up. Ten minutes into the climb, his whole body ached. A mile of this was going to be excruciating. He suspected there were several landings along the way where miners long ago had carved out some cavern perpendicular to the shaft. It took an hour of agonizing climbing to get to that first mining cavern, a much-needed respite. Brill took his time there, nurturing his thirst and hunger. It took some intense will power to get moving. This cycle repeated itself four more times. Twelve hours later, he reached the summit. As Brill crested the top of the shaft, he lay on the cavern floor for some time before exploring his surroundings.

Finding an escape was his primary goal now, as he panned the walls for an exit. Nothing was giving any clues as to how to get out of there. He was thinking this place was so old and long since abandoned that every entrance had to be sealed to prevent people from the hazards of this place. As Brill looked around, he saw the moisture and trickle of water down some of the walls. Though he was hoping for a quick exit, he soon realized it would be a greater challenge than anticipated, so he followed the water.

The incline the water traveled began to narrow as he climbed up, soon scooting on his belly with arms extended in front of himself. He knew the danger of this approach. If he pushed too hard into a crevice in this position, he would get stuck and die there. Fortunately, the channel was maintaining its width, but unexpectedly dumped into another cavern where Brill went head over heels and crashed to floor below. Nursing a few broken ribs and arm, Brill was able to regain his footing. This place showed the daylight from the outside. To Brill's luck, the sun was just rising and provided him the light to the exit. Squinting, he followed those rays of light to a break in the wall where the sun washed over his body and blinded him with pain from the brightness. Overjoyed and still squinting, he made his way out and marked the entrance with some of his clothing, as he did not want to lose this location, or he would never locate his chair and computer. The map he had viewed years ago indicated this area was close to Reno. Based on the travel of the underground stream, he suspected he was just east of it, so he turned his back to the sun and headed west.

5

WHERE IS EVERYBODY?

Over 9 months after the destruction of his underground lab, Brill finally arrived in Reno. The town was deserted, except for the occasional sighting of an animal off in the distance. No traffic and no people, just sounds. He was certain those were something akin to a chimpanzee, but he was concerned he was hallucinating, as chimps could not be here. Brill thought he must be going crazy as there were no wild primates in this part of the world. He went from shop to shop and could not find a soul, so he made his way to a neighborhood. Knocking on door after door, every house seemed dead with no noise and no lights inside. The last door he knocked on, the twentieth, slowly opened with each knock.

An uneasiness came over Brill as he stepped across the threshold. He shouted, "Is anyone home?" No answer, but the smell almost floored him. Walking deeper into the house, the powerful smell of death, feces, and urine turned his stomach. Making his way to the first bedroom, he saw where the origin of the smell was coming from. Two highly decomposed bodies, probably several weeks since death, were emitting the foul odor. His examination of the human like figures showed something gruesome: the entrails were strewn about the floor and feces was all over the walls as if something had ripped them open from crotch to chin and then marked the territory with their feces. He grabbed a dish towel to cover his mouth and nose after soaking it with water, and then he made his way through the remaining rooms. Each one showed a similar scene, dead bodies that were covered with hair and ripped open. The face of one of the bodies looked like it had been eaten off. Not being sure if this was the only house with a death scene, Brill busted down the door of the neighboring houses. Same thing in each house, not one living creature. Even the pets had died, though they looked like they were half eaten.

Brill couldn't understand how such devastation could have occurred. Some type of disease or wild animal on the loose had rampaged this city. At one of the houses, Brill found a smart phone that was unlocked and plugged in, so he started searching the web. Every news site had similar stories: some type of wild animals were on the loose across Nevada and California. Brill sunk in the chair, hoping that Liora and Sirum had escaped the fate of these folks. It finally hit him, what if those animals were still here? He needed to move now.

With little hope left, he found a set of keys. He was able to locate the truck that they were paired with in this home's garage. Realizing he was still a wanted man, he went back into the house and fumbled through the belongings until he located the owner's wallet. This man had no resemblance to Brill, but it would now become his new identity. He paused before he opened the garage to leave, thinking he should cover his tracks. The master bedroom with the two rotting corpses was near the kitchen, making it easy to set up an accidental fire. In the kitchen, he found some candles and matches, which he took to the master bedroom and lit. He roamed the house to make sure all windows and doors were shut. The stove was gas, providing him the opportunity set the house on fire once the gas burners were set to full open and not lit. Lighting the candles and making sure the garage was shut before he left, Brill made his way to a gas station and loaded up on food and drink while the truck was filling up.

As he was finishing gassing up, he caught a glimpse out of the corner of his eye of something running at a high speed towards him. Turning his head to see what it was, a screeching, piercing cry caused him to lower his head on instinct and put his hands to his ears, not realizing that this action probably saved his life. A very large chimpanzee-like primate flew over his shoulders, right where his head would have been had he not lowered it. Instinctively, he jumped into the cab of the truck and slammed the door shut. None too soon, several other large primates slammed into the door and windshield of the truck. Without giving it a second thought, he started the truck and floored the accelerator even with the gas pump still attached, running over several of those animals. The rearview mirror showed the street now covered with these animals, hundreds of them all running after him at a very high speed. His heart rate slowed enough for him to regain his thoughts, realizing that a primate had scratched his arm from the shoulder down to his elbow. The adrenaline must have been flowing through his veins, as he never felt a thing.

The trip to Vegas was a nerve-racking drive, looking out for any of those animals. The trip seemed to last forever, and now Vegas itself was even lonelier. It was a complete ghost town with the occasional sighting of a shadow that may or may not have been those primates. He searched Liora's place and was relieved to not find her. Sirum's place was equally desolate. He broke into a few other random residences to see if the homeowners had the same fate as the people in Reno. There were several decaying bodies in residence after residence, though they didn't quite look human. Some were fully covered with dark hair. The odd thing about these bodies is that they were partially clothed: some in underwear, and one still had a bra on though the hair made this thing indistinguishable from those things that attacked him at the gas station. Curiosity was now getting the better of his fear, and he had to know what happened to these people and what had killed them. Suspecting that the coroner had autopsied the first few cases, he made his way to the morgue. If he was right, those bodies would be in cold storage, as well as the samples of fresh bodily fluids that they would have taken and stored in the fridge as well.

It took some searching, but he finally found the morgue tucked in behind the police station. Entering something that looked like it was right out of a crime scene, hairy bodies everywhere in deep decay with blood and other bodily fluids covering the walls and floor, Brill was dismayed at his hopes for survival. One of the bodies looked like it may have been the coroner, as it was still wearing a lab coat. The smell was overpowering, but he pressed on and found the logbook. He needed to make sure that he found the right bodies, or his efforts would be in vain. The computer screen was in open mode, an unsuspecting break for him as this allowed him to search the coroner's notes and try to understand what was going on at that time. He started five entries above the last on the list, which was a female in her mid-forties who was apparently in good health and then suddenly fell ill. Her family called it in, where they said she came down with a heavy productive cough, which meant she was coughing up phlegm. She had no signs of a fever, but within a day passed out to never wake again. The second day in her bed, her nose started to bleed and never stopped. The coroner did an autopsy that showed all organs had shut down due to her blood vessels losing integrity and breaking open, meaning she basically bled out internally. His notes also said she exhibited some strange skin condition where her skin started growing massive amounts of hair. The coroner noted that he had to shave her abdomen and chest to make clean cuts into the body. Her caregivers, her family, took ill about a week later. They were the last four on the list and also showed similar symptoms of strange body hair growth. Additional notes indicated that the coroner then became ill with similar symptoms of a bleeding nose and rapid hair growth. Quickly after, everything shut down due to the outbreak. The notes in the logbook soon became illegible and ended with a scribble he could not translate. The fluids on the wall and floor must have been from those who worked there and could not get to a hospital, which resembled the feces on the walls in the house in Reno. Brill located the bodies of those last five on the list, pulling them out of the chill boxes. He took samples of his own, tapping into the spine to get at the spinal fluid, as well as tapping into the bone marrow. He needed to understand at the molecular level exactly what had happened, since he was now likely infected after being scratched by that animal at the gas station. He expected to see similar symptoms within a few days. He was now in a hurry, suspecting his time was limited before he succumbed to whatever contagion had infected these people.

With samples in tow, he rushed out the door of the morgue and into his truck. His destination would be his former lab at the hospital. He hoped they had left it untouched, and that it didn't contain any of those animals, as the lab had his dad's notes and former research. The hospital was in even worse shape than the morgue. This time the smell was so strong that he had to grab a heavy cotton shirt to cover his mouth and nose. His first destination in the hospital was the supply room. He needed a mask to cover his mouth and nose, or the smell would knock him out. Rifling through the storeroom, he found a pack of masks and dawned one as fast as he could get it on his face. It helped with the smell but did not make it disappear.

The smell of death had always made him queasy, but this was way worse and very distracting. The elevator was still in working order, which gave him a few moments of needed rest. His office and lab were locked, which did not stop him as he had planned for such a situation. At one point in the past, his office had been a volatile psychiatric treatment ward. Medications were often needed to pass from one room to another without actually entering the room, so there was a door located in the wall. Brill had found it unexpectedly years ago and used it to hide valuables as well as to provide entry into his office if ever needed, as he could reach in and unlock it from the inside. Brill estimated where the spot was on the outside of the office and began punching as hard as he could. After two hits, his arm went all the way through. The door opened with ease, and to his surprise, the office and lab were untouched, just as he left it. He was able to find what he needed and got to work determining the cause of this disease before it was too late.

He prepped the samples and began studying them under the microscope. Nothing obvious. Why would it be? If it were obvious, then the science community would have published it, and everyone would know. This had to be something unknown or at least unknown to the public. He ran through the list in his mind. They would have looked for bacteria, viruses, fungi, mold, and so on. He sat down for a few minutes in deep thought. 'What would they not be looking for?' The answer that came to him was not one he was eager to embrace. They would have started, but more than likely would not have found what jumped into his mind. Prions and nanobots, similar to what his dad encountered all those years ago in Liam's work. This would require an atomic force microscope. The hospital had a state of the art one, thanks to his generous donation a few years ago. Brill grabbed his samples and made his way to the microbiology wing that housed the instrument.

Brill prepped the samples a little differently this time to locate any protein moieties indicative of prions, as well as the sugars that make up the nanobots Liam utilized. The scan did not show any nanobots but did show a type of prion he had not encountered. This prion was the outer coating of something else. Brill utilized methods to rip the prion out of its shell and ran an analysis on the contents it was shrouding, He found single stranded DNA. This was an odd construct, but he found a hit on some of the DNA sequences. They were engineered, some of the ones his former team had used to modify the primates at his old facility. These had some additional modifications he couldn't readily explain. He tried the scanning electron microscope to see what this construct looked like in its native form. It resembled a virus, yet didn't. Brill ran a few experiments, ripping the prion protein off of it and staining the single stranded DNA to see where it was in this thing. The prion created the outer shell of it with the single stranded DNA in its core, which made it very similar to a virus, yet much more powerful. Next, he wanted to see it in action and understand how it infected the cells. The only live cells he had were his own, if they weren't already infected with the stuff. His skin cells seemed ineffective, as it just caused them to replicate uncontrollably. He needed blood or immune cells. He was hoping the hospital still had a blood bank since it would have the living cells he needed, and the immunology lab may have the various cell types he was looking to find.

Making his way to the blood bank, he found slim pickings. The one bag left may be too old, but he took it anyway. He found the immunology lab, but it was locked tight, which was a short-term problem due to the all the staff having died here while on duty. Brill searched around till he found the bodies of what appeared to be several doctors with badges on them, though the bodies were full of hair. He grabbed a few badges, hoping one would gain him access. The first one he tried was rejected. The next one, to his relief, opened the door. Brill slid the badges in his pocket just in case he needed to gain access elsewhere. The immunology lab was still in good condition and the cells he needed were stored in liquid nitrogen. Having retrieved his prize, he utilized the resources of the immunology lab to figure out how this thing infected cells and possibly changed or killed people. The first cell he tried was a macrophage, which was ignored by the thing. He went down the list of immune system cells and finally found the target, two in fact. It was a central memory T cell and a dendritic cell, both from the two different types of immune systems that exist within our bodies: the adaptive and innate immune systems.

It was a fascinating process to watch how these things infected cells and cause other damage and changes. The next set of experiments he ran simulated the full spectrum of immune cells that would exist during a disease response. It looked to Brill that this construct acted like a virus, as it would find its way to the T cell and then in seconds, latch on and inject the single stranded DNA into the cell. With a virus that would be the end of the road, but this thing was different. The prion protein left the surface of the cell and took on a shape of its own and targeted other cells, like those in the skin and brain. The media he was using was blood, and he was shocked at the events that unfolded next. He did not expect the prion to have any effects on blood, but it seemed to target the Heme protein. The thing with prions is that they teach other proteins to take on their shape to become a prion. If this is what it did with Heme, then that would explain why people started to bleed out. The Heme most likely changed shape and lost the ability to hold iron, which would then cause people to not only bleed out, but to rapidly suffocate since they could no longer get oxygen from their lungs to the rest of the body. He had found a few other blood repositories in the immunology lab and tried them to see if it behaved the same on samples from different people. The first few were the same, then he noticed one to where the blood cells seemed to morph and merge into the stem cells in the culture. He kept the cells growing. After a half hour, those stem cells formed into skin cells with hair follicles. Realizing he didn't have time to wait, he ran back to his lab. Later, Brill decided to give the name "Privus" to these things since they were a mixture between prions and viruses.

Once in his lab, the safe was his target. It contained the original nanobots his dad had developed so many years ago, along with a tablet that contained the code for these nanobots. He set out to repro-gram the nanobots to recognize both the prion part and single stranded part of the privus in order to counteract its effects. It took him about an hour to accomplish this and another hour to replicate enough of them for an injection. Towards the end of that second hour, he started feeling light-headed and hair began to grow heavily on his arms and legs. Blood was also oozing out of his nose. Knowing his imminent peril, he took as many nanobots as had replicated in that short time. He injected them into his own heart, as he felt the need to get them to all parts of his body as quickly as possible. Locking away the tablet and nanobots, and hiding the safe again, he lay down and waited until he fell into unconsciousness. These new nanobots would supplement and teach the older ones that his dad had given him all those years ago. They needed updated coding to target and repair the privus and its damage. Until they could fully eradicate it, Brill knew his body would be in a fight for survival. He may even die. The nanobots did their job efficiently and effectively, but the toll on his body was heavy. He needed rest and time to recover. They were designed to quickly restore his blood heme. If they failed, he would die from lack of oxygen. They were to go after and destroy every trace of the privus, reverting its muscular and skin effects back to the original state before the infection. As he was still laying on his office couch after three days from being too weak to move, he thought he noticed strong hands lifting him off the sofa and onto a gurney. Everything after that was a blur.

LIAM'S TEAM had been making great progress on the primate research, so much so that Liam had briefed his superiors of the great things to come. The Swazi twins were his best scientists. They made the most improvements to the rate at which the primates were advancing in their intelligence. They figured out how to increase the size of the neuron connections, the dendrites, which is a hallmark of species that have a higher intelligence. This phenomenon is exemplified in both humans and dolphins who have a slightly higher electrical transmission rate between their neural cells due to larger dendrites. They found that using single stranded DNA to program developing neural cells to make larger dendrites, allowed them to significantly improve the cognition rate of those cells, effectively giving them an exponential increase in intelligence. This was until they hit the memory capacity wall. Increasing the cognition rate was one thing. But, if the mind is unable to store and recall information, having that intelligence did little good unless they could retain what was learned.

Those small steps were a big leap from where they were while working for Brill. The one thing Brill did was never allow them to know what each other's work did. Even though they always talked with one another, they could never figure out what the end goal was. Now, Liam had them constantly running simulations to help them understand how their efforts worked in concert with one another.

Liam gave them access to John Everly's prion research, since it was such an effective means at healing. He thought it may help their intelligence research. At first, they didn't see much of a need for it, until they ran up against the memory wall. A key protein believed to be involved in human memory is netrin, and in primates that protein is significantly shorter. Their view of memory formation and Brill's were entirely different. Brill had found evidence to support his belief that the human brain stores memory as temporal coordinates, points in time and space. He found that certain proteins code memories into spacio-temporal coordinates, a moment in time where the brain can always go back to that point past and watch it live as it happens.

Netrin was a first step in memory retention, but it was unable to retain information by itself. Liam's team was not aware of Brill's work and pursued the netrin protein as the solution. They brought in Dr. Everly's prion research after they had genetically engineered the primate neural cells to express human netrin. The twins saw that the primate netrin three-dimensional shape was different than the human netrin, so they engineered the prion to teach the primate with the genetically engineered netrin to look and behave like human netrin. They were successful with the prion, as the primates soon showed some improvements in memory retention. The twins didn't stop there and wait for things to play out, they continued to tweak and modify various neural genes. Dr. Everly's work utilized the human foamy virus, which was one they had not heard of till they got deep into his work. Use of that virus greatly improved their modifications to the primate brains and work was humming along smoothly... until the shit hit the fan.

THE BUZZING of his phone brought Liam out of his thoughts. As Liam reached for his phone, an uneasy feeling came over him. The number indicated it was from the Area 51 team, likely the Swazi twins telling him of more progress. When the video came up, it was not anyone from his team. "Colonel Rhett, sir."

"This is Colonel Rhett."

"Sir. A situation has begun to occur in the primate facility with your team." He said with a salute over the video chat.

"At ease airman. Is something wrong with my team?"

"The primates have fallen ill. A few of them seem to be sick."

"Wake my team and have them assemble at the lab. I will call there in ten minutes."

As Liam dialed up the lab, his team was groggy at this early hour of the day. He addressed the twins, "These were your experiments. What happened to them?"

"Colonel Rhett, we just started analyzing the blood samples. We will have an answer for you within the hour."

"Have you isolated the sick ones?"

"Yes sir. We are going through the tapes of the last few days to isolate all those with whom they had contact. We don't know the origin of the illness and want to take precautions."

"Uh-oh." One of the other team members exclaimed.

"Don't wait for me to ask, tell me what it is."

"Could be a problem sir. We see one of your staff interacting with the primates about an hour before they got sick."

"Send the video to the rest of team and have base security isolate him. When you get an answer, immediately text me."

"Yes sir," the twins said in unison.

Liam's team identified the enlisted man but were too late in intercepting him before he went on his leave. That sergeant was planning on visiting his fiancée in Las Vegas and had already arrived by the time they identified him. Liam gave the order to immediately get them both and have them isolated. They were hard to find, as they were casino hopping. They had made their way to their seventh casino for the night when they hopped in their RV and headed for Lake Mead. The guards searched and searched but did not locate them.

SEVERAL DAYS LATER, the sergeant's cough was now more intense, but he still felt good enough to hit the casino one more time before heading back. He recognized the card dealer. She had been the one to deal him cards when he was on his losing streak a few nights before.

It was a give-and-take on winning and losing before he was able to win his money back and then some. He and his fiancée bid her farewell and took their winnings to go celebrate. The restaurant was packed, being a Saturday night. His cough seemed to intensify as they waited for their table. They tried to get a corner table near the outside of the room to isolate themselves, so he would not cough on everyone. After dinner he was beat, but before they retired for the night, they capped off the evening as any young couple in love would do. Leaving for the base, he blew her a kiss due to his cough. She watched him leave with tears streaming down her face and a slight tickle in her throat.

When the sergeant and his fiancée had been playing blackjack in one of the casinos that last night, he covered his mouth to restrain a few of the coughs. With that same hand, he touched the cards to see what he had in his hand. This scene was repeated several more times before they left. The card dealer at his table had picked up those cards, as well as the chips he lost in several bets. She then scratched her nose with the hand that had just touched his cards, unknowingly transferring prions to her body. She happened to be suffering from the autoimmune disease lupus and had contracted the Epstein-Barr virus some time back. It took several days for the prion to establish itself in her body, as her lupus medications held it at bay until it synergized with the Epstein-Barr virus. That combination at first had little effect on her, until it combined with the compliment cells of her immune system. With the prion's help, a subtle rearrangement of the Epstein-Barr virus happened. The virus swapped out its protein coat for the prion. Then it made its way to the small intestine where it picked up some of the single stranded DNA that was being shed by the cells that lined the intestines.

The card dealer was on duty for the rest of the weekend. She probably interacted with five hundred people throughout the course of her shifts. With each shift since the second contact with the sergeant, she had been heavily coughing and was ingesting cough drops like candy. Her shift was over on a Tuesday night, where she clocked out and headed for home. Noticing the hair on her arms and legs growing and becoming an obvious sight, she was concerned something was wrong with herself. She began to feel worse and called her mom. The exhaustion of sickness overcame her. In addition to being extremely tired, she now also faced the embarrassment of hair growing heavily on her face and neck. She would not even go shopping for groceries. Her mom and dad took shifts in bringing her groceries and taking care of her.

The cough worsened, and she eventually passed out. When her nose started to bleed uncontrollably, they called an ambulance. She died on the way to the hospital. Her mom and dad soon started showing similar symptoms within a week. Though her brother didn't get sick, the hair began to grow all over his body. They made their way to the doctor before their symptoms worsened, not realizing that those that they came into contact within the waiting room would soon take on their illness and pass it on to others.

⁓

Four Months Before Brill Emerged

Liam had returned to North Carolina where he was meeting with Sirum and Liora to send them on a new adventure. Liam's phone buzzed with an update.

"Yes, Captain?"

"Sir, the sergeant that interacted with the chimps became very ill after he returned."

"Yes, I expected that. Did the twins treat him?"

"Yes sir. Their treatment worked at first, and then he died."

"You did the best you could Captain. I will call the base to order and address them."

"Sir, there is more."

"Go on."

"A similar illness has shown up in Las Vegas, but it is behaving differently."

"What do you mean...differently?"

"Sir, the civilians that are falling ill are reporting heavy coughs, followed by bleeding through the nose, and then death. Yet, some of those contacting it are staying alive, but they seem to be devolving into some type of primate, or at least that is how people are describing them."

"How many?"

"Twenty-four and counting."

"You suspect more?"

"Yes sir. This seems to spread by interaction with the infected, and the first one to fall ill was a card dealer that interacted with the Sergeant."

"So, we may have an epidemic in the making."

"Possibly, sir."

"Do we know the cause?"

"No sir. The team has analyzed everything and cannot find a causative agent. It is different than the Sergeant's symptoms."

"Thank you, Captain."

Liam hung up and then immediately called the Area 51 base commander. "General Tims, this is Liam Rhett."

"What do I owe the pleasure Liam?"

"Unfortunately, not a social call. A situation is developing as I am sure you are aware. I need for you to lock down Las Vegas and the surrounding states and quarantine everyone in place."

"How the hell do you expect us to do that?"

"Call the governors and have them issue the orders. If we don't get this under control, it will wipe us out in a matter of weeks."

The next few hours were chaotic as people panicked and fled the city in every direction. The military had to wait for the governor to issue the orders before they could act, as it was not yet a national emergency. That took many hours and word started to get out, which caused the panic and premature fleeing. During that time, over a thousand people had dispersed to neighboring cities in Arizona, California, and Wyoming. The death toll started to mount, as did those who were changing into some type of animal. Airlines immediately ceased flying, and cars filled with entire families were turned away at state borders in New Mexico and Colorado.

Over the next few hours, the tide was stemmed as weather early on had prevented anyone infected from flying out to the East over the Rockies. It was enough of a delay that allowed for containment of everything West of the Rockies until the airlines could completely shut down flight travel. The unknown contagion, as it was called, killed most and changed many people into animal everywhere West of the Rockies, like a Tsunami emanating in every direction from Las Vegas. Over the next four months, there were more than thirty million dead with five million changed into some type of animal that looked like a small gorilla. There was no way to disinfect the area, so they kept it quarantined until they could figure out the cause and issue a vaccine...maybe a cure. Under Liam's command, the Army was going to burn everything to the ground, as they were fairly certain fire would kill everything.

Four Months Later, Nine Months Since the Destruction of Brill's Desert Facility

"Colonel Rhett, look at this sir." One of his team flashed up a satellite image.

"Is that a moving vehicle?"

"Yes sir, see this movement over the last few days? It started in Reno and then made its way to Las Vegas."

"How could someone still be human enough to drive a truck?"

"Unknown sir. Could be the one in a billion that is resistant to this infection."

"Where is this person now?"

"He or she is at the University Hospital."

"Where did they go before then?"

"They went to a residential area, a gas station, and then to the morgue in Las Vegas. From there to the hospital."

"That is an odd route to take. Where in Reno did they originate?"

"Sir, we traced the heat signature back to an abandoned mine shaft up in the mountains. From there they walked to the city and

made their way to several residences and picked up a vehicle at one
of them. With a few stops along the way, they then made their way to
Las Vegas."

A smile crossed Liam's face when he heard the entry point of this
individual. He thought to himself, could it really be? Could Brill have
survived so long underground? Over nine months? It couldn't be. He
thought to himself, '*this Brill was always a survivor, just like his dad.*'

"Lieutenant, assemble the team and suit up. I want you to recover
this individual and bring him back to the Area 51 base in isolation."

"Yes sir."

With that the team was gathered, and Liam monitored from afar.
They entered the University Hospital in full hazmat gear searching
floor by floor till they found Brill in his office. Liam was watching
remotely as they streamed him the whole event. "Is he alive?" Liam
asked.

"His vitals are weak sir."

"Load him up and get him back to the base."

With Sirum and Liora off to Sri Lanka, Liam was eager to see an
end to this madness. If it was Brill, he would then have a nice surprise
for Liora when she returned.

BRILL STARTED to raise is head as they lifted him off the couch.
Without any strength, he was unable to put up much resistance. They
loaded him onto a gurney and from there into a chopper. When he
came to, he was in a sterile isolation chamber with IV's hooked up to
his arm. Everyone was dressed in full hazmat gear looking at the
dozens of monitors that were taking measurements of every part of
his body. Still too weak to call for attention, he fell back asleep. A
series of painful pinches in his leg brought him out of his slumber
and brought him upright in his bed, which didn't last for long. As
soon as his head made it half-way up, the stars appeared in his eyes
and back into unconsciousness he went. After another half hour, his
eyes opened to someone speaking.

"Welcome back to us Dr. Everly." It seemed as if that soft female voice almost sang to him.

Trying to sit up again, a soft hand kept him down. "I....am glad to be back. Where am I?"

"Dr. Everly you are at Area 51. You have been here once before as I recall."

"Forgive me if I don't recognize you...with the garb and all." Brill continued, "What happened to me? I need some water."

"Certainly. A nurse will bring you some in a minute. As to what happened to you, we were hoping you could tell us."

"I don't remember much after coming to my lab. I was trying to figure out what caused all those deaths. I think I know what killed them, but it was too late to protect myself, so I administered a self-treatment."

"Please elaborate, as we cannot figure out how you are still alive and not infective."

"That is a treatment that will not work on anyone but me."

"Is that the game you are going to play? Well, have it your way. When you are better, you will talk."

Brill's symptoms steadily improved over the next few days, and he was soon eating and drinking on his own. As he convalesced, he began to see his current situation a bit more clearly that he was more of a prisoner, than a recovering patient. He was not allowed to ever leave his room and was under constant surveillance. Two weeks into his recovery, he was transferred to a new room where he had a bit more space but was still a prisoner. Just outside the door were two-armed military guards. Brill was fairly certain they were there to prevent him from leaving, rather than prevent people from entering.

He was paid a visit by his old adversary, Colonel Liam Rhett. Entering in full hazmat gear, "Dr. Everly, it's a pleasure to see you."

"Colonel Rhett, I wish I could say the same."

"Now, now Dr. Everly, let's let bygones be bygones. You have a solution to our common problem, and I need it."

"From where I sit, it looks like your problem not mine."

"Dr. Everly, you know me well enough to know I am quite able to raise the stakes to meet my needs."

"Is that a threat."

"Take it for however you like Dr. Everly, as long as I get the right answer."

"Oh, where to begin. Hmm, let's see. I was accused of murder and hunted by every law enforcement agency in the country. Then you destroyed my lab and tried to take me with it and then left me for dead. What makes you think I will tell you a damn thing?"

"Dr. Everly, I thought you might play this card. You are friends with one Dr. Sirum Lars, right?"

"You know I am."

"Well, he is soon going to be chained to the chair in your office if you don't cooperate."

"You would murder him with this plague?"

"No, Dr. Everly, that would be your decision, but there is also a chance he would survive and become one of those animals."

"I find it hard to believe even you would do something so heinous."

Liam raised an eyebrow at that comment and then his smart phone to show the image of Sirum in a van just outside the airport in North Carolina. "Your call Dr. Everly. It would be a shame if something ill were to fall on him." Brill didn't know Sirum was working for Liam.

"Let me ask you a question, I am curious Colonel Rhett. Why did your team use prions? Those were unique to my dad's work, and I thought all were lost."

"Your Dad helped to design those prions. Why wouldn't they work? And what makes you think my team used them?"

"I found the evidence. Your team's use of that specific prion enabled a harmless virus to mutate into something new, a combination of a prion for the protein shell of the virus and single stranded DNA as the core genetic material. I am calling it a privus, at least until I get a better name for it."

"You are correct. They did use the prion, as they needed it. You know very well they didn't have any clues as to what each other was doing while they worked for you."

"What could they have possibly needed that information for to do their work?"

"I didn't ask those questions, as I only needed them to make progress. So, giving them the prion and keeping them well informed of each other's work was a necessity. Plus, they consulted with the brightest mind in the world on prions."

"My father was the brightest mind on prions, doubtful anyone else would even come close." "Yes, Dr. Everly, as I said, they consulted with the brightest mind on that matter. Let's get back to how you seemed to be cured."

"Well, I am sure you knew my father used your nanobots to heal me when I was young. He also left some that were not coded for any purpose. In the short time I had between figuring out what the problem was and coming up with a viable solution, I went for a Hail Mary. I programmed those nanobots to seek out and destroy the prions while teaching the older nanobots how to heal the damage. That way, it would leave infected cells intact and prevent further spread of the privus. This then allowed the older reprogrammed nanobots to seek out and destroy the infected cells, slowly repairing my body."

"I see. We always thought he used nanbots but didn't have proof till now. I will need for you to recreate that code."

"Once I know Sirum is safe, I will."

"Consider it done. Now, I have to leave. I expect you to honor your word. You know if you don't deliver, the death of those who take your treatment will be on you."

Over the next few days, Brill had recreated the code and given it some modifications to repair damaged cells and organs, but he withheld implementing it till he could chat with Liam.

REUNION

Nine months after Brill's Death

Liam was disconnected from his feelings after Liora left. For a man in his position, this was not unexpected, but for family, he knew he had to show some of those traits that he had long ago learned to suppress. The emotional piece was one he needed to learn to embrace better, especially with family. With the potential epidemic situation that was unfolding in Nevada, he had to reach out to Liora and get her out of there now. He came up with a plan to keep her busy while the present situation was unfolding, but he would need to get her on board. The various projects and special efforts his teams were working on, as well as possible ways to keep her busy until all this was over, were all running through his head. The special secret ones would have to wait, since her role in those would be minimal. The papers on his desk outlined some recent surveillance from the Mao group out of China. There was nothing spectacular about it, but he could turn it into something of interest for Liora. His counterterrorism unit would be the right choice as their efforts weren't being fully utilized presently. He couldn't wait any longer, so he picked up the phone and made the call.

"Liora. How are you my dear?"

"Getting back into the routine of life. What's up Liam?"

"I need for you to come to North Carolina immediately. I will have a driver at your door within the hour. Pack for travel overseas and get your office in order before leaving."

"Wait. I didn't agree to anything."

"I can't tell you the reasons, but you need to leave Vegas immediately. There is a danger to you, and I need you to join me here."

"I need you to bring along a patient of mine."

"And why would I agree to this?"

"He is one of yours, a former Army medic. I am making progress with him, and if I leave abruptly, he may never be fixed. Plus, I think your medical facilities there can do something for him."

"Though I would normally resist this type of request, I'll grant it to you this time. You and he need to be ready within the hour."

She was on her way to Area 51 within the hour and arrived in North Carolina later that evening. When she arrived, she was pleased to see Sirum. She later learned of the illness she just missed and was truly glad that Liam was looking out for her.

LIAM'S TEAM was now fully involved in coming up with every detail of the Mao group and any offshoots they may be spawning since Liora's departure. They turned up the nugget Liam needed to entice Liora to join him willingly. The Mao group was showing increased activity in Sri Lanka. In normal times, this would have been of little interest to his group's efforts. However, a recent discovery of radioactive deposits there had India and Sri Lanka co-developing something. This could pose a risk, as they may be developing weapons, or worse. He knew it was just enough to entice Liora to join him and sending her there to investigate would be the distraction she needed. Now, he just needed a reason to entice Sirum to join. With Brill gone, he had seen how she depended on Sirum. Getting them both on the same project would help him win back her loyalty.

Enticing Sirum to partake was an easier task than he first thought.

Simply offering him the chance to explore the potential situation of a high energy device in the making was enough for him, especially when he learned Liora would be there. He jumped at the chance.

In the pre-dawn hours, Liora and Sirum arrived in North Carolina at the same time. They greeted each other with a long hug, both were concerned that Liam had some ulterior motive. They received the debrief from Liam's team, learning the Mao group had an interest in the radioactive deposits in Sri Lanka. As they were getting up to leave, Liam burst through the door. "I need you both to follow me now."

Rushing down the corridor to his office, he yelled back over his shoulder, "You both got out of Nevada just in time."

Liora grabbed his arm, "What's going on?"

"Not here. When we get to my office," gesturing to the door at the end of the hall which appeared to be their destination.

"Please have a seat. I am just finishing a call with my team at Area 51, and the call will fill you in on the details." Liam motioned to the chairs. Finishing the call, he turned to Sirum and Liora, "As I said, you both got out of Nevada just in time. You just heard, a highly communicable disease has started spreading like wildfire."

Liora stated, "Somehow, I think you have an involvement."

"Perceptive as usual my dear niece, but not directly," Liam retorted. "What do you know of about how Brill was healed when he was younger?"

Liora shrugged, "Not much. Brill never talked about it."

Sirum hesitantly began, "I donated my bone marrow to him."

Liam continued, "Do either of you know more of the details?"

Sirum looked at Liora and she back. Both shook their heads from side to side, indicating a no. Liam continued, "I am not sure how much Brill knew either. His dad is the ultimate genius, and he came up with a novel treatment. It is his development of a prion treatment, not the one publicly released but one specific for Brill, that healed him."

Liora spoke up, "I am guessing you're concerned that this disease has something to do with this treatment?"

"Yes, Liora. As you are aware, Brill's team started working for me at Area 51 after he ended their employment."

With an irritated look, Liora interrupted, "You mean after you ended his work."

A sly smile crossed his face. Liam continued, "My team was making progress in advancing the work that Brill had started, the ability to increase intelligence. The primate work was unique in its successes, as he was showing that the basic learning skills could be improved in them. Why he stopped the team is beyond me."

Liora interrupted again, "Yes, yes, yes, we are familiar with his work. Please get to the point."

Without acknowledging her and not missing a beat, Liam continued, "My team hit a roadblock in advancing beyond the rudimentary intelligence skills. Feeling they needed to modify the genetics of the neural cells, I gave them access to Dr. Everly and the lead scientists from Vassal Biogenetics."

All Liora heard in her anger was the Vassal Biogenetics team, and continued on in her rant, "And somehow it got out of control, didn't it?"

"You have always been quick to the point my dear Liora. To answer your question, no, it did not get out of control. Their work was measured with great progress, as they figured out how to increase the memory retention in a neural protein called netrin. From there, something happened to the primates. A Sergeant inadvertently picked up whatever was making the primates smarter, and it made him sick. Then he spread it through the casinos in Las Vegas. It is still trying to be contained, but time will tell."

"What do you want from Sirum and me?"

"I would like for you two to go to Sri Lanka and investigate what the Mao group is doing and wait this thing out." Liam provided them with enough details to whet their appetite.

"Liam, you have given us minimal details, but just enough to spark our interest. You must promise to keep working with Major Thomas whom I brought with me. His mental illness will require some of your best doctors to work with him. What kind of trouble are we walking into?"

"Liora, this time I really don't have any more details than what I have shared. As to what they are doing there, it is up to you both to find out." Liam walked them to the door, "Whatever supplies, equipment, finances, and cover you need will be handled by my assistant."

"Liam, while we are gone, I would like for your team to try to remove the tiny piece of metal stuck in Major Thomas's brain stem. Do we have a deal?"

"I'll have my team take a look at his medical condition. When you return, I'll let you know their diagnosis."

Within the hour, Sirum and Liora were outbound on a C130 transport to the aircraft carrier located in the Indian Ocean. They were to be parachuted out with the equipment that was a resupply to that carrier, a common practice and would not draw any undue attention to them.

SIRUM AND LIORA arrived in the middle of the night at a desolate spot on the coast of Eastern Sri Lanka. They were given every device imaginable with coordinates to drop points where they could request additional supplies, if and when needed. These devices were equipped with a special laser pulse that would be picked up by orbiting drones. The military loved their gadgets, and so did Liora. She missed this lifestyle, living on the edge with life and death decisions made on the fly. If it were just herself, she would be less vigilant in reducing risks, but she had Sirum to protect. That made her much more cautious and protective.

They had a rough map as to where the Mao group was located, but they needed to establish themselves with a cover. She spotted a tourist group in the forest that was on a guided tour. She spied a couple that they could 'switch' places with, but that would mean she would have to eliminate them and hide their bodies. This was the part of being undercover she detested, having to potentially kill someone to protect herself. Not liking that option, she decided for a different tactic. She and Sirum would join the tour.

To implement her rouse, she would need to check into the hotel and then actually pay for the tour, convincing the hotel staff they would catch up with the guide. This option worked out better because they didn't have to pretend to be somebody they knew nothing about and could keep their current fake identities. The tour was an unexpected gift, as it would last four days and take them across several waypoints that were of interest in observing the Mao group. They were to hit the ancient cities of Anuradhapura, Polonnaruwa, Digamadulla, and then to the cultural triangle in the center of the island with hidden rock caves and ancient sacred temples.

The first day of the tour was full of beauty for the nature lovers, less so for Liora due to the constant "oohs" and "aahs" from the tourists every time they saw some random animal or flower.

The second day was more her style of tourism as they began the tour of the ancient ruins of Digamadulla. On the outskirts of Digmadulla, she spotted the construction sites of interest. It was a massive mining operation. They had already torn up the area and had gone down about a half-mile deep. They were not worried about hiding their efforts. She noted a constant parade of trucks headed out of the area and in their direction, toward the center of the island.

They made their way next to Sigiriya, an ancient inactive magma plug from a long-extinct volcano. The Sri Lankans had beautified this area thousands of years ago, building rectangular fountains and ponds that provided a built-in natural serenity. Once they approached the area, the trucks from the mines faded off into the distance, a place Liora noted for later exploration. She was observant of all activity in this area since tourists and locals should be part of the background scenery.

A few of the folks of Chinese ancestry stood out to her due to their specific clothing. She could tell that they were trying to blend in, but it was obvious to her they were searching the crowd. Their outfits were off from what tourists would wear. She was certain it was standard Chinese military grade clothing, the kind she had observed while in the Mao group's service not so long ago. Pretending to take photos of the area, she made sure to get close up pictures of each of those that looked out of place. On their way to the hotel, Liora was thinking, '*what a stroke of luck to be at the right place at the right time to observe the Mao group and the radioactive ore mining.*' Liam sure knew how to place her where she needed to be and when she needed to be there.

After the fourth day, they were bused back down to the coastal hotel. Liora checked her and Sirum's 'tourism' Visas and saw that it was open ended. She wanted to be sure they did not have a time limit. They needed to blend and not come across as spies, as she was certain that everyone here was under observation by one group or another, and she didn't want to stand out. With that thought in mind, she made reservations at several hotels that they had observed on their tour.

She would take her time in getting to where she needed to be, which she believed was Sigiriya. Plus, she was in dire need of a vacation and was not about to let this trip go to waste. They spent about two weeks at each hotel doing the "touristy" stuff in each town, all the while taking note of things and people that were out of place. By the time they made it back to Sigiriya, she had cataloged over forty military looking Chinese 'tourists,' some of which had happened to show up multiple times where she and Sirum were.

Spotting the same Chinese 'couples' at several similar locations, she decided to always sit close enough to them to be able to listen to their conversations, since she spoke fluent Mandarin and could fully understand every word. Knowing the code words from her time with the Mao group, Liora picked up several that indicated these teams were advanced spies looking for those in power. Having listened to enough of their conversations, it was clear to her that she and Sirum were not on their radar, which gave her the boost of confidence that she needed to stay in the open and remain as tourists.

The area surrounding Sigiriya was full of worshipers from the Buddhist temples who used the pools as their meditation spots. She and Sirum also pretended to meditate, as it gave her the prime opportunity to observe people for many hours. Those from the temples were the ones the Mao operatives were following. An odd thing, she thought, these were simple peasant folks with little to no means and would be low on the socio-economic ladder with no political influence. She also followed those worshipers once they returned to their temples, curious as to why the Mao group would have an interest in them. After several days of this, Liora had enough and decided to enter one of the temples, looking for the monk in charge. Finding her person, she requested time with him to try to understand what was drawing interest to this place. The monk knew her at first sight but remained quiet till they were alone.

"Greetings my child. I recognize you from a few seasons ago."

"Me? I don't think we have ever met. This is my first time to Sri Lanka."

"We didn't actually meet. You were with your friend, the master and great teacher, Dr. Brill, and I was helping him learn the ways."

"I'm sorry, you must have me mistaken for someone else."

"I'm a simple man with little in the ways of the world to cloud my thoughts. I remember everyone I meet, especially those who enter the temple with someone as special as Dr. Brill."

"If I'm who you think I am, then you will understand why I cannot confirm it."

"Child, we all have our disguises that we hide behind. If you are in one today, then far be it from me to remove it. How can I help you?"

"I am here of deep concern for those of your sect. The Mao group has been following your believers and may be attempting to coerce them, or force them, to join their ranks."

"Thank you, child, for your warning. I take very seriously a warning from one connected to the great one. This place, this island, is special. We of the order obtain our energy from the very ground itself."

"What? Is that part of your religion?"

"Some yes, some not. This is one of the special places on Earth where we are able unite with the universe. Our thoughts become one with it, which enables us to exert our will however the world needs it."

Liora left it at that, as she was even more confused. The monk seemed to relish talking in riddles. Sirum and Liora made their way to the road, staying just out of sight, but still able to watch where the trucks were going. They followed them to a deep underground cavern. It was a cave of some sorts that had been artificially widened with a road built right down the middle of it. They came up to the entrance of the cavern and waited till dark to make their next move.

Liora was sure security would be tight, so they needed to come up with a disguise. Having enough food and water to last a few days, they could sit here, as long as needed, but the hotel staff may get suspicious if they didn't return, so they made their way back and settled in for the night, trying to come up with a plan. Nothing immediately came to her, so they slept on it. Her mind must have been in overdrive; she woke up in the middle of the night after having the most vivid dream. As the dream coalesced in her mind, she saw the solution as plain as day. The dream had spelled it out for her; they needed to become drivers of those trucks. Not an easy task, as the driver's union would control those positions, yet something money and influence would take care of. Although, there was another solution that presented the best option.

They would pose as international journalists looking to catalog the hard work of the union drivers. She utilized her military contacts and had an interview with the head of the union later that day. The ruse was received well, and she was sure a large sum of money would help to make access certain. The next day she and Sirum were assigned to two of the senior drivers, each in different vehicles. They took their time really trying to get to know these guys, as they wanted it to appear as real of a story as possible. The military assisted in the ruse by setting up a news blog for them, which was loaded with years of published stories. She and Sirum would post there daily, using specific code words to let Liam and his team know what was taking place. They devised the writing so that Liora's stories in her blog would contain half the code words and Sirum's would contain the other half. In an addition to that, they randomized the words each would use, employing a program Liam's team had devised. That way, if anyone picked up on the codes, they would not be able to make sense of them, as they were positioned within a sentence to correspond to their final position, as well as the paragraph indicating a numerical position, which created a very complex subroutine to decipher. If an individual could put those together, they had a very special mind unlike the rest of the world, similar to the savants of Brill's research.

They spent the better part of two weeks tagging along, making sure every driver knew who they were. After the second week, they were invited to the bars with the team when the shifts were done. Perfect opportunity to get uncensored information, Liora thought. She wove into the conversation multiple queries on their purpose and their orders. The more drinks they had, the more freely they shared. In fact, some were so pleased with their work, they wanted to take them both down into the caverns to show "the great build" as they called it. They mentioned that they were harvesting the metal that was called, "the connection to the universe." It was a unique kind of metal that they could only see in the dark. They were almost fearful of it, saying it seemed to avoid the light. Every time they found a vein of it, they called in the monks to bless it, afraid they would bring some curse on themselves. Finally, she was getting somewhere, she thought. Now to push this one to pull out all the info they had.

"What is the great build?"

"You are a beautiful one, aren't you, asking such lovely questions."

"Why thank you. Have another drink."

"Thanks. Don't mind if I do." guzzling down the beer. "Hell if I know, but it is fancy. Full of gadgets and lights. Something out of a movie. They use the glow in the dark metal in there, calling it the living metal. I'm afraid to ask what it does."

She kept pushing, "Can you take me there? Would they allow it?"

"Well...I don't know, but I can ask."

She handed him another beer, "If you took us tonight, would they let you inside?"

"Of course, I am the shift foreman. They will let me go in any time of day I like. What the hell, let's do it, after a few more beers of course."

Luckily Liora had a van, as they all wanted to go. She drove, since they were in no condition to drive. The couple hundred bucks she gave the bar tender allowed her to buy a cooler full of beer and snacks, plenty to last them the hour drive to the cavern. The guard at the cavern immediately recognized the foreman and was curious why they all came out there so late at night. Before he could answer, Liora chimed in, "We were partying at the bar and they felt bad that you still had to work. He insisted that we come out here and bring the party to you all still working, being a Friday night and all."

"I'm on duty, not sure if I am allowed."

"Take it, take it, take it. We aren't leaving until you join in the fun," the whole crew chanted in unison.

Liora asked, "Can we bring the rest of the crew some of these brews?"

"Hell yeah, if I am drinking, they will have my hide if I don't let them partake in this private party."

Liora and Sirum made their way around the massive underground structure in an intentionally slow pace, observing everything in sight while trying to find those on duty. They had their hidden recording devices taking it all in, capturing every aspect of that place. Each person was given a few beers and invited to join the crew down front. The last man on duty was reluctant to leave, so they gave him a few beers and began to drink with him. About an hour later, all the team came to him, as they knew this man would not leave his post. Soon, there was a party in the center of the massive device. Liora was careful not to ask too many questions about it, focusing more on the people, wanting the appearance of journalist to come through. That tactic worked to open the door for her another time, as she asked if she could come back and learn more about these guys. They were more than eager to invite her back, not giving Sirum much thought, as he always faded into the background. While continuing to go unnoticed, he spent his time poking and prodding the machine to see what it was really about.

The next night, she and Sirum showed up, right on schedule, having an appointment to interview each of the team members while doing their jobs. It was during this time, they spotted members of the Mao group walking around with the South African Swan group without fear or impunity, as if they were invited into the place or had a role there. 'This was an odd turn of events', she thought. Liam's team must have it wrong. Not only was the Mao group somehow heavily involved, but they also seemed to be connected to Connor Swan and his group. She thought, *whatever this is, it can't be good*. This complicated matters, as she was worried, they would recognize her. Fortunately, the Mao group has constant churn at the lower levels, making it so none of these folks were there when she was in charge.

None of the Swan group here were ones with which she had ever interacted. They observed the team from the Mao group and a few of Connor's employees doing the fine details on the electronics. These must have been specialists, recruited for their expertise in whatever this device was supposed to be. Sirum was able to plant a few recording devices, ones that would only transmit when they sensed an outgoing signal from the machine. This would keep them from being detected. They were invisible devices that were made out of a shimmer metal that would appear invisible in visible light. The metal oscillated at frequencies which allowed light in the visible wavelengths to pass through it, making it appear invisible. It would only show under infrared light, even then it was just an outline. Sirum invented this type of metal in his efforts to capture the background radiation of the stars. This was how he was able to 'see' dark matter and pinpoint its location in the cosmos.

His devices were already recording the machine in action before they had left the place. This odd machine was infused with a radioactive material along with this 'living metal', which Sirum suspected was very similar to dark matter. They learned this type of metal only existed in a few spots on Earth, with Sri Lanka being one of them.

The only other places were the bottom of the Bermuda Triangle, Kashmir, Malaysia, and New Zealand. Sirum's intel told him that the machine was bombarding the living metal with radioactive energy, similar to how the super collider works. The best he could surmise was that they were trying to tap into the energy of the subspace universe, or quantum universe, as it is better known. It was a clever device.

Sirum buried himself in the data stream for hours at a time. He knew the more he could learn from their failures, the more he could improve his own research, in addition to figuring out what they were trying to do. Except they weren't failing. They were actually drawing in massive amounts of energy, so much that they had to vent it off into the surrounding ocean. Sirum was so focused on where the energy was going, he missed the momentary flood of solar energy into the device. He put aside the data stream for the moment, since he and Liora were here to 'pretend' to enjoy themselves, and he was going to make the most of it.

With the devices in place, Sirum and Liora spent the next several weeks enjoying the countryside, playing up their role as tourists and journalists. This allowed the devices time to record. The rhythm of outgoing transmissions was limited and of low power. This was the info that told Sirum he needed to install boosters to amplify the signal and package it for transmission to a satellite upload. He also installed several relays and backups, just in case something was to happen to one or more of them. Always good to over prepare when in uncharted territory was his motto.

BACK AT THE HOTEL, they spent several nights going out to dinner. Sirum struggled with the feelings he was developing for Liora. He argued many nights with himself on what he should do. Should he make a move or not, and what would a move even look like? He was not good at this sort of thing and hadn't a clue where to begin. Every dating site he went to for advice had a thousand different opinions and none seemed right. He decided to let it flow and see if instinct would prove better than a well thought out plan, especially since he didn't have one. It was his turn to pick the restaurant, so he decided to make the most of it. He ordered some dishes he thought would be a good aphrodisiac, though he was a bit squeamish when it came time to eat the escargot. He waited and waited for the right moment, then he saw it...she reached for the last slice of bread. Sirum made conversation with her as she made that reach.

"Have you thought much about dating now that you have more time?" With her hand still on the bread, he reached out his hand and placed it ever so gently on hers, just light enough to evoke a tender response.

Sirum's hand was on hers and she kind of liked it. Looking at him to show feigning interest, "I've tried not to think too much about things that may make me sad. Plus, nobody is beating down my door."

Her welcoming smile gave Sirum the courage he needed. "Since we are in one of the romance capitals of the world, let's make the most of it, at least for tonight."

The thoughts racing through her head focused on analyzing the situation all the way to a 1:1 hookup with him. She knew he always had feelings for her, as he was not good at disguising those, and she was the best-looking female he had ever laid eyes on, at least that was what she was telling herself. In her head, the analysis looked like a textbook case of friendly desire. It was not unusual when losing one's best friend, to turn to the best friend's girlfriend for affection, since it is a natural turn of events. The prospect of unbridled passion for a limited time intrigued her. She missed Brill, but also had physical needs, something Sirum could fulfill in this moment. When Sirum made his move, she made it clear that this was for the physical pleasure she needed. Emotional commitment was not even on her radar, but the needs of her body trumped the needs to stay monogamous to a long dead lover.

"You realize why this will never work don't you? Though...tonight some physical relief would do me wonders."

As soon as those first words hit his ears, his hand quickly retreated from hers. He gave up so easily, aggression was not in his nature, "So...that would be a no?"

His hesitation was obvious and she reached out to assure him. "Tonight, it is about our bodies and their needs. If you can set aside your emotions, just focus on the pleasure, let's see where tomorrow takes us."

"Umm...What now?" He stammered.

With her libido fully in control, she took him by the hand, caressing it with each step, as they made their way back to the bungalow and thoroughly enjoyed one another to the fullest extent their bodies would allow.

After several months of this work, it was time to leave. They made plans to depart via a ferry. Aboard the ferry, they would take leave of it in the middle of the night in their powerboat they had attached to the underside of the craft. This was one of those special boats that Liam had built for such occasions, when a boat was needed as an escape. Getting overboard was the challenge and one in which Liora had experience from her past encounters with the Mao group. She placed a small electromagnetic pulse generator near the motor, which was an easy task as the women's bathroom was right next to it.

When she and Sirum were in place, they pushed the ladder over the side and released the underside boat. Within seconds of all that occurring, she set off the electromagnetic pulse and they clamored overboard. The boat that was being towed along had now surfaced as the ferry went dark and lost speed. She and Sirum were able to board the craft after reeling it in and then set it loose from the ferry. Once in the open ocean and far enough away from the ferry, they turned on the electric motor and made their way to the rendezvous point. The aircraft carrier picked them up on schedule, and they were returned to Liam in North Carolina.

∾

LIAM WAS PUZZLED by the turn of events that Liora and Sirum had uncovered, which was a new feeling for him, as he was always one step ahead of most situations. The Mao group appeared to be supplying top notch scientists with Connor's group supplying the manpower in Sri Lanka, all to build some strange device. The recording devices Sirum placed on it were better than having a spy in the ranks, since they were able to record every aspect of the construction and to measure what the device was going to do.

The data they had collected in the short time of their placement indicated this was not an enrichment device for Uranium 235 that could be fissioned into Plutonium, nor was it a nuclear reactor. His team had yet to decipher the end point of their efforts, and Liam was getting deeply concerned, as the amount of Uranium they were packing into this device was more than the combination of all the US nuclear reactors. This 'living metal' had him most puzzled.

$\sim$

PRESENT DAY

The moon was setting over the desert heading into dawn as Liam finished his early morning run. He used these times to clear his mind and focus his thoughts. Today was better than most as he had a lead on the device under construction in Sri Lanka. The data had filtered through on the scientists from the Mao group, allowing his team to put together a working hypothesis. What had his mind turning circles was the finding of one Dr. Brill Everly and a cure to the contagion. The timing could not have been more perfect, as Brill would be able to shed light on the intelligence. Once Sirum and Liora arrived at Area 51, he would tell them about Brill.

7

REAL LIFE

About a week after Liam's departure, Brill finally had enough of his wits about him to be of use. He realized he should have requested of Liam a criticality that would help him later, the clearing of his name. Liam was scheduled to be here next week, and Brill was set on getting him to do just that. Brill worked non-stop the last few days to get a treatment ready that would not only be a cure for anyone infected but would also be a vaccination. He was nearing the final code, which was a bit different than what he used to cure himself. The general population would not have had a previous treatment of nanobots and prions, so those nanobots would require added instructions. Brill decided to use this last bit of code as the leverage he needed with Liam.

"Morning Dr. Everly. I hear you are feeling better and back to yourself."

"Same to you Colonel Rhett. Yes, back to full strength."

"I understand you are nearing completion on your delivery of the cure."

"As you noted, and I wanted to address a bigger issue with you."

Liam looked concerned. "Is there a problem with the treatment?"

"No, not that. When we talked last, I was a bit out of my mind and was not able to tie up all the loose ends of my previous life."

A cautious smile crossed Liam's face. "What did you have in mind Dr. Everly?"

"It occurred to me that you had put my name on the most wanted list and every law enforcement agent in the world was looking for me and likely still is."

"That might have happened. I take it that will not meet your needs to establish your career back to its former glory?"

"Something like that. I wanted to ask, or more like plead with you, to clear my name of any wrongdoing and any other associated negatives with that series of events."

Liam stroked his chin, seeing a great opportunity to see how far Brill was willing to go. "I am not sure I can do that for you."

"Dammit Liam. I am giving you what you want, even with the threat to my friends. I need you to do this or..."

"Or what Dr. Everly?"

"I won't complete the code to make the treatment effective."

"Come now Dr. Everly. You talk big, but could you really have the infection of millions on your conscience, plus the death of your friend Sirum?"

"You aren't leaving me any options Liam. If I have to leave here as a criminal, then I have no life."

Smiling, Liam chided Brill. "Well done Dr. Everly. I didn't think you had it in you. I think you already knew I would do as you desired. Did you really feel you needed to threaten me?"

"Is that a yes, or are you going to double-cross me like you did my dad?"

Liam was impressed with Brill's backbone. He wasn't sure Brill would ever get this far. A lot like his dad, he thought. "Brill, don't go back to the past, it doesn't want you, and you don't want those answers."

"Liam, the past had its treasures, and I needed answers years ago, not now. I take it you are going to set me free when I am done and clear my name?"

"I think you know the answer to that. Stay in the present." As he got up to leave, turning his head over his shoulder, "We can have a very long and successful future with this business arrangement Dr. Everly. I have many resources, so think twice about ever crossing me."

Brill spoke up as Liam was about to shut the door, "You will have your cure by morning." Brill was thinking how much more he was really capable of doing. He knew if Liam ever figured that out, it would be end of his freedom.

SEVERAL DAYS LATER, Liam's team was producing the vaccine/cure on a massive scale. Brill had been flipping through tv channels when he saw an interview of Liam on some news station. Liam was touting how his best scientists had isolated the cause, something he made up, and created this vaccine and cure. Liam then pleaded to the public that everyone in the world should be injected with the vaccination, regardless if they wanted it or not. It soon became a mandate in country after country. Anyone refusing the treatment would be forcibly injected. Liam had used this opportunity to add some extra programing into those nanobots. He wanted to collect information on those injected and tag each individual, so that his team would get periodic uploads to their database of every individual in the world. It was the ultimate spy tech, all in the name of a vaccination. A type of spying that Brill detested, so he would make sure Liora and Sirum were given an injection by himself with a special cure he created just for them, without the spy code.

After two weeks of helping Liam's team, Brill was ready to go. Liam kept stalling, saying he needed to give it a few more days to be sure he was fully healed. Brill began to suspect that Liam had gone back on his word when a knock on his door brought him out of this self-grousing.

Liora wrapped her arms around him, tears streaming down her face. "Dammit Brill, where have you been? I am so glad you're alive... I've missed you so much."

He could barely find the words to express his deep emotion, "...
and I've missed you too."

They embraced each other for countless minutes, taking in the
comfort of each other's touch. After the emotions stabilized, they had
a million questions for one another.

"How are you alive? When I left you, you were dead...with no
heartbeat and no breath."

"A gift from my father." There is time for that story later when less
ears are listening. Referring to the assurance that Liam was listening.
"Tell me what has happened to you."

Raising her eyebrow, "Those stories can wait as well. When you
died...I held you in my arms, unable to believe you were really dead."

"I was, you know...dead, but continue."

"Sirum went up to fetch a battery for your chair thing. I still don't
understand what that is."

Looking worried, Brill put a finger to his lips to indicate to her not
to say any more on that. "It was a preservation device Sirum had
created a long time ago."

Understanding his concern, she continued. "Once he completed
that, we made our way out of the desert and back into the city. From
there, we got back to our lives a bit before Liam caught up with us
and sent us to Sri Lanka. I'll tell you that story later too."

He motioned to her. "Here, stick out your arm. I need to inject you
with a vaccination against that disease that spread throughout this
area a few months ago."

Liora continued on with her story, "When we got back, they gave
Sirum and me an injection."

Shaking his head indicating a no. "Well, I need to be certain,"
swabbing her arm before injecting her.

"Ouch. You aren't very good at this are you?"

"I haven't given vaccinations in such a long time."

"There is someone I need you to look at, someone that needs
medical attention."

"Is Sirum okay?"

"Not him. A patient of mine I was treating before Liam whisked us away. I made sure to bring him with me, since we were making progress."

"If you were treating him, why do you need me to look at him? I don't know much about psychiatry."

"Not that. I believe his mental condition is due to a rock or piece of metal embedded at the base of his brainstem."

"Okay. What happened to him to cause that?"

"He was injured in combat and patched up. None of the field medics were able to remove all the shrapnel, and there is a piece still there. I think that is what's causing his delusional state."

"What delusions?"

"That incident happened two years ago, and now all he hears is 'some dude with a weird name' asking constant questions."

"Sure. I'll take a look at him, but no guarantees I can do anything for him."

～

"Liam, would you let Brill examine Major Thomas, I think Brill may be able to help him."

"Liora, my team has explored every option, and they feel that if they remove the obstruction from his brain he will die."

"Just humor me. Brill is the finest neural surgeon on the planet. If anyone can help, Brill can."

"It's not my call. You will have to ask Major Thomas's permission, as I can't order him to undergo surgery. If he agrees to it, I will gladly let Brill do what he can."

The next morning, Liora was reunited with Major Thomas, who was flown in at Liam's direction. Flying made him agitated, so they medicated him, heavily. Once those meds wore off, Liora was able to get in a clear conversation for a few minutes before his personality fluctuated.

"Major Thomas, welcome to Nevada."

"Shit. You again. Thought I had ridded myself of you."

"Good to see you too."

"What do you want? I was enjoying my nap and you had to fucking wake me up."

"I want you to meet a good friend of mine. He may be able to make you better, but you have to agree to let him operate on you."

"No fucking way. I've been cut on for years and nobody can help. Why the hell would I let him?"

"You trust me, right?"

"Until now, you've not given me a reason to do otherwise."

"Well, if that is a yes, just agree to meet with him."

"What the fuck, doesn't sound like I have a choice. Bring him in."

Liora motioned for Brill to enter the examination room. "Hi Major Thomas, I am Dr. Brill Everly."

"What did you say your name was?"

"Dr. Brill Everly."

"Just your first name."

"Brill."

"You're the shitty asshole who keeps asking those question all the time."

"What?"

"I recognize your name anywhere. You're the fucking dude with the weird name. I remember seeing you when I got injured, and now you won't quit asking me questions."

"You must have me mistaken for someone else."

Liora, realizing this was a breakthrough, jumped in to move the conversation to a neutral place. "Major Thomas, what if you could make Brill stop asking questions? Would you like that."

"Shit yeah. I could finally get a good night's rest."

"Agree to let him cut on you one more time and the questions will stop."

"Just as I figured, you set me up."

"Brill can make the voices stop."

"Your damn right. All he has to do is to stop asking me those fucking questions. Just leave me alone."

Seeing where she was going with this, Brill added to her argument. "I can help, but the questions won't stop until you let me take that thing out of your head."

"What thing."

"A few years ago, you were injured in combat, and that injury put a piece of me in your head. If you let me, I can go in and take that piece out."

Brill knew he was taking a big risk, as his review of Major Thomas's charts showed something buried in his brainstem, not just near it. Surgery outright would kill the man. The only option was to utilize the nanobots. He still had Sirum's vaccine injection where he could pull them. It would only take one, as he could command them to multiply and reprogram them to repair the neural tissue. If this guy agreed, he would operate on him at the end of the day, as long as he could get the preparations done. Realizing a chance to make Liam think he was trusting him more, he would let Liam know exactly what he was doing but omitting that he injected Liora and Sirum with the special nanobots.

Exasperated, Major Thomas relented. "Just make the damn voices stop. Do what you need to do, and next time listen to the answers, so you won't have to ask so many questions. They kept telling you how to navigate the Well, but you wouldn't listen."

Stopping in mid-step as he was leaving, "What did you say?"

Starting to get agitated, Major Thomas was yelling at the top of his lungs. "Get the fuck away from me. I am hungry and tired."

Brill tried to discuss the topic of the Well with him, but Major Thomas had had enough, and his personality switched to the aggressive, angry one. Later that morning, Liam met up with Brill to discuss what he thought was going to be a fatal surgery.

"Colonel Rhett, sounds like Liora has a request of me, and her patient has agreed."

"So, Dr. Everly, I thought doctors took an oath to do no harm?"

"I have and will cure Major Thomas."

"How do you figure? My team has evaluated every treatment option, and they guarantee with one hundred percent certainty that this man will die if he is operated on to remove that mass."

"You are right about that, but I offer another solution."

"Do tell."

"I can program the nanobots to heal the brain tissue almost instantly."

"If what you are saying is true, why would I agree to let you?"

"For the knowledge of how to do that."

"You must really care for Liora to part with such a prize."

"Yes, I do. It means a lot to her to heal Major Thomas, and I will do everything I can to make her happy."

"So, you would do it for her and not the patient?

"You are clever with your words Colonel Rhett, but the patient is healthy today, just not mentally. I could do nothing and not cause him any harm. So, yes. I do it for her, not him."

Tapping his fingers in almost eager anticipation, "What do you need from me?"

"I need access to the computer my father left your team. The code for the nanobots is on it. I can show your team how to access it and then how to modify it."

"Done. Follow me."

Liam led Brill to a large lab bustling with activity. When Liam entered, the whole lab stopped what they were doing and stood at attention saluting him. "At ease soldiers," he commanded the room, and then showed Brill the prize he was seeking.

Brill did not use the nanobots Liam's team provided, but carefully removed a hair from his shirt or so it seemed, as the hair housed the nanobots Brill intended to reprogram. Brill acted like he was carefully moving the hair from the arm of his shirt, going over the dish containing Liam's bots, and slightly tapping it as he did so. That was a signal for the bots to jump off into the dish. A simple command Brill was able to program into them with the limited resources in his room earlier. With his dad's computer and code, Brill was able to access their core code, a tidbit he conveniently omitted from what he shared with Liam's team. To them, it looked like nonsense code, as Brill was showing them how to wade through the layers and layers of code to get to the command sequences, which were purposely separated from the core operating code. The position Brill put the 'nonsense' code in created a series of commands that enabled him to activate the core code and override any ghost programs Liam's team was sure to try to embed into these bots. Brill knew what he was doing and had developed a strong coding ability to rival even Liam's best. Since Brill was pulling in commands his dad had programmed into Brill's nanobots so many years ago, it only took half an hour to do what he needed. The tricks he showed Liam's team would keep them busy for years to come.

The surgery on Major Thomas went smoothly. Brill injected the modified nanobots into the tissue around the shrapnel before he excised it. As Brill made the first cut, the Major convulsed violently, which was not unexpected when cutting into the brainstem. As quickly as it started, the convulsions stopped, indicating the nanobots were doing their job. Knowing the rate of replication of the nanobots, Brill made sure not to go faster than they could replicate, since he needed them to fill in the shrapnel void with active brain tissue, and that took time. The surgery lasted for six hours when Brill finally removed the shrapnel. As he pulled it out, it glistened unlike any metal he had ever seen. Given what the man said about the Well, Brill wanted to study this piece of metal and understand its properties. He acted only slightly interested, so as not to draw attention to it from Liam's team.

Holding the shrapnel up to the light with the forceps, he made the off comment, "Odd that nothing adheres to the surface of this. Please save this for me. I would like to understand what type of metal it is."

Liam's team didn't give it a second thought. They dropped the piece of metal in a zip lock bag and tossed it on the shelf for Brill to retrieve later. After he closed up and put in the last stitch, Brill grabbed the bag with the piece of metal and left. This was one souvenir that Liam didn't care if he had.

∼

LIAM WAS true to his word in clearing Brill's name and sent them on their way. Getting back to a normal life was not something Brill could readily dive into, as he just wanted to be in Liora's arms and she in his. They spent the better part of the next few weeks getting to know each other on a much deeper level. As the weeks ebbed into months, life got back to somewhat of a normal routine. Brill was eager to retrieve the chair. He tried to come up with a scenario that would allow him to do so, when it finally hit him. The three of them, Liora, Sirum, and himself, would plan a hiking trip to the northern Nevada mountains. Instead of making it a clandestine event, he decided to work it into his next conversation with Liam. He thought it would draw less suspicion that way. Before that, he realized he needed to hike many times to show that as a pattern, the location would just be different each time. Plus, Liora was teaching him to rock climb, something she practiced regularly while he was gone.

The ruse worked better than he thought. The first few times hiking, Sirum brought some tracking devices to spot drones and the like. Sure enough, in the first five hikes they spotted drones monitoring their activities. Each time after that, the drones faded, and soon they were hiking in solitude. Of course, Brill suspected the satellites were recording their activities. They had run the calculations on how long it would take them to get the chair up from the lower levels of the old mine and made sure to camp out a few days longer than their projections.

Brill was amused that Liam had brought up their hiking and camping in a conversation, phrasing it like a guess, rather a surety. "Brill, glad to see you are enjoying yourself again. What are you doing in your free time, going on camping trips?"

Brill was smiling internally as he answered, "Well, as a matter of fact I am. It has given me time to catch up with Liora and Sirum. I think we'll keep it up on the weekends, since it allows us to clear our heads."

Liam seemed to accept that answer. Had they been in person and not on a video chat, Brill suspected that Liam would be able to notice he was only telling partial truths.

They made a trip to just outside of Reno to locate where the mineshaft was and to drop off the equipment they needed. Spending most of their time hiking and camping to hide everything they left behind. In order to mask returning trips to this spot outside of Reno, they hit several other hiking sites again over the next few months (returning to the Reno site every third or fourth one) to keep it randomized. During the fifth hike there, all the equipment was set in place. Their sixth visit to that place proved to be the most productive in that they made their way to retrieving the chair and quantum computer.

Over the times they had dropped off equipment to the mineshaft, they had put in place a series of winches and pulleys. A very simple system which was easy to install, only needing the pulleys to be mounted into the rock wall on a staggered basis. That way, as the chair and computer were lifted up, they could easily be connected to the next set of pulleys and have them up in about an hour. It took only thirty minutes once they were able to open up the old mine-shaft, as Sirum had automated the connectors, allowing for quick transfer from one pulley system to the next. On each of these camping trips, they had driven a truck with an oversized bed and covering. This allowed them to easily keep the chair and computer from any spying satellites and drones. With everything loaded and covered up, they headed back to Sirum's place in Vegas, a house with a large garage where they could hide the chair and computer.

The trip back to the city was uneventful. Pulling into Sirum's garage, Brill could not believe they had pulled it off. Probably because Liam had no idea of what the equipment allowed him to do. To further hide the transfer of the chair and computer to Brill's house, they put in place a series of texts and emails which established that Brill wanted Sirum to bring him some of the belongings he had stored there when he was on the run. After a few weeks of this back and forth with several trips of pseudo equipment, the chair and computer were finally in Brill's house, ready for him to use.

∾

ONE THING on Brill's mind was to analyze that piece of metal he took out of Major Thomas's head. Brill suspected that this metal somehow gave him the ability to hear what was going on in the Well. It emitted a low level of quantum energy, which reminded Brill of the energy patterns of X-points, those elusive tears in space where the enemy of the Knowledge Well had broken through in the beginning of existence.

Brill had also analyzed Major Thomas's genetics as soon as he returned home and had access to the quantum computer. Major Thomas had one of the genes necessary to access the Well, but not the rest. Odd Brill thought, that he could gain that link to it without the dark matter and chair. Had to be the metal. He gave it to Sirum, since he had all the fancy physics equipment and would be able to readily identify it. Two days after the start of the analysis, Sirum couldn't find any known metal that it matched, though it did seem close to the shimmer metal he had invented.

When they were in Sri Lanka, Sirum had shipped home some of the samples of the radioactive material and odd metal that the Mao group was mining there. The radioactive material was the typical Uranium, but the odd metal was also not identified. Curious, Sirum ran the Sri Lanka sample in parallel with Brill's sample. They came back as a perfect match, neither of which provided a hit of any known metal. The samples were placed in a resonance chamber to try to understand if they had any harmonic frequencies. As Sirum adjusted the frequencies bombarding the odd metal, he rotated through one where his mind was blasted with noise, but only for a second. Not realizing it was the metal causing it, he kept going without showing any results. The resonance was set to cycle back down automatically, and he turned his attention to other items when Brill showed up.

"Any progress Sirum?"

"Nothing yet...Damn that noise again."

"You heard it too?"

"Brill, did you also hear something?"

"Not really hear with my ears but perceive in my mind. For a second there, I thought for sure I was in the Well."

"All I heard was loud static."

"Are you still running the experiment on the metal?"

"Yes, that was why I called you down here. That metal you took out of Major Thomas is identical to the one Liora and I took from the mine in Sri Lanka."

"Very interesting. I see it in that chamber. What are you doing to it?"

"Running a resonance scan to see if it vibrates at a specific frequency."

"Stop it where it is and step it back little by little."

As Sirum stepped it back, it hit on a frequency that was just above gamma radiation yet supplied it with a full spectrum of quantum energy when Brill yelled, "Stop. That's it."

"I can see/hear the Knowledge Well. This must be what Major Thomas heard all of those years, driving him crazy. I don't understand how this would connect one to the Well. Are you still hearing static noise?"

With his hands covering his ears, he stammered, "Yes, can we make it stop?"

Brill adjusted the setting to the point where Sirum could no longer hear it. "I guess we know why the Mao group was harvesting that metal. Someone in their group must be able to hear the Well with the help of that metal, and they are trying to use it to explore the Well. Why would they need radioactive material?"

"Well Brill, my guess is that the radioactive material is something they hope will boost their abilities, maybe give them a mental boost?"

"Maybe you should let Liam know of this little finding. It will really spark his interest." "Really? I thought this would be something you would want to keep to yourself."

"Under normal circumstances, yes. With the Mao group trying to tap into the Knowledge Well, that could give them an unparalleled advantage and abilities to defeat anybody. Liam needs to know, but I won't let him know about my abilities. That has to remain secret, as well as the genetic link to the Well. I doubt that the Mao group even knows that link."

"You got it Brill, but this is going to have him in my business for a while."

"As the old saying goes, keep your friends close, but your enemies even closer. Do it. I'll be playing with my chair, since that's the only way I can control what I do in the Well."

HE HAD BROUGHT the piece of metal back from Sirum's, the one he removed out of Major Thomas and set it on the shelf near his bed. With the chair all setup and ready to go, Brill was not sure what he would do first once back in there. Thinking back through the events of the last few months, he had so many questions and so few answers. He would go into the Well once he was sure nobody needed him for several weeks, since he was not sure how long he would be in there.

When Sirum and Liora had been briefed by Brill on what the chair enabled him to do, they were in awe and a bit scared he may not be able to return again. Brill assured them that each time he went in there, he learned more and more about how the Well worked and would eventually be able to control it, or at least direct it the way he wanted it to go. Liora was hooking him up with the IV bags and various electrodes when Brill reached out to give her a comforting kiss, assuring her that this time was different.

"Liora, we have taken more precautions this time and accounted for any power failures. I should be fine. Just keep Liam busy while I'm in here."

"Brill, I worry for you and can't go through you dying again."

"Not to worry my love. As you saw last time, my body has some built in safeguards to at least delay that inevitability."

"Sirum my friend, please connect the remote monitoring device and give that to her so she can know my condition no matter where she is."

With that, Brill closed the canopy and plunged into the quantum world, now seeing the X-point that enabled him to get into the Well and return. His consciousness ebbed and flowed with a purpose now, meandering beyond the threshold of life itself, near the deeper parts of the Well, ever cautious of that ancient enemy and ready to quickly back out to the edge. His sense of self in this place was stronger this time, as it was still connected to a living, breathing body. He gained a sense of a foothold on the edge of what he knew to be the Well, not coming with any directive or specific questions. He had more curiosity this time than he did when he was previously here.

The Well as a place lacked definition, yet it was massive, as best he could decipher. Something in him just knew about this place, a place he should not be able to enter without the aid of a machine, but the possibility existed that he could. He wasn't sure if this was a want or a reality, so he explored the thought a bit more. How did he get here? The question resonated as if he had a voice and shouted it at the top of his lungs, though none of those things existed in this place. He was just a consciousness, though not entirely in full. He was more than the sliver of consciousness, as he knew the others in here to be, yet not as much of a presence as that enemy at the core. His entry into this place was unique, since the Well as much told him so, this entry method gave him more 'abilities' in this place.

As he pondered the thought of how he arrived here, images and equations materialized about the X-points and dark matter. He explored those, vetting out their viability, until he landed upon one that stood out from the others. Those others were capturing how a living being could push their thoughts into this place and then return with some answer. The mechanism of how this place worked was that it seemed to be anti-neural energy that attracted neural energy of a specific frequency. This was likely the reason only so few were able to access it, and even fewer have the genetics to generate that type of neural energy. They also described the amount and type of energy those bodies utilized to push their sliver of consciousness into this place. The solution to how he arrived here was one of several different components that happened to be present in his body.

First, he needed highly specific genetics, utilizing the output of multiple chromosomes and multiple genes on those chromosomes, all working together in unison to isolate the consciousness of him in his mind. Then something like excitation energy pushed his consciousness out of his mind through the dark matter in the chair and into a quantum tunnel that narrowly bridged the macro universe where his body resided, crossing down through the anti-matter, the X-point, which looked like some type of connector to the Well. The best he could describe it was a 'bridge'.

That's when he saw it. The bridge was the key, he just needed to 'see' it with his consciousness and then push himself through it to here with the help of the dark matter. He then realized that 'bridge' was an X-point, and the dark matter was a premature state of the living metal. Without the aid of his chair and quantum computer, the dark matter alone would not have been enough to get Brill in here, yet that odd metal would.

The Well was all that existed in this small corner of the quantum universe. The picture appeared to him of how to get back, instead of a bunch of equations. A particle he recognized, anti-pions, were freely flowing between where his body was and where he is, he just needed to hitch a ride on one of those to get there. They were following the quantum tunnel through the X-point leading back to his body. He might later regret learning this, as the Well was also being taught this bit of unknown information, and those beings at the Core were observing it all.

The anti-pions appeared to be the exact quantum structure of the frequency of his neural energy. So, this is how these solutions occur to him, he realized, sometimes as equations and sometimes as images. Exploring this a bit further and looking at the quantum universe was when he saw it was not the asymmetrical version of the macro universe. Brill observed images of pockets of energy dumping into areas of the quantum universe, which appeared to have no discernible reactions. There were pockets of the quantum universe that appeared to be active with matter annihilation, the combination of matter and anti-matter without the buffering effect of the dark matter and the use of the X-points. The Knowledge Well was a recipient of the dumping of quantum neural energy from those genetically linked individuals, and then it returns to that user an ability to solve complex or impossible problems. This all happened in the form of images, not equations. Must be one of those abilities of having his full consciousness here he thought, being able to see equations in addition to images.

Now that he had a solution and explanation on the bridging between his body and where he was, he would try to figure out how to come and go without the need for the chair. He 'saw' the dark matter was one of the keys and one he could overcome, yet the metal that gave access here was still a puzzle to him. He knew this metal was one of the other keys and would keep trying to flush it out. The X-point would be the most challenging obstacle to figure out. If he could merge the dark matter with his mind via that strange metal to facilitate the transfer of his consciousness to this place, then he might stand a chance, at least that was one fleeting thought.

He was deep into a solution when some consciousness or thought seemed to slam into him again, sucking him into the mind of the person who was projecting this thought. To Brill, it was as if he were seeing a million images in a fraction of a second, none of which were decipherable. He was being drawn deeper into the mind of this being, though this mind had a familiarity to him. The thought of returning to the core and the evil that resided there helped his mind pull himself back like a boomerang returning to the hand of the person throwing it. He seemed to fly through the Well, brushing across many of the threads of consciousness that littered the place and skirted the edge of a few of them. Each time he skimmed the surface of those threads of consciousness, he got a glimmer of their questions, but only a glimpse. Brill felt like he was falling into the core of the Well again, when he regained control of his movements. His will to command his direction seemed to drive where he went, a newly found skill he learned from that mind that slammed into him. Without a real purpose here, he aimlessly wandered about until the desire to return was too compelling to ignore.

Before he returned, he got a glimpse of a disturbing thought. This

Well, this place of seemingly immense knowledge, was not all that it seemed. He saw something akin to a prison where all those connected minds were being used by the beings at the core. He now believed the Well was the prison of those beings, but somehow they had pulled at the minds of beings across all time and space to utilize that collective intelligence for their purposes. It started to make sense to Brill. Those beings at the core had been trying to escape since the beginning of his universe. Brill was drawn back to that image of when those beings first invaded the proto-universe and their use of the X-points. That image slowed down to a frame-by-frame progression, then he saw it. Those beings were only able to make their way to Nurizzi in the form of single celled organisms. Everywhere else across the cosmos they were only able to insert a few strands of RNA via viruses through the X-points. Finally, Brill felt like he had a "Eureka" moment. This was a literal version of hell for those beings, yet they managed to entice others to unknowingly to come here with the lure of easy knowledge. Outside of Brill's awareness of this place, he suspected none of those beings realized that a portion of their consciousness was trapped in a very real version of hell for all of eternity.

The return trip was an education for him, as he gained images the ability to move through each level of the quantum world, to go through the X-point, and then back to his body. With his conscious-ness back in his body, he stayed in the chair while connected to the quantum computer. This allowed him to start to understand and process everything he had just learned.

The computer allowed for the overflow of information while in the Well and a much more rapid recall and assessment than his mind alone could give him, all courtesy of the nanobots in his mind. Images from that mind that had collided with him while in the Well were now unfolding in his brain, much like a dream state. One of the images that jumped out to him was of the exploration of X-points. With his mind linked to the quantum computer, he had captured so much more of the information on X-points than he had realized while in the Well. He now understood them to be nexus points which the dark matter linked to allow him entry into the Well, and those were points where the Nurizzi progenitors that blasted themselves into our existence.

AFTER OPENING the canopy and then removing the IV, Sirum was the first person he called.

"Sirum, come over quickly."

"Is something wrong? Liora is here with me. I'll bring her."

"Nothing wrong. Definitely bring her along as well, she was going to be the next person I called."

They arrived with much anticipation, wondering what was so urgent. "Glad you are both here. What do you know about X-points?"

Sirum being the astrophysicist, chimed in first. "Everything that the scientific community would know. Why?"

"When I was in the Well, I saw these X-points and thought they were only the entry points into and out of the Well. Something is bugging me that I can't put a finger on, as I feel like these could be so much more of use. I just cannot place how and need to bounce some ideas off of you two."

Liora was the first to respond this time, "Is this another one of those things that is going to have you hiding from Liam?"

"Good point my dear. I had not given any thought to him yet."

"Sirum, the why is because there is an alien race out there somewhere, the Nurizzi, that are controlled or manipulated by those eerie things at the core of the Well, and they seem intent on doing something to Earth, or so I gathered by my encounter with them in there."

"Brill, I've studied X-points a bit, mainly due to the curiosity of their natural formation, and I really see no use for them. The ability to move an object from Earth's orbit to the middle of the sun is incredibly exciting, but not doable with those."

"Ah, my friend. You did not have me around when you were studying them."

"Brill, I'm an engineer, and I just cannot see how to make a machine that could do anything with them."

"Ha! First mistake of every inventor, giving up before you even start. You didn't internalize everything I just said. Recall how I said those things at the core are using them and may have created them?"

"You also said something collided with you in there. What else did you learn?"

"I seemed to absorb a massive number of images from that mind. It was familiar and different than the Nurizzi. I have not been able to make sense out of most of those yet, except for this image of the device and the X-point. That mind had a familiarity I have yet to pin down."

Curious now, Sirum let out a few explicatives before getting to the point. "So, what is it you want to bounce off of us?"

"What if we could generate those X-points using a machine and then control the entry and exit from them?"

"I would first question what you are drinking or smoking. Are you totally serious or pulling our leg?"

"Dead serious. There is something to this, I just know it."

"Brill, I know you are smart, but I just don't see how to make what you want."

Liora had watched the back and forth for a bit before putting in her two cents worth. "Brill, what if those things at the, what did you call it...the core...what if they were purposely deceiving you or leading you on?"

"Not sure I understand you. Why would they deceive me?"

"The point is that something so easily obtained may come with a higher price. You just haven't paid it yet."

"I still don't see how that applies. I narrowly escaped those Nurizzi progenitors and barely found a way back through the X-points."

"You are making my point Brill. Think about it. You are too smart for your own good sometimes."

"Didn't you say those things were likely the cause of the "Big

Bang" and were labelled enemies of the Well by something in the Well?"

"Yes, so what."

"How come I can see this as plain as day and you don't? Sirum, help him out."

"Not sure I follow you either Liora."

"You guys are too analytical and not looking at this from the deception perspective. The way I see it, those things have been trapped in there forever, and the thing they wanted most was to get into our universe, or so it seems from what you described. All of a sudden, you show up, and they see a new player to the game who was not invited. They don't know how you got there. But if you can leave, then just maybe it gives them a way to leave as well. They might have just guided you along to the X-point just to see if you can get back through it. As you mentioned, they and the Nurizzi can only access it through a genetic linkage. You are different, not one of them, yet you are there. Maybe you are showing them how to invade our universe. Maybe it really is the biblical version of hell and those things that are trapped are true demons."

"I did say those things, yes. Let me see if I can build a good counter argument. If that place is the hell as described biblically, then it doesn't fit. I didn't see any fire and brimstone. On their being trapped, I got the sense that they are still coming and going from wherever they came from, but they just can't get into our universe. It's possible I am showing them a way out or in from their perspective. It is a risk I will have to take."

"Brill, if they are those things of legends, then you are playing a dangerous game just to get knowledge."

"I always love your perspective Liora, but I just don't see the danger. As long as I avoid them, even when I'm at the core, I should be able to learn to master that place."

"Brill, every fiber in my being says this is a bad idea, and you should stop while you are ahead, unless it is already too late. Didn't you mention that the beings accessing the core for knowledge are used by those enemies at the core?"

"Fair enough. I did think of a way to try and create X-points, but it will require some fancy engineering."

"Brill, before you shift gears, tell us about those images from that thing that collided with you."

"The only one that I haven't mentioned is one image that has me troubled." With that, Brill went silent and wouldn't say more.

Liora tried several times to get him to elaborate, but Brill would only say he was still processing that troubling image, and that it had nothing to do with X-points.

BRILL SKETCHED out a device he thought may work to make X-points. Looking at this, Sirum saw the problem right away with trying to create a stable X-point on Earth. The problem had to do with the magnetic fields of the Earth and Sun colliding at their apogee, where X-points have been explored by NASA. The science community called these things flux transfer events, and the magnetic fields had to be pure so nothing could interfere with them as they collide. This would be a big problem if one were to make the device on Earth, as the magnetic field of the Earth would interfere with any generated magnetic fields, unless the Earth's field could be dampened.

The extremely detailed device that Brill had developed, something he pulled out of the Well for a different use, looked like the devices that are used to generate a magnetic monopole. The monopoles of each device would collide together so that the fields from those identical monopoles would rip a hole in the atomic fabric that makes up our universe. Sirum pondered this for a long while, perplexed as to how to do anything with it. He could possibly make the devices, but it would go against conventional physics dating back to the early eighteen-hundreds when James Maxwell first explored the theory behind magnetism. Maxwell's theories still hold up even under the rigor of today's modern physics, yet the Well seemed to have a more robust solution. Magnetic monopoles have been elusive, ever since the physicist Paul Dirac proposed their existence in the early part of the twentieth century, but his theories only allowed for it as a quantum particle. Sirum took up the challenge and decided to try to build it. He worked several months on it before showing Brill a prototype.

"Brill, I have something resembling the device you depicted, but I am not sure where to go with it from here."

Brill looked it over very carefully. "This is brilliant! Tell me more about your concerns."

"Well, I can generate something that looks like an X-point, though I am not sure where it goes. It could be the middle of space or somewhere here on Earth. I was hoping you could provide some guidance on what to do next."

"This is the perfect problem to take into the Well."

"I'm not sure I believe that, but if you can keep coming back with solutions, then I'll have less doubt."

∿

BRILL WAS HOPING to find a way to access the Well without the need of the chair and computer, since he may need it when those items aren't accessible.

With Sirum's help, they began to process the dark matter, essentially creating an ionized form of it, so that it would bind to his mind when injected. Brill wasn't sure it would do much, but it was a risk worth taking. Brill insisted on injecting himself with the dark matter in case he didn't survive. After he injected himself, nothing happened. Brill gave it a few days and still nothing.

Disappointed, Brill was exploring the strange metal to see if it would offer any additional clues. The metal was still in the microscope when Brill reached in to retrieve it. As Brill's hand was just above the surface of the metal, the metal jumped up and slammed into Brill's hand. Reflexively, he jerked his hand out. In that split second, his mind was trying to process what it was seeing when the metal flew from its attachment to his hand and right into his forehead. The metal started to dissolve into Brill's brain. He fell to the floor and started shaking violently before anyone realized he was in jeopardy.

The metal caused the dark matter to blend with every cell in his body while every nerve ending screamed in pain. Then the strange metal dissolved into every neuron in his brain. After two agonizing hours, he finally stopped shaking and the pain subsided. He was unconscious for almost two weeks.

When he awoke, the world looked different to him. Colors were more vivid, sounds more distinct, and emotions were heightened. Brill started sobbing uncontrollably, then laughing hysterically, and then shouting in rage. It seemed the dark matter and strange metal had minds of their own and they examined every facet of his psyche. Exhausted, he staggered to his bed and slept for another twenty-four hours straight.

Not giving up on his first efforts to explore the Well without the chair and computer, his first efforts were like a dream state and not of much use. Every time after injecting the dark matter was a failure. He was just not able to access the Well. He and Sirum had many an argument on the why, but eventually settled on the X-point as the roadblock. They were of a mind that the chair was able to access that quantum tunnel into the X-point with the help of the computer. Its processing power allowed the trip to the Well and back to be focused and was somehow directing the dark matter energy into the X-point, something Brill's mind had not yet learned to do. Brill also suspected that the strange metal that was thrust into his brain was playing a role but had yet to pinpoint what it was.

Brill tried other techniques to get there, like focusing heavily on solving the paradox of generating magnetic fields on Earth that are not influenced by Earth's magnetic field. This high degree of specificity and his complete focus on it started the process of activating the dark matter/neural interaction. It was almost enough, but he needed more practice. Needing a solution more than a way in without the chair, Brill went back to the tried-and-true method. He decided to stop trying to enter the Well without the chair, for now.

Once in the Well, solutions started to come to him. He focused deeper on the frequency of neural energy that he was sure his mind was generating. Visualizing in his mind what that energy would look like, and how it would travel down the quantum tunnel through the X-point to the Well. This was the entirety of his thoughts, and he was sure he could make it happen when he returned.

In the Well now through the chair, he focused on what to do with the magnetic monopole device and how to solve the magnetic field problems Sirum outlined. At first, he pushed out the images of the device and the equations around it. What unfolded next gave him a sense of immense beauty. The dim light of the Well seemed to boil with activity, like watching the electrical energy of the Aurea Borealis. Time had no meaning here, and he seemed to watch this phenomenon for a very long time. He was 'watching' the great minds of history at work on a problem they had never encountered, a truly beautiful sight, even if they were held here against their will. An occasional image materialized before him revealing a tantalizing series of equations. As he 'read' through those, he realized they were close, but not what he wanted. They gave him more theory, but no plan of action. After many of these failed attempts, he took a different approach. He was still learning how to use this place.

Instead of trying to get a simple solution to a complex problem, which is what he did at first, he broke down the series of problems they had defined into individual queries. This proved far more fruitful. With the individual parts of the problem broken down into a series of smaller problems, he had all of them solved after a bit. With a complete series of solutions, he then posed the query back to the Well on how to build the device.

Almost instantly, a series of images and equations materialized, with each one building on the previous. At the end, he now had a workable solution to take back to Sirum. Now to get out of here. He was focusing his will on returning when a consciousness slammed into him again. This time, he was not drawn down into that mind, but was bombarded with more images. Those images were of a message of needing help and one of great doom. This consciousness had the same familiarity to him as before, but he still couldn't place it. It was trying to possibly warn him of something or asking for help, building on that troubling image he saw from the earlier encounter. He couldn't tell which it was. There were images of a planet on a collision course with Earth and spaceships unlike anything he could have ever imagined. Just as quick as that transfer occurred, it ended, and he was now traveling back to his body.

The discussion with Sirum was a flurry of activity. Brill could hardly contain himself as he was downloading all this information. He used the quantum computer to run all of the scenarios, and by the end of the week, they had a working plan on what to build and how to do it. Whether it works or not was anyone's guess, but Brill had confidence it would work.

THERE WERE several critical pieces of the path to success that were missing, but they had to start somewhere, and this gave them a big head start. Being able to build a device that could create magnetic monopoles would enable them to open an X-point anywhere they choose, simply by forcing a collision between the magnetic fields from two opposing machines. This generated a magnetic monopole of the same oscillation and frequency of magnetic field. Cancelling out the Earth's and other interfering magnetic fields required shrouding the magnetic monopoles in a quark absorbing type of metal, one Brill had created with the help of the Well. They created an identical device to be the receiving point of the X-point. Using the frequency of the monopoles, they being unique enough, would enable the devices to be connected across any length of space, as the X-points travelled on the quantum scale and distance was irrelevant there.

Brill envisioned these devices being placed all across the Earth to eliminate the need for cars, planes, or any other form of transportation. He wanted to entice businesses to use these devices to transport their goods from their warehouses to the distribution centers, saving them on transportation costs and time. As he looked across the global distribution system, saving that amount of transportation emissions would cut global pollution by a third. Brill was wealthy enough that he was pursuing this from the standpoint of helping out the future generations and not wanting to do this from any monetary standpoint, plus he was eager to see something from the Knowledge Well put into practice. As he got older, though one could hardly say a person in their thirties was old, Brill was feeling the need more and more to help others, as he did not have kids or any other relatives. He needed an outlet to make him feel whole.

THE STRANGE METAL was a perplexing issue to Brill, especially since it was now part of his body. He went back into the Well to try to figure out if it was the key to utilizing the dark matter and accessing the X-points without the aid of the chair and computer, especially since it was a state of dark matter. The Well was a disappointment on this topic, as Brill really couldn't describe what that metal was.

Returning back to his body, he sat up frustrated. The question kept bouncing through his mind as to why that strange metal adhered to his hand and then dissolved into his brain. He still had one of the pieces of metal, the one Sirum and Liora brought back from Sri Lanka. It was still in the scanner, so he tried a different tactic. Instead of the harmonic resonances they had been running, Brill tried pulsing quantum energy through it. He was hoping it would access the quantum tunnel his consciousness used to get into the Well, similar to the dark matter transition. Setting that on auto, he walked across the room to the quantum computer, looking to see if he could use it to analyze the signals coming off the metal. As he started entering commands into the computer, the most intense pain he had ever felt flashed across his whole body. Panic started to set in when he realized he was frozen in place. His hands seemed to be locked onto the keyboard and his feet wouldn't move. The pain...so intense now that it caused him to black out while standing up.

∾

SIRUM WAS WORKING on building the X-point device when an extremely loud noise pulsated through the building. He couldn't imagine what it was, as it sounded like a sonic boom and continued for some time. Exiting his room, the noise intensified and reached a deafening level as he approached the room where Brill was working. Seeing something was wrong, he scanned the room for Brill and couldn't locate him. There were several aft rooms from this main chamber, and he thought Brill may be in one of those. The sound was too intense to keep going. He needed some ear protection, so he ran to the wall to grab some ear plugs.

Sirum entered the main room that housed the motors and cooling equipment for all the scanners in the next room. Brill had equipped his place recently with the equipment Sirum needed, and this series of rooms was the best spot in the house for it. The rooms were not designed for such large machinery, and it was a tight squeeze to get from one room to another. Sirum was certain noise didn't seem to emanate from here, as the passageway shook his body the deeper he went. In the next room were scanners and other instruments, but no Brill. The light coming from the scanner was blinding. Curious at this oddity, he tried to get close enough to it to see what was in there.

The light was now so intense that he knew he risked blinding himself if he peaked in there. The process of trying to get close to the scanner also showed him that the sound was coming from there. Confused, he turned his attention to finding Brill who was nowhere to be seen. The only option now was to push through that blinding light to get to the next room, since that was the spot Brill was most likely trapped. Turning his head to the side, he spotted exactly what he needed, a pair of welding goggles. Brill had been welding some of the equipment previously and fortunately had left the goggles. That stroke of luck gave him confidence that he could find his way through. In the next room, he observed the strangest phenomenon. The intense light was now a focused beam. He took off the goggles, with eyes squinted, and followed the light beam.

Once his eyes adjusted to the lighting, the image that unfolded made his heart stop. The light seemed to be a focused beam right into the back of Brill's head, and the sound was pulsating off the wall right into the frontside of Brill. Sirum was now panicking with no understanding of what he was seeing; and no idea of what to do. '*Have to call Liora...she will know what to do*', was the only thing that came to mind. The phone was inoperable in here, so he dawned the goggles and made his way back.

Liora, seeing Sirum's number, answered right away. A hundred words seemed to erupt from in an incoherent string, until he finally got out. "Help. I don't know what to do."

"Slow down. What's wrong?"

"It's Brill. Something is happening to him."

"What! Is he okay?"

"I don't know. There is a beam of light coming from the scanner and pointing directly into the back of his head, and there is a deafening sound pulsating into him."

"Sirum, is the power still on?"

"I think so. Yes, the light still works. Please help."

"That's it Sirum. Turn the power off."

"I can't get close enough to the scanner to do that."

"Then turn it off at the breaker box."

"Where would that be?"

"Seriously, you're the mechanical one. I'm not sure where it is. Try the garage."

Sirum found his way there, still on the phone. "Not sure this will work, but I'll give it a try."

"Just turn the damn power off and hurry. Hit the main one, as it would take too long to figure out the breaker you need."

"Already done. Now finding my way back in the dark is going to be a challenge."

"You definitely don't do well under pressure. Use your noggin and open the flashlight on your phone. I'll be there in twenty minutes."

Sirum got back to Brill as fast as he could. He observed that the light was still coming out of the scanner but was way less intense. Curious as to what would do this, he looked at the scanning table and his mouth dropped. It was that strange metal they couldn't identify. His hand reflexively went to his ears, causing him to realize the sound had stopped. 'Well at least that part worked,' he thought.

Brill was slumped on the floor, yet the light had followed his head down to the floor and was still focused on it. Sirum was hesitant to do anything till the light stopped. He couldn't tell if Brill was even alive, though he knew Brill's nanobots would do all they could. Frightened, he sat down next to Brill, pulled his knees up to his chin, wrapped his arms around himself, and began rocking back and forth. All he could do know was wait.

BRILL FELT HIMSELF EBBING AWAY. Something was pulling all his consciousness out of his body. To where, he could not fathom, only follow. The light had a beauty so strong it wrapped up every bit of his being, pulling him onward.

8

THE BRIDGE

Brill looked around at his new surroundings, thinking back on what had just occurred. The last thing he could recall was typing on the keyboard and then hearing a loud sound. This place was abstract to him. He could not sense any other consciousness, and his perception of this place was much different than the Well...this was different somehow. Everything in here was coming at him at a furious pace, like being inside static noise. Images/thoughts, or whatever he was perceiving, were like viewing the colors of a kaleidoscope, but from the inside with no point of reference.

He tried the tricks he had learned in the Well, by using his consciousness to slow down the colors coming at him. At first, Brill could only deflect what was bombarding him. Though the more he focused his will, the better he got at it. He was able to start controlling the flashes of colors he was seeing/perceiving, as he was certain he was just a consciousness in here. Slowing down the set of colors flying at him, he could see those were planets and stars. It took many attempts to learn some control in this place.

The first one he was able to slow down showed it to be a planet similar in appearance to Jupiter, minus the red spot and ring. He reached into that image with his consciousness and was surprised to find himself zooming in on the surface of it. His field of perception changed to the surface, as if he was standing on, or more like, flying across it. Something up ahead of him caught his attention. It appeared to be a pulsating light or reflection off of a surface.

Focusing in on that light, he soon was hovering over it. The area looked to have been swallowed up by volcanic lava sometime in the past. It looked to Brill to be the remnants of the top of a building of some sorts. Brill focused on the building, but could not make himself get to the surface, at least he had yet to figure out how. He turned his attention to the surrounding area, focusing on distant mountains. In what would have been the blink of an eye, Brill was now right over the mountains. Some wildlife was observed meandering through the mountain meadows. He started to get the hang of commanding his movements and was able to see anywhere on the planet he desired. After countless hours of moving around and observing, he was certain this world no longer contained any life, at least sentient life on the surface. Brill then turned his thoughts to returning to the nexus point.

The knowledge of how to return was still a guessing game to him, so he thought back to that point in space where he entered. That seemed to be enough to get him moving off of the planet, into the upper atmosphere, and then into space. His focus was on the entry to this place and how to find it. Brill was hoping the entry point would also be an exit point. Entering the upper atmosphere, Brill observed many a structure off into space orbiting the planet. One in particular caught his attention, since it appeared to be a type of machinery that was encased in stone. Once he spotted it, an instant later he was hovering right over it. Able to inspect every facet of its surface, Brill noticed a structure that resembled a doorway, so he entered.

The terminal was an eight-sided obelisk structure in the middle of the room he just entered. His focus was on activating it and seeing if he could learn something. Nothing happened, so Brill tried to use his focus to lift an object off the floor. To his surprise, the object levitated when he thought it to do so. With this bit of confidence, he turned back to the obelisk. Every side of the object contained buttons and lights that were flashing periodically. One area near the top was something Brill hoped was a monitor, even though it wrapped around the whole obelisk in a circle. It was the right height for a being measuring eight or nine feet tall to easily see and access.

Brill focused on pushing buttons to see if anything would happen. One or two would depress and then rise back up, yet nothing happened on the screens. The pattern of lights that occasionally flickered now had Brill's attention when it hit him on how to access this device. Those lights were pulsing a well-defined sequence of colored images. Brill noticed those images were also present on several of the buttons, a few of which he had already pushed in and out. He tried pushing the buttons that resembled those sequences, but nothing happened. He attempted a few more before moving and was on the last two. Commanding the second to last sequence to activate, the room came alive once that last symbol was pushed.

Lights started pulsing in a multitude of areas, not only in this room but across the whole structure. The wall in the place to where Brill was focusing pulled back to reveal a live image of the stars. Brill was now certain this room was a control room of some sorts to whatever this structure was. Brill turned back to the obelisk and commanded the last sequence to be entered. That allowed the terminal to come to life, displaying a language he was unable to translate. It resembled hieroglyphs set in a multi-dimensional cube with many of them arranged in rows and strings of sequences. Slamming his imaginary fists down, Brill was frustrated as he had worked for some time to decipher the symbols and couldn't make sense out of any of them without a key. The obelisk seemed to power up the whole structure, allowing Brill the opportunity to explore deeper into its function.

Passing from room to room, Brill came upon a cavernous area. The walls were lined with lockers. Brill went to one that had powered up for a closer look, and to his surprise, there was a being in there. If it was alive, he couldn't tell. His focus of will allowed him to pass into that locker to see the being up close. It was a biped with two arms and legs similar to humans, yet its head was wide and flat with eyes that went completely around. If it had ears, he couldn't see them, and the brain was an unknown. Brill went back out to decipher how many of these lockers there were. Too many to count, so he went on to explore a bit more of this structure. It contained a few more cavernous rooms filled with similar beings. Brill came upon a room with something akin to video monitors. On them, Brill could see they were tracking other structures, much like the one where he was. Brill decided to continue to find the exit.

Having had enough exploration, Brill turned his attention on returning to the image place. The sole of his focus was to find the point where he entered, in the hopes it would also be an exit, though multiple passes around the planet left him empty handed. The next vector he took was to head towards the sun. Just as he started to move, a momentary flash piqued his interest. With that as Brill's focus, he zoomed in on it before the spot disappeared. Brill was dazzled by a burst of energy emanating from that exact spot.

Approaching the spot, no larger than a grain of sand, Brill's focus had him getting smaller and smaller until he was as tiny as the entry point. Brill was soon realizing that he had a lot to learn to master his control in this place. Just as he was about to enter the spot, now the size of a doorway, the flash of light burst out as Brill reached to go inside. The light was like a river of energy as it flowed against the backdrop of space. Curiosity overtook him and he jumped right in, only to be surprised at the symmetry of the place. He was part of every bit of energy flowing outward, and yet he did not move. In his current state it just flowed on by. Brill visualized waves of energetic particles. The mathematical representation of the sine wave, that undulating up and down, was the term Brill could immediately place on it.

Then it hit him. He had seen this before. And in this state, he could readily recall everything he ever knew, plus what the Knowledge Well gave him. This was the X-point and what it looked like on a subatomic level. Eager now to get back to where he started, Brill pushed on into the X-point.

Entering the X-point, Brill thought to himself, '*Where the hell have I gone?*'

'*Lost, I must be lost.*' Was the last thing he thought.

∽

SIRUM WAS STILL CROUCHED next to Brill when Liora found him. He was in a state of shock, muttering to himself.

"I killed him. I killed him."

Liora was shaking him and yelling at him, "Sirum! You did what you could. Snap out of it. I need your help."

Sirum just sat there rocking back and forth with his arms wrapped around his knees continually saying that phrase.

Liora had enough and slapped him to bring him out of this funk. Nothing. He just kept rocking back and forth. This time she didn't hold back and gave him a slap so hard it knocked him over. She didn't have time to wait and needed his help.

"Get off your ass and get the power back on."

"What the hell did you do that for?"

"You were stuck in self-pity, and I needed you to snap out of it. Desperate times require desperate decisions."

"Fine. I will help, just don't beat me again."

"Done, now get going. I'll tend to Brill."

When the power returned, the scene was a chaotic mess with shattered equipment everywhere and Brill laying slumped on the floor. Checking for a pulse, Liora was getting worried now, as Brill was going cold. '*Think*' she muttered to herself, '*what did I do last time?*' Last time Brill had a plan, this was unexpected and nothing in this place was designed for that purpose. She would have to improvise.

"Do you know where Brill keeps that chair?"

"Yes. It's near the quantum computer. Why?"

"We need to get him into to it. Help me carry him."

They made their way to the room with the quantum computer, finding the chair right behind it. They carefully placed him in the chair and closed the canopy. Sirum punched in a command sequence to be sure the chair would activate, since he had programmed those in as a failsafe if he ever needed to work the chair on his own. He was glad Brill had not changed those out, as the chair immediately came to life. They hoped it would keep Brill's body alive until they could figure out what to do with him.

THE SEQUENCE of events that unfolded next were a topic of discussion between them for months afterward. Shortly after Sirum activated the chair, the quantum computer began emitting a multi-colored light that circled them and the room. Liora noticed an image in the light, it seemed to flap back and forth, similar to a movie reel where the black and white shot in the reel showed one after another on the screen. Sirum had a different take. He thought he viewed a doorway and in it were images that moved so fast he could only catch a glimpse. A blue sky here, an image of stars there, an image of some city, and so on. Then the computer levitated into that light. The massive quantum computer was actually moving and neither Sirum nor Liora could believe their eyes, until it floated right through the doorway Sirum visualized. Liora's view was of it merging with that hazy image in the light.

Then everything went sideways. The light where the computer disappeared sprung up again and intensified to that of a blinding sun with electrical charges sparking off the walls, almost catching the both of them. Out of the corner of her eye, she caught sight of the chair with Brill in it, ripping off the bolts that were holding it to the floor. As it levitated, the arcs of electricity emanating from the light encircled the chair, as an explosion ensued. Then it went dark. The image burned on her retinas was that of the chair flying into the light followed by the computer blowing apart, so quick it seemed to be between breaths.

Darkness. Not a sound to be heard. Everything just stopped, all power and noises. Liora called out for Sirum, unsure if she were imagining this or living through it.

"Here...Over here."

Fumbling through the dark, following his voice until she grabbed some part of his body. "Do you know if there were any flashlights in this room?"

"Already on it" Sirum spurt out, just as his hand landed upon the flashlight. "Got it."

Liora snatched the light before Sirum could get another word out. She was quick, as she had the light and was searching the room for any sign of Brill.

"He's gone. How's that possible?"

"I had hoped you would find him on the floor and this would be all my imagination."

Liora combed every inch of the room, hoping she might find him. Then she slumped to the floor, bursting into tears, only one of two times Sirum ever saw Liora cry. He wasn't sure if she wanted comfort or to be left alone.

Sirum sat beside her and clasped her hand. She embraced him with tears flowing everywhere. "Not again...not again," between sobs.

BRILL TRIED everything within his grasp to escape. This place, he was certain of it being inside the X-point, was connected to something he couldn't place. The images, they looked different from the one he had just encountered. They weren't just of places, many looked like they were stars of different colors. Though some were dark. Brill noticed there was more to this place than the images. Something was flowing through him, coming from behind his presence. It took all his will to turn his attention to the source of that flow. As he turned, he could see stars, more than he could count, projecting out in every direction. The 'flow' was energy, more specifically radiation on every spectrum. He simply knew that's what this was, though he was unsure how. He followed the flow of that energy to the exact spot where he was now. Once the energy flow hit that spot, Brill saw it split into a few images, and it flowed with those images as they passed by his view. The flow of one specific stream of energy was his focus, as it was changing color, going from a blueish white hue to a deep red. As he was concentrating, the stream began to expand until it washed him over and then his physical body in the chair slammed into whatever he was there, capped off by the computer blasting into him. His essence in this place was being pulled into his body that was now in the chair. At first, he fought that pull until he realized what was happening.

His body, being whole now, was revived by the chair. As Brill awoke, he was unsure of what to do next. Laying in the chair with the canopy closed, Brill accessed the environmental sensors, hoping that he could at least breath. To his surprise, the environment around the chair was a balmy room temperature with plenty of breathable air.

'*Well, what do I have to lose?*' He muttered to himself, exiting the chair.

The chair canopy opened, and he raised up with due caution. Now that he had eyes, he truly visualized the surroundings. He could no longer see the flow of energy, but he could feel it as a steady hum or vibration. Turning in a circle to take in his surroundings, Brill stopped in his tracks as he laid eyes on the computer. The questions of how it and his body got here were still far from his mind, but the attention getter was what the computer was doing. Brill had a diffi-cult time deciphering if the quantum computer was exploding or taking on a life of its own. Still questioning exactly was he was seeing, the computer began to break apart into smaller pieces, each one a replica of the larger self. Then those pieces broke apart again into even smaller pieces. This went on and on, until it was like grains of sand, with the exception of one piece. That piece was the size of a quarter.

Within a fraction of a second, all those pieces literally exploded outward, zipping past Brill into the images. Only one went into a specific image and they never duplicated. Brill watched this unfold as until only the quarter sized one was left. That piece flew into his forehead, burying itself in his brain. The momentum of that collision carried Brill back into the chair where he fell perfectly flat and the canopy closed.

Eyelids popped open. On instinct, he checked his pulse to be sure he was still alive. A heartbeat convinced him he was not dreaming, but to be sure he pinched himself. '*Ouch, guess I'm still alive.*' He stammered. He opened the canopy and sat up with caution, unsure if he had the strength to stand. Upright now, he was glad to have his legs under him. Remembering the last few minutes he was awake, his hand went to his forehead. No hole, nanobots must have healed him. Hoping all the drama was over, the images were now the obvious choice of study in this place, as these were the only likely way to get out of here.

The moment he stepped out of the chair, into whatever place this was and onto the unknown floor, the flow of energy coursed through him with the intensity of a lightning strike, except there was no pain. Understanding soon arrived with that flow of energy. This was the X-point nexus that linked to every X-point across all creation, billions of them. A gateway of sorts, long unused, which allowed the energy consumed by blackholes to exit into stars and planets. It was the energy that gave earth-like worlds their habitability. Brill could see back to their formation from his knowledge gained in the Well. The black holes were the rips in our universe made by that ancient enemy and this place was the gateway they created to make the X-points. The X-points were then formed to balance that energy drain by funneling the energy out into space via stars, a perfectly balanced system.

Looking at this beautiful place with his newfound knowledge, Brill saw the opportunity every science geek dreamed of, being able to travel the stars. This place was that gateway and could enable it, he just needed to figure out how. The first order of business was for him to get back to his house, back to Liora and Sirum.

The quantum computer piece that was embedded in his head was just beyond his comprehension. He could sense it but didn't know how to use it. When he came across an image of what looked to be Earth, the throbbing in his head from the piece of quantum computer stopped. It was a serene feeling. When he moved on to other images, the throbbing started up again, more intense this time. He went back to the Earth image and it stopped. Realizing this was a clue, Brill approached the image. Just below the top of the planet, there was a faint dot of light. Focusing on that point of light seemed to be what it took to draw him into it.

LIORA GRABBED A FLASHLIGHT. Illuminating her surroundings still didn't help her to make sense of the events that had just unfolded. She still wasn't sure if what she had seen was real or her brain tricking her. Glass was everywhere and smoke was still spewing from the pile of debris where the chair and computer used to be. She stared at that pile for a while until she realized that was just the remnants of the wires and other attachments to the computer and chair. Not sure what to do next, she turned to Sirum in total exasperation.

Tears started to build in her eyes, "How?"

Putting his arm around her in a show of rare compassion, "It'll all work out. He always seems to find a way back to us."

"Maybe. Thanks for not trying to console me with meaningless platitudes."

They both just dropped to the floor and sat in silence for countless minutes. Just before Liora was about to break the silence, a blast of cold air rushed at them both. In tandem they turned to see what was causing it. As they did so, a blinding light pierced the darkness. They both covered their eyes as Liora pushed Sirum's head to the floor, covering her own in the process.

BRILL HAD BEEN DRAWN into the light, like a fish on a line. The light was washing through him and around him. His brain was trying to process everything it was seeing and not seeing but feeling. The light moved in waves which throbbed through him. The wave told him about the place it originated. Brill interpreted those waves as images of points in time on Earth, each telling its own story. The light gave him more information than he first processed, and he was slowly putting the pieces together. There were temporal coordinates embedded there, but he could only go back as far as to when he was born. This was his life and every point along it. As he watched his story unfold, the point at which he entered this place was being displayed. Brill was able to slow it down and take it moment by moment or go backwards. Once he got to where he left the Earth, the images stopped, just the blinding light. Not knowing why, he saw that light as a doorway, something buried within his consciousness that finally emerged. He followed that light and was now in a familiar place, the X-point that bridged the Well and Earth. Curious if he could go back to the memory place, his focused turned back to that spot. The landscape changed and he went back there. With more confidence in his ability to control this process, he went back into the X-point leading from the Well. While there, he could see that the energy from this place could be directed to anywhere on Earth, hope-fully allowing him to enter and exit as he chose. This was just the push he needed, and he focused on that point in the room where he was snatched away.

The dormant quantum computer in his brain began to emerge right beneath the surface where it entered his forehead, though it never broke the skin. Combined with the nanobots and dark matter coursing through his neurons, the quantum computer bits were directing some type of quantum energy out of his forehead. That neural focused energy allowed Brill to essentially create a doorway or bridge between the X-point and that point on Earth, one in which he was able to freely move through. Brill could see the room coming at him fast and furious. He was elated to see his friends as his vision focused in on them.

BRILL STEPPED through the light into the room. Liora looked up at the shadow now shielding her, realizing this was a familiar figure. She jumped up and gave him a big bear hug.

9

NEW TERRITORY

Brill was eager to recreate the mechanism that allowed him to travel from where he was into the X-point and them back to reality. The magnetic monopoles were the way to go, and he helped Sirum to refine the nuance of the device, tailoring it to allow for travel from one spot on the planet to another, as long as they were connected via the monopoles.

THE FIRST TEST of instantaneous transport of an object from one side of the building to another was a dismal failure. The device was monstrous, and they needed two, and Brill was no help in miniaturizing it. One device to send and one to receive, kind of like a phone call with the difference being that mass is moved, not a voice. Though the concept was familiar to Brill, just energy from one site to another, it proved much more challenging than he thought. His panacea that the Well had given him all the answers was being tested and proven to be a false belief, even though he was able to do it. He just didn't know how the quantum computer bits in his head were able to create the doorway. When he went to the Well for answers, it simply gave him the tools and he was now learning that it required much more than equations and creating a device to make this work. It needed a mind to focus all the connected neural energy in the Well into one action, as those connected minds feeding the Well needed direction. Other than the Nurizzi and that ancient enemy, he had not yet encountered another in the Well that could utilize its information.

SIRUM STARTED simple in building the matter transport using X-points. The first effort was to move a basketball a hundred feet across the room. The sending device consisted of two giant magnets generating similar monopole magnetic fields with the distance between them far enough that the fields would not contact each other. To engage the transport mechanism, they would push the magnets towards each other till the magnetic fields collided, ideally the collision would be directly on the object trying to be moved. As the plates moved closer together, the ball started to roll away from one magnet and then back to the other. As they approached each other, the ball bounced back and forth so fast the eye couldn't keep track of it. Then it exploded once the fields collided when there was no more room between the fields.

They reviewed every scrap of data they had collected, with none of it making sense. They slowed down the video, looking at it in nanosecond increments. From everything they could tell, the machines showed the ball disappearing from its current location and reappearing, as if it transported away and then immediately transported back, yet the accepting site for the ball never showed it appearing.

So where did it go? That question nagged at Brill for many weeks without any answer. Brill went into the Well several times, now that he was able to get there without a chair, but no results were generated. The Well helped him to quantify what he saw, but not how to make it work. Brill was starting to realize the limitations of the Well, it needed a lot of fundamental information to advance an idea, or a mind that was directly connected to the idea. Brill suspected that the reason some ideas were so full of information is that a mind or many minds over a period of time or in some other part of the galaxy, had already developed the idea and learned how to make it work. The Well seemed to be the gathering point for information from those minds, when those minds presented an idea and solutions to the Well. Those minds could solve it if someone had seen some part of the question before. Brand new ideas, like the one Brill was advancing, were outside of the mental collective's analytical capabilities, simply because none of them had ever seen anything like it in action, nor had those minds figured out how to make something like this work. They could work on small bits of the problem if it was a thought they had or would have at some point in their future.

Realizing the limitation of the Well, he began to focus more on what he now had in hand, a working theory and devices that were close to what he needed. The data was where they focused their attention. When they stepped back and analyzed what they had accomplished, the confidence in their own abilities began to surface. The creation of magnetic monopoles was nothing to sneeze at, since it was an engineering feat that had had eluded even the brightest of minds. The analysis showed that the X-points were not entirely similar. They had to look down to the trillionth decimal place to see the variation, as the magnetic fields in those different spots had just enough oscillation out to that precision level, that it seemed to impact the ability to transfer the ball from one site to the other. With this in mind, Sirum went back to his shop to work on a device that would create dampening fields. The Earth's magnetic field was highly stable, but something else was interfering. The detectors picked up neutrino emissions. If this were the problem, he would need Brill's help.

"Brill, I may have found the problem."

"And?"

"Sorry, I am trying to understand the data. The neutrinos seem to be causing fluctuations in the magnetic field. I need someone to bounce ideas off of."

"Glad to help, but I still don't follow. My understanding of quantum mechanics has always taught it to be the other way around, that neutrinos are influenced by magnetic fields."

"Yes, that is the classical teaching."

"Would not be the first time that we have seen classical theories on quantum mechanics be lacking in their substance. Let's play out what you have observed and see if we can put some effort behind making it work."

"Thanks Brill. The data is very clear. The magnetic fields were aligning from the sending site to the receiving site. Then a single neutrino passed through the detector at the receiving site. That followed in a variation in the magnetic monopoles of both devices there, collapsing the X-point. The next time we tried, there were multiple neutrinos that disrupted the lining up of the monopoles."

"Sirum, how in the hell are we going to block something that can pass through anything?"

"Well, that's not entirely correct. A neutrino is a fermion, which means it generally has a weak subatomic force and gravity and is also electrically neutral. It is generally thought that its mass is so small that it doesn't interact with the mass of elementary particles. Since it is a half spin, it is a lepton and comes in three flavors, the electron, muon, and tau neutrino. Some of those flavors are high energy, depending on their origin, such as the collision between photons and protons, resulting in pions and muons that decay into high energy neutrinos."

"Dude, you lost me there. Though I appreciate a good lecture, I have no idea what the hell you were trying to tell me."

"Sorry, but I get on a roll with that stuff."

"Sirum, maybe you need to look at it from a different angle instead of as a physicist."

"You'll have to elaborate, as I don't know where you are headed with this."

"If what you are saying is the problem and the high energy neutrinos are interacting with the magnetic monopole, then maybe we are not viewing the data as to what could be really going on.

What if the monopoles are attracting those high energy muon neutrinos?"

"I hadn't thought of that way. I was looking at the neutrinos as the problem."

"Maybe you should look at the data again and see if the energy of the monopole matched the anti-energy of the neutrino?"

"The detectors weren't designed to detect that level of detail. The only reason I knew there were neutrinos there, was that I had put in place a Boson detector, looking to see if the Higgs-Boson particle would interfere with the monopoles."

"Even better. We now have a course of action and don't have to rely on the Knowledge Well to lead us down a useless path. How long before you can build the detectors and a neutrino collector? If this continues to be a problem, then we need to understand how to shield the monopoles from attracting subatomic particles."

"Give me a month and I'll have the detectors in place. It may take a few more months to build a collector as that is new territory."

"Great. Let me know when you are ready to start up."

It took a little longer than originally anticipated, about a month more. Sirum had to create a new metal to absorb not only neutrinos, but any other subatomic and exotic particle that existed on the quantum level. He found that the dark matter was a great starting point to develop something that interacted with everything on the quantum level. It naturally was a neutralizer of quantum particles, but was too strong, since it also neutralized magnetic fields.

Sirum had not only developed a high energy micro super collider to surround the monopole fields, but also was able to make the monopole generator a whole lot smaller. Within the collider, photons were bombarding the dark matter. This created semi-dark matter, similar to what Brill injected himself with, and it generated just enough of an in-between state as to not interfere with the monopoles, but strong enough to absorb not only neutrinos, but Boson particles as well, if they ever showed up. The final device was something of a work of art. It looked like the Olympic Rings turned on their side to form a triangle with the floor made of the super conducting metal

Niobium. The monopole generators were the upper three rings and the lower two were the super collider. This was repeated on the opposing side, but with a separate monopole generator. The fields converged at the direct center point of the triangle. Simple in design, yet powerful in function. If these worked as planned, they could revolutionize travel across the planet.

BRILL WAS LEARNING MORE and more about the Well and its power or lack thereof. The first time he found his way there, he was bombarded with too much information, too much to make sense out of it. Then came the understanding of how it could help to solve or advance a specific problem, equation, or theory. That approach was actually the most difficult, as he learned through the exploration of this place. Then came the let down on learning it was not the knowledge equivalent of the fountain of youth, as it had limitations on what he could gain from it. In his latest explorations without the need for the chair to get there and was in his full human form there, knowledge was easier to obtain and understand. His body was firmly planted in that bridge between the X-point and the Well, yet he was able to fully see and hear in this place, as well as to move at will any spot in the Well. Now he truly saw with his eyes the patterns of the Well when a question was put to it. The patterns were like roads, as with any road, some were dead ends and others led to an abundance of activity.

He found the roads to be patterns of civilizations, both past and present. The more intently he focused on the patterns, he caught a glimpse of an image his brain could only interpret as a faint image. The structure and outline of it were foreign to the human way of thinking. Once he had the glimpse of it, his mind could follow it and try to bring it into focus. Every part of his being said what he saw/perceived was wrong or improbable, as it didn't fit any conventional human way of thinking. To Brill, this was exciting, as he knew he was seeing something his mind was not trained to learn and that made him want to know even more. The closer he got to those patterns he could see why his mind was having trouble defining it. This was an entirely alien civilization and the thoughts of this species moved or oscillated at a frequency his mind was unable to define. In here, he could make his mind learn and begin to understand everything about this civilization. From his chance encounter with the Nurizzi in here, he knew that alien societies had to exist out there, but until now, he had not figured out how to find them.

The oddity of the knowledge of this alien civilization became more familiar the longer he observed them. After some time, he began to see the patterns of their language and ways of thinking. This culture seemed to be focused on art and beauty. Their 'problems' they were trying to solve centered around what it took to build massive structures. These were not stone and mortar, but structures of energy and other forces he didn't yet comprehend. The longer he observed, the more he realized he had started at the early point in their civilization. Their knowledge seemed to blossom as more minds joined the fray and the back and forth between them across time brought advances in their medicines, buildings, transportation, and science that eluded his understanding.

This species lived on gas giants, hence the mammoth structures they built, indicative of their size. The form of these beings involved a 'body' of charged particles that formed the outline of their semi-fluid existence. Those particles housed the equivalent of organs, nerves, and was the equivalent of skin, with all the sensory inputs similar to the human body. Their minds operated on a level that was much faster than a human mind and they seemed to advance from their early development into a highly advanced society. Brill learned about avenues of physics that the human mind could never comprehend.

On the large world in which they lived, a year on their planet was the equivalent of five hundred on Earth, which is why they seemed to advance so much faster. In the Well, temporal measures had little meaning and all Brill could see was the rapid influx of minds in what seemed a short span of years on their planet. That would have equated to millions of years on Earth. Through them, Brill saw how to manipulate the matter transport device he and Sirum had built, which is why he guessed he was brought here. This society had learned to travel the stars with something similar to what he had devised. They were massive species that required the ability to contain their form, so spaceships of the kind developed on Earth would not work for them. They had discovered the X-points early in their development, as these places existed across the surface of their planet, since the moons around this gas giant imparted such high gravitational fields that collided with the planet on its surface. They had learned how impart a high energy plasma stream into the corona of the X-point to direct where it went on the surface of their planet, enabling them to 'move' around the surface without exerting much energy, a must have for a semi-fluid being. Just the bit of info he needed to take back and apply to his efforts.

Brill had finished with that alien race for now, getting ready to move on, when his mind had him pause long enough to call up an image. The image was one he first encountered in the bridge, as they scrolled past him. The image was connected with spatial coordinates in Brill's mind. Brill turned his attention from the entry to the Well and focused on the entry to the X-point. He brought up that image in his mind to see it now unfold in the X-point entry. The question that came up in his mind was how far away from Earth was this alien society. In the span of a neuron firing, the image was now side by side next to the Earth X-point, along with some type of symbols. Brill was not sure what those symbols were, but guessed they were spatial coordinates. This was a curiosity that would suffice him at a later time, as he was too focused on getting back to the Well to solve his immediate problem.

GETTING BACK into the Well from the bridge, Brill moved on from that species, learning how to pick up the noise of alien minds, since his human mind could only hear other like-minded beings. Each time he saw where these pockets of noise were, much like a weather radar on

Earth, he could 'listen in' and learn about these alien societies. He soon found out that it took too much effort to pull any nuggets of information out of those societies, as their thought patterns were so different. He had to start from the beginning, if he could find it, and take it to the end to see what they knew and if it would be of use to him.

The Nurizzi were the constant mystery for him. They must be close to human thought patterns, since Brill was unable to pick out where they were in the Well. Much like the human thoughts in the Well. When Brill homed in on one of these other alien species, there were so many individual minds over the course of their history, it was extremely difficult to find the beginning and end of these societies. The Well seemed to merge them all together making it difficult to find a single mind. Occasionally, he was able to jump in at the starting points in their history and follow their course of development, but those were rare instances. Most of these species were so different from the human way of life that their medicines and that type of technology was of little applicability.

Brill would come across some new physics occasionally, like X-points, but for the most part, they looked and lived so differently that nothing they did would apply to the human way of life. If he ever found the Nurizzi, he would be able to see if they were oxygen breathers or something else. Carbon based life forms were common, but many used photosynthesis type reactions as the equivalent of oxygen based redox reactions. Being gravity bound was also an anomaly, humans seemed to be in the minority on that front, as nearly every species he encountered could live in the void of space as easily as the surface of planets. Yet there were so many Earth-like planets across the cosmos...This was a bit sobering to Brill, as he was expecting far more humanoid like races. The Well seemed to have infinite capacity, so he would eventually find more human-like species, that he was certain, but for the moment, it was not the case.

∾

Navigation in the Well was becoming easier now that his body was in the bridge. Every time he entered, his mind was constantly mapping and cataloging everything he had seen. He was observing about the hundredth space dwelling species, when he inadvertently stumbled across an oddity. He noticed he could push the thought patterns around if he concentrated on just the single thought the alien mind was casting. Brill found this fascinating, since these minds were already pieces of history and he was an observer, so he thought. Somehow, he saw he was interfering with their thought transmission, but not likely their history. He wondered if this could change the history of this species. Curiosity took the better of him and he began to focus his consciousness on blocking this individual's thought. Brill watched his efforts domino outward. Regions of the Well here that were connected to this individual began to wink out, similar to blowing out a candle. Once he let go of the blocking, those areas began to return, though not as wide spanning as before. Could he have influenced the history of this alien race. He needed more confirmation, so he set out to block another individual mind when something hit him. At first, it gave him the experience of a merry go round, as he was spinning and not able to focus in on any area. Once the spinning stopped, Brill realized he was back in the region of human thought. Brill needed more data, so he found his way back there and tried again to influence the first mind he encountered. This time Brill was looking around when he saw an unusual scene unfolding in front of him. What looked like a small cube with a man sitting on it was steadily growing larger at a rapid speed. When it was close enough to get a vision of the man, he saw it was no man at all, but an outline of a human and the 'man' seemed to jump off and grab ahold of Brill's consciousness and send him flying back to the human region of the Well.

What was that? Brill said to himself. His perception was of a being that slightly resembled a human but was made of light. He thought back to the events he had set in motion and he suspected that being was some type of guardian of this place, something like a keeper of the garden. Nature always seemed to provide some mechanism of balance or order. He guessed this place was no different. The more he pondered this, the Well started to provide answers, and it told him the Well was always in balance, knowledge in versus knowledge out. A second answer appeared to him: The Well needs the creative mental capacity of those minds connected to it as they are used to serve a higher purpose. No further explanation was provided on the higher purpose, as it seemed to be the Well itself telling him this information and it did not appear to want to yield any more information.

Brill thought back to his newly found abilities in here. How could he use those to learn? The thoughts/his need to learn what this place was kept tugging at him. At first he brushed aside that need, continuing to focus on what that thing was that moved him around in the Well. The question on dark matter bubbled to the surface of his thoughts and was now consuming him. The Well itself began to provide these answers, as the minds connected here were not aware of dark matter, at least not the kind he and Sirum had discovered/made. Dark matter was a created substance, made for the purpose of drawing into the Well, the unique cognitive abilities from each generation of the universe. Brill's mind erupted with more questions than he could field at one time. The first was who made the dark matter. The answer that returned had him even more puzzled, as it was short, to the point, and made little sense to him. The Well told him, '*From the other side*', before the enemy, in order to draw in the *parts of the enemy.*' The barrage of questions that explanation generated went unanswered. Aside from those unanswered questions, his others were answered with a word here an image there, nothing more. Brill's mind finally processed the last piece the Well had told him, '*each generation of the universe.*' He questioned what was the meaning of that?

The answer, '*The universe is infinite yet has a beginning and ending. Every ending starts a new beginning, and every beginning starts an ending.*' Brill didn't know how to process this. Somehow it fit with his understanding of how the Well was created, maybe the why it was created, an infinite prison for that enemy, so he saved it for later. He could spend an eternity here and never achieve a full level of understanding, even as brilliant as he was. Having filled his mind with new topics to ponder, he made his way back to the bridge to take home the information on the transport portals.

WHEN BRILL RETURNED to the Well, he started where he did the first time, on its edge. He decided to take a different tactic. He wanted to see if he could see the Well from the perspective of its topside or bottom side. The Well seemed to show him the means to do this and Brill faded back to a perspective of seeing the Well as it existed in its whole. His mind could now see how it could span every aspect of the universe many times over and all at the same time. It showed him the universe was like looking at a vine that grew around the inside of a sphere, where the leaves were a Mandelbrot series that would touch another Mandelbrot series at their ends and then dissolve into each other, the literal beginning and end of two universes. The vine though was infinite on itself, as the outside of the sphere was the inside of a different sphere. Brill perceived these as anti-spheres, a never-ending line of bubbles of spheres and anti-spheres with an infinite number of universes like his that were made, progressed, and died and then reemerged as another universe. This was so confounding and difficult to perceive, Brill almost bolted out of the Well, as his mind said this is not possible.

Brill took a step back even further, as he was so caught up in trying to analyze what he 'saw' and didn't take the time to think. Now he stopped and let everything soak in and asked the Well what he was seeing. The images of chemistry analogies began to surface. He wasn't sure if it was chirality, no those are right and left hand, must be enantiomers. Yes, that was it he thought. Those are mirror images and once he hit upon that, the term asymmetry surfaced. Now he was certain that was it. He was looking at a mirror image, but through the context of mirrors within mirrors, like a carnival funhouse. With that image in mind the multitude of images began to shrink and show what was driving the multitude of previous images. Those were his mind's inability to process what he saw.

With the context now in focus, he was able to narrow down and see what it really was. There was one Knowledge Well that was the vine and those Mandelbrot series that branched off were looking into a mirror image of themselves, so that once they collided with themselves, they collapsed back towards the center of the vine and then started over. This was the beginning and end of universes, so that there was always conservation of mass and a constant turnover of universes being created and then destroyed. Wherever the Well, the vine, went it must be this 'need to imprison the enemy and keep it from invading'. He tried to find the end of the vine but could not locate it. Maybe he was looking at a neuron in God's mind? As that thought surfaced, the Well seemed to give him something else to ponder, more like a nudge. That was the idea of parallel universes and that nothing there was infinite, as everything came full circle. He realized what that meant, in that if one looked at infinity straight on, the end of it would be the spot directly behind him that he could not see, always there, but always out of reach. The physics term that Brill had surface was the lensing effect of time. Brill could not see or perceive it and he could not understand how there were beings to take care of such a massive extra-verse, as he had no other term for it. The extra-verse meant everything outside of his known realm of understanding. He realized even if he had the equivalent of eternity, he would never be able to learn all that was contained within the infinite. He may not be able to perceive this on its whole, but he could tap into the multitude of intelligences that existed within it and he would definitely do so, possibly even figure out a way to travel to those places. Though the thought crossed his mind, *'what if those beings, those enemies, are using the minds linked to the Well to try to escape?'* A thought he quickly dismissed as nonsense.

BRILL RETURNED to the bridge only moments after he left, yet his mind was processing the equivalent of years in the Well, further evidence to him that time had little meaning in the Well. The first thing he did upon his return to his lab was to bring Sirum up to speed on fixing the X-points. Brill liked the idea of calling the X-point devices portals, as they could move matter from one location to another on Earth. The first test he and Sirum ran was to transport a bunch of empty boxes from a location in California to the one in Nevada. Success! They were thrilled as every box arrived in the condition it started and not a smidge out of place. They moved on to more complex items, like electronics and vehicles. All were instantaneously moved from one site to the other. Then they tried a vehicle that was running in idle. They placed all kinds of sensors across the engine and exhaust, wanting to see if anything was interrupted while it was transported. The analysis took a few days for Sirum's backup quantum computer to analyze every measure down to the trillionth of a second and everything was perfect.

From there, they progressed to the bigger test, a living being. They started with bugs, fruit flies, then moved up to mammals. Monkeys were always the favorite for this type of experiment. Brill was concerned about genetic mutations and the like, so he created a complete genome and protein map of all five primates both before and after transport. The primates went through unscathed. Brill immediately took blood and bone marrow samples for analysis. Even with the quantum computer, it took two months to complete the analysis. In the end, everything was perfect, no anomalies. They repeated the test several times on the same primates looking for everything that could go wrong. For the first few days after the transfers, everything seemed fine until the first primate started seizing. The rest soon followed, and each died with minutes of one another. Autopsies revealed organs slowly turned inside out and parts of their insides completely missing or twisted up with other parts.

Brill's heart sank when he heard this news. He had so hoped to transport people without the need for fuel or traveling for hours, sometimes days. He and Sirum poured over the data for months on end and still no solution. Brill frequented the Well often, but no answer would come to him, as he suspected. Brill had found that anything entirely new that had never been invented was something the Well could not help them advance. If there were parts of the idea related to something already invented by others or based on mathematics, then the Well could propose many solutions. Brill's X-point portals were entirely different than X-points used by that semi-fluid species. He couldn't understand why the Well would not connect his problem to ones they had encountered, if they ever did.

The 'trick' Brill developed was to break the problem down int smaller bites and this was how he put the pieces together to create the portals. So, now he did the same approach with these results, backing out each observation and trying to associate that with some theory or problem someone associated with the Well had solved before. In the multiple trips to the Well on this problem with the transport and the primate physiology put Brill onto the trail of quantum entanglement, a theory that had never been fully proved, until now. Discussing these possibilities with Sirum, they arrived at quantum entanglement as the only solution and guessed it was the transfer from the magnetic monopole gate through some type of quantum tunnel to get to the other monopole to exit. During that quantum venture, they guessed that exposed the genetic material of the primates to various quantum exotic particles which may have instigated the rearrangements.

The solve that he and Sirum figured out was to trap the traveler and its contents in a dark matter bubble. The theory was solid but creating and implementing it was far from easy. The first step was simple, generate the bridge between the monopoles. The next steps were unclear.

"Any ideas Brill on how to safely generate a bubble of dark matter inside that magnetic bridge?"

"Well, not really. I will go out on a limb and say let's see if we can push energy into it."

"Won't the energy interact with the quantum particles and cause an explosion."

"In theory, yes. It may however give us and idea of what won't work and help us home in on what does."

Every type of energy they could generate resulted mostly in destabilization of the magnetic fields. They did this through the night without incident and took a break till midday. They fired up the devices just as the sunshine was blazing in the sky. Just as the device was at full capacity, the sunlight reflected off a shiny piece of metal right into the portal. Nobody noticed the reflection and probably wouldn't have cared had they noticed. The beam of sunlight had been reflecting into the portal for about five minutes when Brill approached to bombard the portal with high energy radiation. Just as he was about to hit start, the surface of the portal began to oscillate like a wave on the ocean and then began to spark. This caused Brill to instinctively take cover. No sooner than he jumped behind the protective shield when all hell broke loose. The loudest boom he had ever heard reverberated around and through him. Then fire soared around the shield, leaving him gasping for air, as it consumed nearly all the oxygen around him.

In that peril, the pieces of the supercomputer in his head activated and transported him to the quantum bridge between the X-point and Well. While there, his body consumed all the oxygen needed to return to normal. While his body was coming out of shock, the solution came to him, something akin to music washed over him. This was different than music as Brill could see the harmonics of the sound waves and their rhythmic patterns. It was the background of the universe. The noise that many dismiss, and none have discerned a reason as to why there is background noise in the vacuum of space.

This was it. So simple Brill would have never arrived at that as an answer. Use a sound wave as a way to push the dark matter through the portal and create an atmosphere and shield from one side to the other. Had he not been in this state with a clear mind devoid of any thought, he would not have noticed the sound, more or less come up with a solution to his problem.

Now armed with a potential solution, he and Sirum set about seeing if it would actually work. The first few tries were met with failure, much like every other attempt they had tried. They cycled through every audible frequency and then combined one after the other, hoping they would land upon the right combination. They set the computer to try every single combination. After four weeks of this and billions of combinations, still nothing worked. In a rare outburst of anger, Brill turned to the portal and yelled obscenities as loud as his voice would allow. Several minutes of this had his voice cracking like a prepubescent male. He stopped yelling as a pinging sound on the monitoring equipment caught his attention. The monitor showed a successful bridge had been created. Brill was at a loss as to what had work and was too tired to care at this point. He called up Sirum, elated with the success and had him pour over the data to find what had worked.

"Brill, it was sound alright, but it needs to be at a specific decibel."

"I'll be damned. You mean that outburst of anger I had actually was productive? Guess I should do that more often."

Now that they had a solution, they began the tests to prove it protected the travelers. Test after test yielded positive results and they were ready to go public with it a few months later.

The rollout to the world was met with skepticism and trepidation. Brill started with personal care goods manufacturers, showing them that they could transport their goods from their manufacturing site to their distribution warehouses instantaneously. It took about a year for that to catch on, and when it did, it was like wildfire. Once businesses started showing massive profit increases from not having to transport their goods, almost every business was beating down his door to get the portals installed. After he had thousands of businesses signed up, Brill set up a news conference to let the world know of his successes.

～

"Thank you everyone for joining me today. I have some exciting news to share with the world on my company's efforts to reduce world pollution," was Brill's opening statement and he continued to present the work he had put in place over the last year.

A reporter shouted out a question as Brill paused in his dialog, "When will this transport people?"

"Thanks for asking," Brill intoned, "not for some time, as we want to fully show its safety before moving people around."

"Yes, and..." then another reporter interrupted, "Will we be able to go to the moon with this?"

Brill was getting a bit agitated with the interruptions. "No, that's a complexity we have not yet taken on."

"So it's a possibility?"

"Again, thanks for asking. Anything is possible if we can think of it. At the moment, it is so complex to move people and things around the Earth that we don't yet want to take on space."

Brill finished his presentation and took several more questions before calling it a night. With the public now fully aware of what he was doing, Brill was less concerned about Liam's team stealing the work and making him keep it secret. Brill couldn't figure out why Liam hadn't already taken it. '*He must have plans that require the public's acceptance of this.*' Brill thought.

10

THE RETURN

S*ix years earlier – The Day Brill's Dad Was Killed*
Liam returned from the ceremonies with a heavy burden on his conscious. Today he had ordered the hit of one Dr. John Everly, effectively ripping a family apart and setting his son on a course that could never be reversed. This was the hardest decision he had ever made. Dr. Everly was not an assassin, nor was he even military, but he committed the ultimate crime, treason. Liam had definitive proof that Dr. Everly had stolen state of the art nanobots from the military installation at Vassal Biogenetics. If Dr. Everly had just told Liam he had taken them, they could have worked something out, but his superiors were insistent that Dr. Everly be eliminated.

At Liam's urging, the body of Dr. Everly was ushered to area 51 without autopsy and placed in cold storage. As far as everyone was concerned Dr. Everly got his due. When Liam got back to area 51, he brought his second in command, Dr. Les Clancy, into the morgue containing the body of Dr. Everly.

"Les, do you have the serum prepped?"

"Yes, Colonel Rhett. I am ready to proceed."

"You are certain the serum will hold?"

"If Dr. Everly's theories were correct, then yes I have it right."

"Well, Dr. Everly better hope his theories were correct, but now is not the time to find out."

Dr. Clancy placed the serum into an IV bag and proceeded to inject that into Dr. Everly's lifeless body. "How will we know if it worked."

"All in due time my good friend. Please make sure to change out the bag every few months. Only you will be allowed in this room, so no worry about discovery of our efforts here. Just be certain to never mention this place nor your actions to anyone. That's an order."

～

Eighteen months earlier

Liam met up with Dr. Clancy in the morgue only he and Les could enter. "Les, did you find all the equipment and missing code?"

"Yes sir. What am I supposed to do with it?"

"No formalities here Les. It's time to see if a legend wakes."

"This thing looks like a fancy headgear with a tablet computer attached. Haven't seen one of those in years."

"As I recall, Dr. Everly planned to hook up this headgear and then use the tablet to enter the command sequence, assuming that is the code you found. From there who knows if it'll work."

"All right Liam, all is hooked up. I will leave you the honors of throwing the switch."

It was not really a switch per se, but a command sequence on the tablet, which was now also connected to a quantum field generator. Liam had glossed over the explanation Dr. Everly had provided so many years earlier. All Liam got out of that conversation was that this would repair any battlefield injuries, as long as the soldiers had the nanobots in their system first. If they were injected later, the bots would not have time to infect every cell and their treatment would be ineffective.

Liam really hoped Dr. Everly had injected himself with those stolen bots all those years ago. He really needed his intellect with the illness spreading across the Western states. Liam held his collective breath as he punched in the command code. He was not sure if something was supposed to happen right away or days from now, so he strolled over to the fridge and pulled out a six pack.

"Les, would you like one?"

"Sure, why the hell not. He's already dead, not much worse we can do to him."

Laughing, Liam handed him two. "Not sure how long this will take, so I brought refreshments."

They started bantering back and forth talking about their exploit's years earlier, when Les touched upon a delicate subject. "What happened to you after Africa? I didn't see you for several years after you left. The crew thought you died in some covert ops."

"Hmm. Even though you have high clearance Les, that's one area even you aren't cleared to know."

"Come on Liam, it's just the two of us, nobody else to hear."

"You know there are some things that are need to know and that is one you really don't need to know. Just let it go."

Les was going to push a bit further after a few more beers when the heart monitor started the slow beep of life. They both jumped out of their chairs looking to see what his vitals looked like when Les piped in, "Shit, I don't believe it, guess his theories were correct. How in God's name is he alive?"

"Les, that's one of those things you don't need to know."

"Alrighty then. His pulse and core temperature are steadily increasing. Starting to see some brain activity. Not sure how this is possible. Have we created a monster?"

"If his theories were correct, then he will be the same man he was. Though I am not sure if his memories will be intact."

About five hours later, one Dr. John Everly was as alive as the day he was shot. He had not yet woken up but was showing movement in his toes and fingers. His face twitched often as his color returned. Liam found this hard to believe, as none of the bots his team had could ever achieve this feat. Liam was happy to have Dr. Everly return but was also irritated the more he thought about what he had lost in having to 'eliminate' him. His superiors were kept in the dark to this little venture he was now undertaking. If Dr. Everly returned to his former self, he would be given a new identity, more to protect him from those who long thought him dead.

Dr. Everly sat up in his bed after several days of consuming multiple IV bags of nutrients. "Where am I?"

"Welcome back to the land of the living John." Liam greeted him.

"Is that my name?"

"What do you remember?"

"I...don't know."

"Well, let's get some food in you. Maybe some things will come back to you in time."

Liam was about to leave when the tablet caught his eye. After he had punched in the command code, he had thought it of no more use and placed on the table next to Dr. Everly. The screen on the tablet was now blinking in bright pastel colors with the words scrolling across the screen hand me to John Everly. Odd Liam thought, but then again Dr. Everly was always one to plan for contingencies, so he handed him the tablet.

"Here Dr. Everly. It says I need to hand this to you."

Liam backed to the side to let it do its thing, but not too far back so he could see what it would do. At first nothing happened. Liam suggested, "Try touching the screen Dr. Everly." After doing that, the screen went into a different mode and projected a light, as if it were scanning his face. Then it projected an LED beam to the headgear that was still on his head. It pulsed varying colors and intensities over the course of an hour, at which point Dr. Everly's head fell back on the pillow, as if he were unconscious. Not knowing what to do, Liam left things as they were and he and Les went into the adjoining room.

"What do you make of that Les?"

"Umm...I really don't know. You know more than me here."

"I think John planned for something akin to him needing to be 'rebooted' at some point. I am hoping he will have his memories when he awakes as I was not aware he had developed any of this tech."

Dr. Everly slept for several days in varying states of sleep, some restless and some deep and unmoving. As he sat upright in his bed looking around, Liam saw he was up and joined him in the room.

"Welcome back Dr. Everly."

John looked up and all the muscles in his face tightened up to hold back the emotion. With jaws clenched, he barely got the words out, "Liam, you shit hole what have you done?"

"You were dead for a few years and we just revived you."

"Are you fucking kidding me? A few years?"

"Please tell us what you do remember. Do you know who you are and any memories of your past?"

"I know what I know, and I know the tech was never designed to keep a body in suspended animation."

"Do you remember more?"

"Did you not hear me? I designed this tech to repair a battlefield wound and not more."

"And yet here you are a few years after being shot."

"You mean after your team shot me. The bots were designed to repair near death. That means that I have been revived and died thousands of times while in your makeshift stasis."

"You seem fine."

"There is a cost for what you put me through. The bots were designed to take healthy neurons and repair those that were dying. If you kept me in stasis that long, that means that I have lost more than half of the neurons in my brain."

"Again, you seem fine. We will talk more later. I have to go for now."

Liam had John transferred to a medical ward and ordered his staff to help him recuperate and get him back to health. Dr. Everly tried to convalesce but was in a steady decline of health and mental function.

"Dr. Everly, glad to see you are still alive. Has all of your memory returned?

"Liam, I am dying. Seems like it is coming faster each day. If you have a need of me, you better ask it soon, as I can't imagine why you would have brought me back unless it was a dire need."

"As much as we were at odds in the past, I was hoping bygones could be bygones and we start fresh. If you are dying, I regret not having revived you sooner and really need your help now, so let's get down to business."

~

LIAM PRESENTED Dr. Everly with the chain of events that led up to outbreak and how it was somehow related to the work his team was doing on primates.

"Dr. Everly, do you recall your prion research?"

"Certainly, that is one of the things I remember best."

"My team was modifying your prions to try to advance intelligence when something went wrong."

With the anger building in John, he blurted out, "You power hungry son of a bitch. Why the hell would you do that? They were designed to fix damage. Low or lack of intelligence is not damage."

Unphased by John's comments, Liam continued on, "One of the primates fell ill and then it passed to one of my men. From there, he ended up spreading it to a card dealer in Vegas where it changed, mutated somehow. How it changed is what we need to know, as it is causing people to either die or turn into some type of animal. Something not quite human, but not primate either."

Still angry, John composed himself and replied, "Damn you Liam. I am not sure I can help but I'll try for as long as I can. Show me the lab. I hope you have tissue and blood samples. I'll start with the prion and see if I can figure it out."

John's progress was slow. Now that he was physically debilitated, due to the reduced brain function, he tired easily and found it difficult to concentrate for long periods. Dr. Everly's slow start found him doing what he did best, understanding how this disease affected the infected people, much as he used to do with cancer patients. He felt like he was making progress, albeit slow, until one day when he noticed that the prions were not behaving as he recalled them. They seemed to be only carriers, not really having any of the prion function he designed them to have. This was all petri dish work and he was realizing it was leading him to a dead end. Animal research was not his desired form of research, as he much preferred working on people. The primates were his last and only resort, so he gave in and used them to get what meaningful data he could. John was gingerly moving around the primates, as his bodily functions were barely within his control and it took all he effort just to move a few steps. He approached the primate that was named Shama. Slowly approaching her, she reached towards him to take the food he offered. They told him it was a peace offering that would allow the animal to warm up to him. All was good until Shama caught sight of the syringe in his other hand. He was told to keep that well-hidden, but his memory wasn't all it used to be. Shama burst out in a hysterical fit and bit a chunk out of his arm. Fortunately, his caution had him wearing a protective covering over his arms and face, though he had missed pulling the cover over the very section of the arm that was now missing part of what used to be there. John fell back in pain as blood sprayed everywhere. The cage attendants were too slow to intercept and rushed to his side as he hit the floor.

As John lay in the recovery ward, he felt the changes occurring within himself. At first, he wasn't sure if it was the degradation of his neurons due to being in stasis for so long or if was just degeneration. Then his body started to physically change. Hair started to grow on his arms and legs where it used to not be. He knew then that he had been infected. Now he had his human subject. Not sure if this was preferable to the rapid deterioration his body was experiencing before the infection, he put his effort towards finding a cure before he could no longer recognize himself.

For most, the disease resulted in a rapid transformation into an animal state or death. For John Everly, it was a different path. He body was in such bad shape to start, the prion infection worked more to repair his failing muscles than it did to change him into an animal, though he was still changing. Now that he could observe the changes in their native form, he started to home in what was happening to the prion. It began to pick up nucleic acid matter, either DNA or RNA,

John wasn't sure. Before he could progress further, he fell into a deep coma and was unresponsive from then on.

∽

THE NEWS REACHED Liam that John had succumbed to the disease and was now unresponsive. The work John had completed was enough to give Liam's team a direction. Before this, they were spinning their wheels. Liam had his doubts that they could devise a cure, but hope was all he had. Then word came that Brill was spotted back in Vegas. When his team finally caught up with Brill, he had a cure in hand and had administered it to himself. Brill was now on the road to recovery. He may still yet be able recover the great Dr. John Everly. Liam was eager to have John continue his research and expand the scope of what those nanobots could do.

"Leverage", Liam kept saying aloud to himself, "Leverage, I need leverage." He used to hold all the cards with manipulating John, but now he had nothing. Somehow, he would need to entice John into working for him, instead of against him, assuming he would wake up from his coma.

∽

PRESENT DAY

A knock on the door from Liam's staff sergeant brought him out of deep thoughts, "Colonel Rhett, may I enter?"

"Please come in sergeant. I take it you have news for me?"

"Yes, sir." As he saluted.

"At ease, sergeant. What do you have?"

"Two things sir. First, Dr. Everly responded to the treatment from Dr. Brill and has fully recovered from the virus, though he is as still deteriorated as before. Second, the unknown substance that your niece and Dr. Lars brought back from Sri Lanka has unique properties that match sample Eqypt-1."

Liam started to raise from his chair at that comment. As he

headed out the door, looking back over his shoulder, he said to the sergeant, "I'll be in the lab. I need to see the analysis."

When Liam entered the lab, the lab tech looked up from the bench, and immediately jumped to attention with a salute. "At ease lieutenant, what do you have for me."

"Yes, sir. We finished the analysis of the Sri Lanka sample." Handing it to Liam. "We were just getting ready to analyze this unique shrapnel that Dr. Brill Everly sent to us from that metal he took out of the head of Major Thomas."

"Why would he do that?"

"Sir, Dr. Everly mentioned that it was an identical match to the Sri Lanka sample."

"You also mentioned that it also matched Egypt-1?"

"Yes sir, a perfect match. We are setting it up now to see if the metal Dr. Everly sent matches it as well."

The lab tech looked up a Liam, "It's a fucking hit...Oh, pardon my language Sir."

"Show me." Liam barked as he quickly made his way to the screen with the data.

The technician typed in a flurry of keystrokes and the screen rapidly changed to show three separate graphs that slowly merged into one where the different color lines of each analysis merged into a single series of peaks and lines. "See here Sir. All these on the left are the separate analysis, each done in triplicate. Then on the right, all three are overlaid on top of each other. As you can see, not a single deviation. All lines are the same."

Liam stammered with a quiet voice, "So what I am seeing means that Egypt-1, the Sri Lanka sample, and the metal from Major Thomas' head are identical."

"Yes sir. If could tell us what is in Egypt-1, maybe we might be able to make more sense of what this metal is, since it does not register as any known substance we have ever seen"

Liam looked up at the tech and said on reflex, "Egypt-1 is eyes only and you do not have the clearance to know more about it."

"Apologies Sir. Awaiting your orders."

"Doesn't look like you will easily determine what it is, so focus on what it does."

Liam proceeded down the hall to John Everly's quarters. He needed Dr. Everly to remember his work on the nanobots, as Liam was stymied at every turn on getting them to work like they did in John. He was thinking, 'Even if he were only to get them to revive a half-dead soldier, then all the work and sacrifice would be worth it. Then he would be ready for his next phase.'

A short knock on the door brought John out of his thoughts of the past. He looked up, "Enter". When he saw who it was, he was less eager to engage in conversation.

"Dr. Everly, I am pleased you are back to your old self."

"My old self? Are you fucking blind? My body is crippled and slowly dying."

"Minor pains given what you are fortunate enough to have recovered from."

"If you had just left me dead, I would be in a better place than here."

"You can always terminate your nanobots. I assume you built a suicide code into them. Though I doubt you would last long, and I would be sorry to see you go."

"Yes, that is always an option, especially if I don't like what you will ask me to do. If only I could remember the command for that sequence."

"Details, details. We will get to that in due time. For now, I want you to put your impressive intellect to a problem that none of us can figure out, including your son."

That last bit changed his body language enough to tell Liam he had hit upon a topic that may eventually give him the leverage he needed.

John tried not to react to Liam's comment about Brill. The cure he had received seemed to have unlocked those emotion areas of the brain, and he was working to suppress those since he knew Liam would use every single thing he could to get him to bend to his will.

"What is this great mystery you have?" John was eager to do anything but sit in this room and remember the past.

Liam could see this was going to be easier than he thought, boredom has a way of influencing many a stubborn mind. "Glad you are on board. Follow me."

When Liam entered the lab with Dr. Everly lumbering behind, all the techs rushed up to greet him. Dr. Everly was well known among their team and any nuggets of information they could get out of him could boost their careers. After the greetings and introductions, they shared with John everything they had and waited for him to reply.

John was quick to make suggestions, as his previous work on analyzing the nanobots while in Guantanamo had stuck with him. John had a suspicion on the function of the metal, since it could not be welded or joined to anything other than itself. About a month into the work, John was debriefed on the intel that Liora and Sirum had gathered since their return from Sri Lanka. Once he heard this, he was furious and determined he would give Liam an earful next time they chatted. John viewed this update as a delay that could have helped move him in a different direction from the start. Seeing how the Chinese scientists were using the metal, he directed his team to set up a similar set of experiments.

The metal, nobody could think of a good name for it other than 'the metal', so John kept calling it that. John was reviewing the results of the latest experiments, where his team was bombarding the metal with different forms of energy emitted by the radioactive Uranium. The team had viewed that experiment as a failure, but something caught his eye. The area with the background radiation seemed to grow as the energy was ratcheted up and grow in a very sharp area of the background, almost exponentially. John compared this area to other experiments and noticed a pattern when the radiation was in a specific energy range. The historical norm was that this area of the analysis readout was noise due to the background energy of the universe, so it was uniformly overlooked. It was very clear to John that a specific range of energy frequencies were driving an amplification in this region. The thought that came to mind was this was a previously unknown form of energy, yet the pattern looked familiar. He would gather more data before making a big deal of this.

Several restless nights brought John awake in the wee hours of the morning, constantly thinking about that background radiation pattern. He could sense it in the periphery of his mind but could not land on the specific memory where he first saw this pattern. He was now obsessed with finding the memory. His daily work proved nothing more than a distraction, as he was constantly trying to recall that memory. This specific day, he was working with the nanobots to try to modify some of the internal architecture to make them more resilient, as a dead man would not produce enough neurotransmitter to keep the nanobots functional, so bringing a dead soldier back to life may prove impossible. This was the fundamental paradox he was trying to solve. A particular scan, elemental scanning electron microscope (SEM) he was running, one he had not done in years, was looking at the energy patterns of the nanobots in response to different food sources. Then he saw it. The pattern from the metal was identical to what this nanobot was showing. He tried different analytical techniques and equipment, but the pattern did not emerge until he went back to the elemental SEM analysis. This memory had escaped him as it reckoned back to the time he spent trying to find a cure for Brill. Now he had it, almost. He had the match, but not the specific type of radiation that was being amplified. He recalled a paper, on physics of all things, he had read at Vassal during that time years ago. It talked about Cleon waves, a form of background radiation that is attracted to Muon particles. Those particles were particularly dense in this metal and that had puzzled his team since they started analyzing the metal. Now he felt he was making progress.

John assembled the team to announce his findings. Liam arrived with Liora, as she had arrived earlier in the day at Liam's urging, regarding an uptick in activity at the Sri Lanka site. As they were seated, John started presenting his findings in such a hurried manner that he accidentally tapped the go screen on the Cleon wave generator. He had brought up the screen to show what Cleon waves were and the start button happened to be right in the area where he pointed while he was touching the screen. Just as he finished, not realizing what he had done, he opened the door to the bombardment chamber and was literally pulled to the now radiant shimmering metal. As his hand touched the metal, the world seemed to come apart. He was fighting with everything in his power to let go of the metal. Nothing worked and now he felt like he was being pulled into the metal itself.

The team watching Dr. Everly was eagerly taking notes. Liora and Liam both were intently listening. Right about the time John had started the Cleon generator, she received an urgent text. She excused herself and made the call out in the hall. Moments after she left, she came rushing back in to grab Liam. As she reached for Liam, out of the corner of her eye, she could see Dr. Everly being absorbed by the strange metal. On instinct, she rushed to his side and reached for his hand.

WHAT HAPPENED NEXT WAS a blur to both Liora and John, as well as everyone in the room. In a fraction of a second, Liora and John were no more. They vanished. The metal kept glowing, and parts of the room were now being drawn to it and they vanished also. Nobody in the room knew why the metal was doing this, nor how to shut it down. With only seconds to react, Liam was on his coms ordering the power to the base to be shut down. The suction to the metal had those left in the room hanging on to anything they could, and it was growing stronger. Once the power was cut, the five minutes it took for the metal to stop pulling things into it seemed like an eternity for those in the room.

When they were able to gather their wits. Liam finally realized that Liora and John were gone. He ordered the base to be shut down and searched. If they were there, he would find them.

11

LOSS

The Mao group had stepped up their efforts after completing the construction of the device in Sri Lanka. Liam was perplexed at their mission, even with the spy tech in place. He could see what they were doing, but not the why. As much as it pained him, he would fall back on his last resort, send in Liora. She was well known in that group and thought to be dead. If she suddenly surfaced there under fake orders from their leaders, then they would embrace her, albeit reluctantly. Liam did not want to send her in, he knew Brill would never forgive him if she was killed.

Liam had asked Liora to join him in Area 51. This time, he would ask a high price of her, if she agreed. With Brill in her life now, he wasn't as persuasive as in the past. Infiltrating the Mao group in Sri Lanka would take all he had to convince her she was the one. First though, they would listen to the news Dr. John Everly was so eager to share, as he seemed rather excited about it. Liora was escorted by his office where they exchanged pleasantries and then made their way to John's presentation.

Dr. Everly's presentation of his discovery about the Cleon waves had Liam wondering on the possibilities, and now more than ever he wanted Liora inside that facility. He noticed Liora get up to leave after she received a text. "Is everything okay?" Liam asked.

"Yes, I just need to give Brill a call. Be right back."

A few minutes later, Liora came back in, drawing his attention. The next few seconds were a blur, even for Liam's well-trained eye. Out of the corner of his eye, he saw the metal glowing and John being sucked into it. Liora had rushed to Dr. Everly's aide, too fast for him to react, as the word stop was coming out of his mouth, the world seemed to fall apart. He barely grabbed post in the middle of the room when everything was being sucked into the room with the metal. After everything calmed down, neither Liora nor John were anywhere to be found.

"Lock the base down." Liam barked. "They have to be here somewhere."

~

LIORA BRIEFLY LEFT the presentation to take a call from Brill. Not an urgent matter, but she wanted to hear his voice, as she had been away for several weeks. When she reentered the room, the metal caught her eye with its blinding radiance. She immediately saw that Dr. John Everly was in trouble and instinct took over she rushed to help him. His hand was stuck to that glowing metal and she could see him trying to free it. She grabbed his arm with little effect, so she reached for his hand. As soon as her hand was on his, something happened. With all her might, pulling as hard as she could, her hand would not release from the metal, being affixed to his. The metal seemed to pull on both of them. No amount of resistance could stop it. The wind rushing past their face didn't help either. The glow kept growing until it enveloped them both and the wind pushed them right into the core of the metal.

~

THE LIGHT WAS BLINDING. On instinct, she tried to shield her eyes. That's when she noticed her hand was now free of the metal. None of this made sense. Her mind was trying to process these events when the light finally ceased. Looking to her right, her eyes fell upon Dr. Everly. Something was off with him. As she watched, the worst headache ever hit her. To her horror, Dr. Everly started to literally come apart. It looked to her like his skin was coming off as droplets of sweat that would roll off someone exercising, except it was more than his skin. It was all of him, every part of his body was being pulled apart. Those droplets were attracted to the high intensity Cleon waves bombarding the metal. When those stopped, they sought out the nearest living tissue, since they were nanobots designed to protect and keep it alive. They headed towards Liora. From her perspective, something like a swarm of those droplets of Dr. Everly's body surrounded her, clouding her eyesight, as these nanobots recently ripped from his body completely encased her. In that moment, there was nothing left of the great Dr. Everly.

Liora thought she saw a familiar place right before the swarm covered her, she was in the main chamber of the Sri Lanka facility. Then she was moving again, and she could barely make out the images beyond the swarm, but the intense light still made its way through their protection. The pressure on her head grew and grew until she fell over in unbearable pain, except she never hit the ground. It felt like she was tumbling head over heels, an odd sensation she thought. Her mind processed this sensation as she began to wonder how she could do this, since gravity usually took hold when one fell. As she tumbled, the next experience was like traveling straight up in an airplane. Her cheeks began to pull towards her ears and the force on her was so intense she blacked out.

WHEN SHE CAME TO, this place was unlike any room she had ever seen. The air was sharp to each breath with the taste of metal and each breath was a labor to take. There was a purple haze that filtered through the opening in the wall, she guessed was a window. Over her head was a giant arch with glowing strands of metal, very similar to the one Dr. Everly had latched onto. She tried to right herself, but her equilibrium was off, and she fell back to the floor. To her good fortune, the floor was some type of cushiony substance that absorbed her fall, as if she laid her head gently onto a pillow. That sheen of nanobots that had encased her on her voyage here, now absorbed inside her, deep into her cells. They took on the function they had served for Dr. Everly, repairing damage and protecting her cells right down to the DNA.

She sat there for the longest time, although that word didn't seem to have much meaning anymore. Propping herself up on her elbow, the room started to take shape, though that irritating purple light was making it difficult for her to see with clarity. Something, many some-things, were approaching her. '*Dreaming, yes dreaming. This can't be real*' She thought.

The creatures had heads that resembled hers, but with deep black eyes the size of silver dollars. Staring hard at them, they had some familiarity, what exactly didn't readily come to mind. Her gaze was fixed on those giant eyes. She then noticed what was missing. They had no pupils in their eyes, just coal black without definition. Her eyes moved from theirs to the rest of their face and then to their bodies. They looked human, though the hair was more of a second skin than hair like hers. They were about the size of humans, though their skin looked more yellow than brown in this purple light. The clothes they wore were form fitting, showing they had two arms and two legs. Their height was considerably shorter than hers. She stood at six feet and guessed they were about five feet tall, though they were too far away to make an accurate assessment and her vision was still clouded from the nanbots that continued to coat her from head to toe.

The resemblance to the Roswell grays finally surfaced in her mind, those reported aliens from the 1940's in Roswell, New Mexico. 'What had just happened to her and where was she?' were thoughts resonating through her mind. Her senses were telling her she was someplace else, not in Nevada and not in Sri Lanka. This place had some semblance of familiarity, 'Brill's transport things, yes that was it', she mumbled to herself. If she were 'here', where was here? Fear took root in her heart, a feeling she rarely had, but it grew intensely as the creatures approached.

The sounds coming out of these creatures may have been words, but it sounded like birds chirping to her. One that appeared to be in charge came closest and helped her to her feet. It was trying to communicate she was certain, so she said, 'Hello'. With that, they went into a rapid series of exchanges between themselves. Liora was straining to make out their language, even though she was a bit of a linguist with the multiple languages she spoke. This was unlike anything her brain could decipher. As she focused on their every exchange, the nanbots surged into her, her hands flew up and pressed as hard as she could on her temples. The pain in her head was immense, seeming to go on forever. At this point, these creatures all stopped and stared at her, now seeing she was human, since the nanobots had obscured their vision and now she was fully revealed.

The nanobots mistook Liora's tense thoughts as neural damage, though she was only trying to understand the language. This intense thought created distress in the frontal lobe of her brain, specifically the Broca's and parieto-frontal areas. This was the first place the nanobots targeted as her reasoning, problem solving, and learning due to trying to understand the creatures were in overdrive. They did more than just aid the neurons there. Their design was to rebuild entire neural networks, so they added new neurons to each of these areas of the brain and lesser associated regions. The result was a significant boost in Liora's ability to understand the language, along with so much more. The rebuilding of her entire brain lasted for several hours, the pain of which caused her to lose consciousness in the process.

After waking, she found herself in a sealed room on something resembling a bed. The room was round with the bed in the exact center. Testing the waters to see if she were restrained, her head edged over the bed, followed by her feet. Gaining some confidence in her ability to move without restraint, she gingerly sat up. She was a bit dizzy with thirst and hunger starting to take hold, so she was hoping these creatures were at least able to meet those fundamental necessities, though the lavatory did not seem to be included in this room. The room seemed to go up without end, yet there was light coming down from somewhere, that annoying purple light that was more intense now that the nanobots were no longer clouding her eyes. Liora noticed her vision to be exceptional, better than it used to be. Her eyes scanned the wall for any signs of a door, and something caught her attention out of the corner of her eye, a slight haze. As she stared where that haze first appeared, her vision began to change, almost as if she were zooming in on the defects in the wall. The image that appeared in her mind was something akin to a door handle, so she thought, 'why not', and reached in her hand in to give it a try. At first nothing happened. Something in her head said to focus and imagine opening it. Her mind processed that image of her opening the door and it moving outward, and then the strangest thing happened. She could feel her mind pushing the door, and it opened, actually opened. Standing there with her jaw agape, amazed that she could do such a thing, it took her several minutes to realize she had an exit.

She made her way down a corridor with dim lighting, heading towards chirping sounds that told her those creatures were ahead. She cautiously peeked through the open door to see those creatures sitting eating and drinking. She observed how they made specific gestures on the wall panels. Squares of different shapes appeared, along with a cup of some fluid. As she watched and listened, their language started to materialize in her mind. Those chirping sounds began to take shape and the rudimentary nuggets of their speech were building a foundation in her mind. Realizing she could not keep this position for much longer, lest she be discovered, she continued on down the corridor. Finding a similar room with tables and no occupants made the perfect place to try to scrounge some food and drink.

Liora gestured in a similar manner around the wall panels, yet nothing happened. After about the fifth try, with frustration and hunger raging, a calm voice in her head said to visualize in her mind what she wanted to happen. This was close to what she did for opening the door to the room earlier, so she gave it a go. It took a bit longer than the door did, yet her reward was several multicolored cubes and a cup of fluid. Thirst was a driver now, and the cup was at her lips before she could think otherwise. Before the fluid made its way to the back of her throat, the bitterness of it almost caused her to spit it out. Now sitting at the table, recalling how the creatures took a bite of the gray cube before drinking, she did likewise. The gray cube had no taste. When the fluid crossed her taste buds this time, the bitterness was gone, and it was sweet tasting. Eager to get some nourishment, the rest of the cubes were consumed without thought. The fluid started tasting bitter, so she took bite of the gray cube and refilled her cup. With thirst and hunger abated, it was time to explore further.

The exploration of the various corridors was proving fruitless, nothing but empty chambers and eating places. Frustrated, she sat and leaned up against one of the walls, trying to get some strength back. Her thoughts drifted to her arrival here, wherever here was. One thought crossed her mind she couldn't shake, '*think your way there*'. Feeling she had nothing to lose, she gave it a try. A thread of thought, more like a sense of direction, drifted into her mind. The longer she sat there, the stronger that thought became, until it was an urge to action. Following what seemed to be instinct, arriving at a dead-end hallway, '*now what*'. That thought was no sooner expressed than the image of another panel hidden in the wall appeared. Similar to her actions before, she reached a hand in and imagined opening it. She went through an opening leading to another chamber, though it started to close in on her before she could gather her wits. The air around her started to thicken, creating some type of physical barrier, and then it was like the best roller coaster she had ever ridden. Up, down, sideways, back up, and then a long sideways travel left her dizzy and disoriented. As she regained her senses, it was apparent her destination was successfully reached. Not sure what to do now, she began looking around. If she could figure out this equipment, maybe with her mind, then home may not be too far away.

The equipment to the portal device did not have computers as Liora knew them. There was a large oval shaped maroon structure, about three feet high and two feet wide, centered geometrically at the center of the device. Without thinking, Liora made her way to that structure and placed her hand on it. This time her thoughts centered around the return trip home. As those thoughts took shape, the room began to glow. Something was happening, so she concentrated harder. The portal window began to open, about the size of her hand. No sooner than that process began, she knew something outside of the portal was off. A low droning tone that reverberated her skull, brought scores and scores of the creatures rushing into the room. Realizing she must have tripped some alarm, she tried to hurry the process, though it didn't want to speed up. Liora kept pushing on when tendrils of energy wrapped around her and yanked her off the platform and away from the maroon structure. 'Damn, captured again', she thought.

The creatures brought her to a different room and had her securely bound to a table. One of the larger gray creatures approached her with a device in its hand, its long bony fingers wrapped around it. She heard the chirping sounds that her mind was starting to translate, when the device spit out the words in perfect English.

"Earthing, how have you traveled here through this Eukema - the word wouldn't translate for her, but she guessed he meant the portal?"

"I am not sure how I got here or where here is."

Ignoring her reply, it went on, "how have you mastered our technology?"

"I don't know what you things are and I have no idea about your technology."

"We have visited your world and you are nowhere advanced enough to develop such transportation."

"So, you are the Roswell grays?"

"What do you intend? What world has helped you advance so far so quickly?"

With the most vehemence she could muster, standing up to tower over them with her arm still bound to the table, "You have a lot of questions and so do I. How about we start over? I am Liora. Who are you?" She almost let the sounds coming out of her mouth be in their language, but held that back, realizing that would be her advantage to spy on them without them knowing it.

They immediately backed away from her, now seeing her as a threat. Still using the translation device, it went on. "The Nurizzi will not be intimidated by an Earthling. What is your purpose coming to our home world?"

Now getting irritated, Liora jumped into soldier mode. "Look you gray bastards, I am not here to harm you, I just want to get home."

The chirping sounds now were immediately translating to words in her brain when they spoke next. "Human, you are a very long ways from your home. We are the Nurizzi, and you are correct, we have visited your world many times. How did your people build this device? We observed your people building it and we replicated it here. Until you came through, we have not been able to activate it. Tell us what you know and how it works."

"I told you I don't know anything about this Eukema. I was brought here by accident."

"Earthling you clearly know how to use it. How? What is your purpose in coming here? Did you trick us into building it so you could invade?"

Realizing she was getting nowhere, a different tactic emerged in her mind. "Everyone has enemies, including your people. Earth has been reached by many of your enemies and we are allies now with many worlds." Lying was a skill she had mastered when it was to other humans. She was not sure if the Nurizzi could be fooled as easily.

The reaction she observed in her captors spoke volumes and she saw clearly that she had hit a nerve with them. The tone of their chirping was now less harmonious, and Liora's mind translated that as nervousness. "Who? The Bleeva or the Shirnna or was it the Neptali?"

Now feeling a bit more in control, Liora kept her body language in tight control. On the last name, Liora squinted her eyes and made her heart rate increase. With the increased heart rate, the desired effect was achieved. The Nurizzi began chirping amongst themselves so rapidly that she could not keep up.

"So, the Neptali are helping you. Your people don't know who they have invited into their lands. We have been at war with them for many thousands of your years. If they are helping you, we must try to convince you of your error. We will show you what your people will suffer if you continue with them."

Liora followed the gray bastards, as she liked to call them, to a wall that she could tell had one of those hidden levers in it. She watched their hand sequences as they not just opened a door but called up something that resembled an elevator. Once all ten of them were in the elevator, they went up. The journey up seemed to last for several minutes, with many sideways movements until they were at their destination. When the door opened next, they pulled her out of the elevator onto a high overlook of a valley below. To Liora, it was beautiful, green everywhere, and her lungs told her the air was rich with oxygen. A bit confused, she turned to the lead gray bastard and asked what was wrong with what she was seeing?

"When you look out, it may at first resemble your Earth, but not all is as it may seem."

They grabbed some type of furry creature in a cage and brought it with them. Looking over her shoulder from where she emerged, the landscape took her by surprise. Nothing but rock and water, no green anywhere, though she did see creatures scurrying about the rocks. They were leading her by the hand down into a stairwell into the valley below and the quickly approaching the greenery. The closer she got, the less she was sure what she was seeing. It looked to her like giant blades of grass, some were hundreds of feet wide and countless feet tall. They pointed at the base of the greenery, urging her to watch. One went right up the base of the giant blade and drew a line in the dirt. The movement seemed to cause agitation within the blade, as dirt with the line in it started churning around and soon the blade was where that line was. Then they took the small animal out of its cage and set it right next to the blade on the dirt. Then the gray bastard spooked it, causing it to run along the edge of the greenery. Liora's eyes were following the animal when she noticed the greenery alongside its path began swelling out, just over head of the creature. Then she heard a loud yelp as she watched the grass thing essentially 'eat' that creature.

They turned her around to see all the land behind her and began explaining why the Neptali were supposedly bad. Liora picked up some nuances in the tone of language. If they were human, she would have thought they were extremely angry. They went on and on about how these Neptali destroyed all the plants on their continent and forced them underground. They were also incensed about the animals they had let loose, as those things did something she couldn't translate, she just knew from their tone that it was not good for the Nurizzi. They kept talking about all the atrocities the Neptali had committed against them and never provided the information as to why they had done those things.

'*Why were they at war with them?*' The question resonated through her mind but didn't get an answer.

Seizing this point of conflict as a way to learn more about her enemy, "Tell me, why did you and the Neptali first go to war? Are you both from the same planet? If so, you each should each have a right to exist here?"

With the most ear piercing chirping she had heard yet, the leader of them spat at her, "The Neptali have no right to exist, here or anywhere."

"I get that they destroyed your land, but you travel the stars, so why are they so threatening to you?"

Back in the building with a flick of their wrist, they motioned her to a different chamber of the eating room, where they all sat and offered her some type of drink, indicating for her to sit as well. Their leader started talking in a calmer voice, "Many years ago, we lived as one people across this great planet. We both call this world Nuir. The Neptali were genetically different than us, both in physical attributes and intellect."

Liora chimed in, "Earth had a similar dichotomy eons ago. We called them Neanderthals, and they were thought to have bred in with the Homo Sapiens, which became the dominant race and they died off."

"The Neptali believed they were intellectually superior and began to modify themselves to increase their intellect and physical strength. They soon lived ten times as long as a Nurizzi. They viewed the Nurizzi as genetically inferior and forced us into camps. This continent was our last refuge, so we burrowed underground and fortified our cities."

"If you are able to travel to Earth, why didn't you relocate there before humans exploded in population?"

Continuing on as if he didn't hear her, "Not long after we relocated here, out ancient ancestors found a way to communicate with us from the great beyond. They assured us we were the chosen race, the direct lineage of them and the Neptali were outsiders who didn't belong. Our people soon became greater than the Neptali, both in longevity and intellect. We were able to infiltrate the Neptali with mind devices that allowed us to learn what they knew as they advanced. Eventually the Neptali discovered these connections and located us. Then they destroyed the land as you witnessed. We learned enough from our ancestors to develop space flight. We did not discover Earth until you began mastering the atom. Those bombs your people made allowed us to track you to your location. We approached your leader, but you proved to be as vicious as the Neptali."

That last bit raised the hair on the back of her neck. Liora thought, '*So, they view me as an aggressor.*' Seeing that line of questioning would go nowhere, she tried a different vector. "What are you exploring in space?"

"We constantly search for a home that will allow us to live in peace. Your people seem to be advancing faster than we anticipated, developing the Eukema as an example."

"I told you I know nothing of these Eukemas."

Their leader slammed his cup on floor. "If you don't willingly give us the means to operate this technology, we will take it from your mind."

One of them came running into the room and relayed a message to their leader. Not knowing she could easily understand them, they openly talked with each other. "Director, Commander Laage has returned from his trip to Earth. He is several months ahead of schedule and indicates he has an urgent message for you."

They all rose and ushered her along a different corridor to a cavernous room. When they all looked up, Liora did likewise. The roof, several stories up, opened to the sky and a spaceship descended. It dropped like a leaf on the wind, not making a sound and gently floated to the floor. Something akin to a stairwell protruded from the ship and out came several dozens of those gray aliens. All fell into some type of military formation and the obvious leader, she guessed was Commander Laage, approached the director. He relayed a message that Earth had utilized those Eukemas to send someone off world. How he didn't know. As he uttered this last sentence, his gazed fixed on Liora.

With his gaze fixed on her and she on him, time seemed to stand still. Then he marched over to her, slapped some type of restraint device on her and ordered her to be taken to a room and put under guard. Before she was taken away, he grabbed a translation device and began yelling at her. "You! You are connected to the one that built these. The one we know from the field of light of our ancestors. Why have you chosen to go to war with us?"

Not sure exactly the best path, Liora decided to the stir the pot a little. "We have shared this technology with the Neptali, and they will soon be here to rescue me."

She was no longer able to walk, as this detention device immobilized her and moved her down the hall to a small room, one that was barely big enough to fit her. It must have been a closet of some sort, as it was a tight fit for her. With nothing but her thoughts to entertain her, she focused on the device and how it could do what it was doing. Several colors flashed through her thoughts, similar to seeing stars when one is about to pass out. She wasn't sure if she was losing consciousness or hallucinating. Then equations started to rise to the surface of her thoughts. She asked herself '*Why? What do those equations mean?*' The answer seemed to float into her conscious mind, electromagnets in a harmonic resonance with the signals her muscles use to contract. The effect was to render her immobile. The nanobots began revealing themselves to her at that moment. The memory surfaced of Dr. John Everly designing and manipulating them. The second memory they showed her was Dr. Everly's use of them to enhance neural cells. Several other memories of his also were downloaded to Liora. Now she had a firm grasp of why she survived the trip to Nuir and was quick to pick up their language, she had the help of nanobots in her brain. That was the final gift Dr. Everly was able to give her in order for one of them to survive.

The nanobots were showing her Dr. Everly's memory of delta waves and then of surgeries he did on specific muscles. They helped her to see that the delta waves were the key to defeating this device. The image they showed her next was the Mandelbrot series. She needed to focus on solving that unsolvable equation, as it would generate the delta waves that would help her to escape this restraint. Her focus was complete. Her mind was in near complete calculation mode. At the side of her thoughts, she could perceive what looked to be a wave that was building in strength until it was massive and then poured out of her with a force that would have knocked her back if she were able to move. All went quiet as she blacked out. When she revived, her hand instinctively brushed the hair out of her eyes. It took a second to sink in.

She was free. Now escape was on her mind. The lever hidden within the wall was easy to find. This time, she was instructing the wall panel with different commands, or the nanobots were. The schematics for the base appeared on a hidden monitor in the wall. Her destination was clear, the portal. Another series of commands showed where the Nurizzi were on her route to the portal. It must have been an hour that she explored the information in the database she was now accessing. She used the device to scan for life signs and saw only two of them were between her and the portal. Avoiding detection, the room with the portal was easy to access. This time, she took effort to lock the door to the room and then jammed the opening mechanism by telling the door to close, even though it was already closed. She heard the grinding of metal and tried to open the door. The effect was as desired, since the door could not engage to open. Turning her attention to the portal, she sat at the control panel not sure what to do next.

The panel stared back at her, patiently waiting her commands. Not sure how she got here in the first place, she hadn't a clue as to how to return. She mulled ideas over, having discussed with Brill many times on how the portals could transport, but they needed a receiving portal. Unless...Yes, she remembered now. Her and Brill had discussed using these to travel the stars and Brill was stuck on that very point and now she recalls a potential solution he devised, though never proved out. Though, she was not sure even he thought it would work. Brill had thought each earthlike planet across the universe had X-points above their planet, just as Earth does. If you knew what to look for, you could tap into the unique exit points and enter the planet from there. What did he say was the unique feature of these?

She lay her head in frustration on the console, as that bit eluded her. She just lay there in desperation, her thoughts completely focused on that one problem, as the threads of a solution filtered into her mind. It was the planet, yes, that was it. Brill had said each planet would generate a gravitational wave unique to itself from any other. That unique wave would allow the portal to 'harmonize' with it and create a lock to allow for transfer from the starting X-point to the X-point above that planet. She thought this was all fine and well, but how was it going to help her? That solution filtered in as the others had. She was on the planet, so finding that harmonizing wave would be easy, and each continent would have a slightly different frequency.

She would have to use the X-point over the planet to slingshot herself to another point on the surface.

With a solution of exit, or at least a plan. One that may prove fatal, if she were to emerge in outer space and not on the surface somewhere else. Thinking back through her conversations the Nurizzi, they had mentioned that the Neptali were in the Southern continent, or so she guessed, as they mentioned them being on the bottom of the planet. Even if they weren't there, anywhere was better than here. The Southern continent would have an opposing magnetic resonance, if it were anything like Earth, so she started with that. First, she looked for the harmonics of the magnetic pole under her feet. Having found that, she used the console to locate the opposing magnetic field. Sure enough, she located one in the Southern region of the planet. Not sure how to program this information into the portal device, she hoped the nanobots could guide her. Before they did that, she was moving autonomously to start up the power source, that odd glowing metal from Earth, and then came programming. With the portal now active, she could see the X-point over the planet. Essentially using this as a mirror, she put the coordinates in for it just above its surface. If she hit the center dead on, it would transport her to the sun of this solar system and that was not her desire. By focusing just above the entry point, her energy would 'bounce' off its surface, like light reflecting off a mirror, and could be directed or attracted to the opposing magnetic field. This would complete the resonance loop and allow her to exit somewhere on that Southern continent.

Everything was powered up and she was about ready to step through when one more thought occurred to her. Sabotage. She should destroy this device. The power source was the first that came to mind, but she suspected they had built in a failsafe to prevent an overload. A smile came across her face. She went back to the console and set the device to activate again when her travel was complete. The next time it would aim for the center of the X-point and create a stable opening. She hoped the results would be devastating with the pure energy of the sun bursting into that room until the portal was

consumed by the sun's energy. The banging on the door got her attention and she stepped up her pace. With everything programmed in,
she ran into the portal.

Then, nothing, no sound, no air and immense cold. The lack of
air ripped at her lungs as she struggled to keep her eyes from
popping out of her head due to the vacuum. This was only for a split
second, but enough for every nerve in her body to scream in pain and
then she was on solid footing. Blood had begun to fill the void in her
lungs when the vacuum of space had pulled the air out. She gasped
for air, bent over coughing up blood, trying to stay conscious.
Collapsing in exhaustion, the nanobots began to fulfill their primary
function, restore and repair her cells. Days later, Liora lifted her head
off the ground, soaking up the sun. Thirst was now gnawing away at
her parched throat. Liora mustered enough strength to get on her
feet, for a brief moment before the world began to spin and her face
hit the dirt. The smell of rain told her there was water to be had, and
that drove her to crawl in the direction her nose guided her. The
muscles in her body screamed at her with every inch she moved.
Slow was the pace, but steady. When her ears picked up the gurgling
sound of running water, her body seemed to find the strength to
press onward. At the water's edge, Liora hurt too much to dip her
head in the water, so she managed to roll her body over the bank into
the water and drank till it hurt.

The water refreshed her inside and out. Her lungs still burned
with each breath and she could barely see. Mustering enough energy
to climb the water's edge, Liora lay there and looked up at the sun.
For the longest time, she thought she may have made it back to Earth
with the moon starting to rise in the early evening sky. Her eyes had
trouble focusing, yet when the second and third moons rose behind
the first, her heart sank, as she knew she was still far from home,
somewhere on Nuir, hopefully. She climbed out of the water barely
able to move further. With her spirits in despair, her eyelids grew
heavy and much needed sleep was a welcome exit from her troubles.

The night had a chill to it and the shivers racking her body roused
her from a deep sleep. She tried to sit right up, yet every muscle in

her body revolted and locked up in objection. When the spasms stopped, she rolled to her side, brought her knees to her breasts and managed to get them underneath herself. From there she was able to get her upper body righted and the world hadn't yet started spinning. With her feet now under her, looking around unsure of the direction, anywhere was better than here she decided. Her course of action was to follow the water. Water was a needed resource everywhere and she suspected Nuir was no different in its use of water. She hoped the inhabitants of this land were friendlier to her plight than the Nurizzi.

The journey down river was a slow walk for her aching body. Along the way, she found several bushes of berries. The berries that looked most delicious were very inviting to her empty stomach. As she reached for a handful, her hand jerked back right as she was about to touch them. Unsure why she did this, she stood there looking at them until her logic could make sense of the situation. The thought that crossed her mind was the wildlife, 'watch the birdlike creatures and see what they eat'. Those creatures flocked to another bush that had very few berries. Those were of a different color and were the target of those flying beasts. Not a single one of them went for the other bush.

Now she understood her reaction, as the nanobots must have given her a subconscious warning to the danger of those. Still cautious, she approached the bush the creatures were harvesting and began to fill her belly. The creatures were too large to get to the interior of the bush and there was an ample supply of the berries there. To Liora, these berries were sweet, juicy, and packed with a pleasant flavor. A handful of them made her full and she couldn't stomach more, so she crawled up under the bush and slept. The morning brought about another long day of journeying with no civilization in sight. She had packed her pockets with those berries and would refill them when needed, as she found bush after bush with ample berries along the river.

The area she had landed seemed to be the upper edge of a large plateau. Several weeks after her landing, she made her way to the edge of the plateau that dropped down into a valley and then eventually to a sea or ocean, if she were to believe her eyes, which were still having trouble focusing. As she scanned the valley for signs of life, her heart was sinking low and then her nose caught scent of a familiar smell. She was sure she could detect smoke from wood burning. Her eyes had yet to locate the source, but her nose told her the direction. With little else to lose, she scanned the plateau edge to find a way down. There was no easy path and it looked to be a one-way trip. The valley below was several thousand feet, and it would be a hell of drop. With few options, she looked to the river trying to see over the edge, hoping for a deep lake below. She grabbed a log that floated by and without hesitation, took the plunge. Down, down, down, seemed to go on an eternity. The drop was unlike any free fall she had ever experienced. Counting the seconds in her head, trying to guess where the bottom was. Right before she estimated where the plunge into the lake would occur, she took as deep a breath as possible and hoped it would be enough. A few more seconds went by and then splashdown. The water was ice cold, chilling her to the bone. When her head bobbed above the surface, getting air was the priority. Fog was everywhere with no direct sight to a shoreline. The falls behind her were pushing her back further out into the lake. Hoping for a cave behind the falls, she swam towards them will all her might. The progress swimming on the surface was a futile effort, so she took a different tactic and plunged beneath the surface. She could tell she was making progress when the force of the falls pushed her deeper than she hoped, indicating her progress had brought the journey directly below the waterfall. With lungs screaming for air as she crested the surface behind the falls, the putrid air that was now filling them and the echo off the wall, told the story she was hoping to hear, a deep cave. Getting out of the frigid water was the first priority, swimming along the edge and finally spotting a crevice that would allow her to crawl up onto the rock ledge. Now out of the water, she laid there till the shivering woke her out of the slumber that had overtaken her. Now to explore the cave and find anything to make a fire. Time had no meaning here, estimating it was several hours to find a dry spot and wood that may burn. Up on the plateau, flint like rocks were in abundance and she had brought several along for the ride. A fire was finally roaring, allowing for her clothes to be hung out to dry while a bit of sleep could be had. Getting up after several hours of fitful sleep and making her way into the valley in the hopes of finding the Neptali was now the sole focus of existence in this place.

THE GRAY LEADER was roused from a deep regeneration. "What is the urgency?"

"Director, the prisoner has escaped."

"Escaped? That is not possible."

"Yet it is so. See, the monitors show it going into the portal."

"Bring Commander Laage to me. This is his area."

Commander Laage was already attempting to break into the portal room. His team was diligently working through every option to get inside. The room was designed to seal off, in case of an energy surge. As such, once sealed, it was nearly impossible to open, and the prisoner had sealed it from the inside. They were certain the device would not work, so they were in little hurry to get inside. In their minds, the prisoner had effectively imprisoned itself. Even so, Commander Laage ordered his team to power up the recording devices. If in some unknown way the prisoner was able to use the device, they would at least be able to observe every aspect of it and potentially use it against the Earthlings. His team worked for hours to break through, but to no avail. Laage was undeterred and set up rotations to work every angle. As his team got a small hole into the room, one they made having been able to bore through a metal rod. An energy beam tore through that hole and burrowed through to the lower levels of their structure.

The sun's energy poured through that tiny hole, now heating up and melting most of the hall. The panic that ensued was unlike any the Nurizzi had experienced since the Neptali invasions many generations ago. Commander Laage was corralling the inhabitants to exit ships in a mass evacuation. Less than a quarter of the inhabitants of this city made it out. The whole structure seemed to melt. Laage had managed to get the director aboard the escape craft, frantically ordering his staff to upload any data they had collected before it was lost. Laage's body had begun morphing into the war phase his species would grow into when provoked. He was now bent on destroying Earth and every human in existence, especially their prisoner.

One of the smaller grays, the science staff, rushed up to the director with exciting news. "Director. We may have a way."

"A way for what?"

"To destroy Earth, but only if they have enough of the Eukemas active."

"Explain."

"The Eukemas emit zirge beams and muon particles are attracted to zirge beams."

"How will this help us attack them?"

"If they are using enough of those Eukemas, the zirge beams will propagate into space, many parsecs from the planet."

"Keep going, as I still don't see how this will help us."

"Our junction five station is a quarter parsec from Earth and it a structure highly dense with muon particles. If we coat the surface of that station with enough muon containing asteroids, we can make one the size of their planet and then set it on a collision course. The zirge beams will attract the muons from there, pulling the station to them, all we have to do is put the station in motion."

"Brilliant. I will let Commander Laage know. Start the preparation."

It took the Nurizzi a year to build the muon packed Earth-sized asteroid. It was set to always point towards Earth and keep on track to collide with it. They set it on full power and used their spaceships to push it to a fast-enough speed that it would collide with Earth and cause total annihilation. Laage was pleased with the work of his team. Every morning, he would rise to look through his telescope and watch the progress of the asteroid. Finally, the Earth would be destroyed, long overdue, he thought.

12

PANIC

The day had been one of success for Brill. He and Sirum had made significant strides in point-to-point transfer, the first successful commercial human transport.

The text was flashing on his watch as he crawled out of the pool, "Brill, come quickly." Short and to the point. That is why he and Sirum always got along, never any fluff and they always knew where each other stood. Not halfway finished with his swim, he was half inclined to do a few more laps. If he knew Sirum, a gap of ten minutes between the text and no response would have him send another. If that one didn't receive a response, then Brill could expect a phone call. He really needed this exercise, as his mind had been clouded lately with Liora running off to help Liam in some urgent matter. Normally this wouldn't have bothered him, but something at the edge of his consciousness was telling him something was off, a premonition maybe. He had those from time to time, but they were usually out of his control, so he never put too much thought into them. This time though, the bad feeling kept nagging at him and his day was just beginning. As right as rain, the next text followed ten minutes to the second. Brill lumbered grudgingly out of the water and hit a reply back, *'will call after I clean up'*.

Brill called up Sirum on his way over to the lab. "I am headed your way. Are you going to tell me now or make me wait?"

"Brill, my friend, this is one you need to see in person."

Scratching his head, Brill couldn't think of anything they were currently doing that would generate such excitement. "You always like to hold the cards till the end, don't you?"

"Really, this is something you have to see to believe."

Brill arrived at the lab about fifteen minutes later. He was halfway up to the building when Sirum came racing out. "On time as usual. Follow me."

"Guess your day is going better than mine then." Brill followed in lockstep and they didn't say a word until they were staring at the monitor that Sirum had set up next to the portals.

"Sit here my friend. Recall when we first developed the transport devices? Well of course you do. What I mean to say is do you recall the one thing we wanted to do most, but were unable to because of the quantum entanglement we were seeing?'

"No, you haven't been testing that have you?" Answering his own question, Brill continued. "I guess you wouldn't have if you were this excited. Please enlighten me, as I am at a loss."

"Well, I haven't done any galactic transports, just simulations. I had been working this on the side until all the pieces fell into place for me. I could not figure out why the quantum entanglement is occurring when transporting over such a long distance. Then it hit me."

"Hope it didn't hurt."

"No, it's a metaphor. Nothing actually hit me."

Brill was trying to repress the laughter at this point, as Sirum was deadpan serious. "A joke my friend."

"Ah yes, that humor I never get." Sirum continued on without missing a step. "The entanglement was always our trip up on living things passing through the portals. We were able to solve it with point-to-point transfers on Earth but could not go beyond its boundaries."

"So far you are only telling me what I already know."

"I'm getting there. It occurred to me that you are likely going long distances to get to that bridge and yet you are fine."

"I do have nanobots to protect me."

"Bingo. You hit right on my idea."

"I don't follow. How does that help transporting people without nanobots?"

"I first had to figure out what the nanobots are doing for you. I realized they are generating some type of protective barrier around you, most likely an energy field."

"You were never able to detect any energy around me when I go, at least that's what I recall from the last time you measured."

"Right on Brill. Then I realized they are making your cells reflect the energy hitting them. That is the answer we needed."

"How?"

"We generate an anti-energy field around the travelers. Essentially creating a large version of your nanobots to protect a bubble containing the traveler inside the portal chamber."

"As you recall, the point to point here on Earth are essentially instantaneous yet is still a lengthy time in the quantum realm. Because they are staying on the surface of the Earth, the crust of Earth likely absorbs the quantum exotic particles that may cause the entanglement. When we go through outer space, we don't have that buffer to protect us."

"Wow. How long did you spend thinking about it before you came up with a solution? I would not have connected the Earth's crust with any benefit."

"Funny thing is I did not spend any time thinking about it. The idea came to me in a dream last night and I spent all this morning flushing out the details."

"Just shows how brilliant you are. When do we start? I am eager to try space travel."

"Well...That is where I need your help. I have no idea where to point the portal for an exit. How do I find those X-points out across the galaxy?"

"One step ahead of you Sirum. Recall I told you there were odd symbols associated with each window to a place in the bridge?"

"Yes, did you figure out what they meant?"

"Maybe. I think those may be the signatures of the gravity wave emanating from the specific celestial body, as you know there are likely X-points in the center of every star."

"Do you remember one we can try?"

"I remember them all. I just don't have any idea where they are in the galaxy or if they are even in this dimension of existence."

"Okay. You're in the lead on this Brill, as I need the specifications of your nanobots in order to scale them up to the size of the platform."

THE PUBLIC WAS hesitant to embrace the new transport technology. Rumors started circulating that the device gave the government the means to tag each individual and possibly change their genetic material. Brill was constantly running experiments to show the public that these were safe devices and that it would help to eliminate their need for cars and planes.

It was a slow ramp up over a year before widespread acceptance of the device. What helped Brill was him making it free for the first six months of everyone that signed up for a two-year pass and then it was only the price of a few tanks of gas that their car would take. Giving people the ability to travel anywhere in the world for the equivalent of pennies was a big draw. After a year about half the population of the world was using these. Brill had set up a company to install these globally, so he didn't have to think about the logistics. At the end of the first year, there were half a million of these installed all across the globe with some cities having thousands of them. Car travel soon declined to very local use and airplane travel became nonexistent.

BRILL AND SIRUM had turned their attention to figuring out how to travel to the stars. Figuring out how to access the X-points to a planet halfway across the galaxy was no easy feat. The initial difficulty had to do with no receiving device there. They needed to figure out how to get their equipment to the place first, otherwise they wouldn't be able to return.

"Brill, just give me a destination point and we can push through a return portal."

"Maybe. What if the portal is damaged in its travel there? We would be stuck."

"As much as it pains me to say this, you will have to be the one to go and test it out."

"Always the sacrificial Guinea pig, eh?"

"No...That is not what I meant. My thinking is that you have the ability to get to the bridge, likely from anywhere you are. Nobody else will have that luxury. Once you are at the bridge, you could easily return to Earth."

"My friend you have to learn to take a joke. I do see your logic and agree with it. I will likely be protected no matter what the conditions are at the exit point. Hopefully I never have to test that out."

"So, that brings me to my initial question. What are the first exit points?"

"Let me go back to the bridge and see if I can find some nice-looking worlds and then we will figure it out from there."

This quest to find other worlds to visit was a nice distraction from the bombshell Liam dropped on him a few months ago. Somehow Liora was taken away by that strange metal. Brill pressed and pressed Liam for weeks to show him what had happened, but Liam wouldn't relent. Shortly after Brill's press conference on the portals, he got a surprise call from Liam.

"Dr. Everly, I think it's time we talk."

"Glad to hear from you to Liam." Sarcasm was ripe in Brill's voice.

"Not over the phone. It has to be in person."

"I can be there in 10 minutes. We just completed a portal near your base. Please have your men pick me up there."

Brill arrived within the time he suggested and was quickly whisked away by Liam's men. Brill had to wait longer to see Liam than it took him to get there.

"Dr. Everly, welcome to Area 51."

"I wish the circumstances were better, but I brought you here to see the events I had described in Liora's departure."

Liam brought Brill to a room that was sealed off with top secret tape and do not enter placards everywhere. Liam led Brill deeper into the room, which was littered with debris and showing signs of damage. There was a lab of some sorts in the interior that showed the most damage and was where Liam began to describe everything.

"Dr. Everly, this is where Liora disappeared. I brought you here, as the video I am going to share with you required some explaining that could only be done in person. Please sit over here." Liam motioned to some chairs nearby.

"Okay, let's have it."

"I need to take you back to the events of your father's death. Shortly after he died, I had him brought here and kept him on an IV, just in the hopes he was not dead."

"You son of a bitch. I know you are the one that had him killed."

Before he could get another word out, Liam cut him off. "Yes Brill, I played a role in that. I am not proud of that but was following orders. Your dad was labelled a traitor for stealing state secrets. I am sure you know what I am referencing."

"Liam, nothing your sorry ass says will ever make that situation better."

"I understand and I am not asking for forgiveness. Please listen before I show you this video."

"Just get on with it."

"When the pandemic broke out, I revived your dad. His revival confirmed that he not only stole the state secrets but used them on himself. When he was revived, he helped to point us to a possible cure, at least until we found you. Though he almost succumbed to the disease and remained crippled."

A hint of excitement in his voice, "Is my dad here? Is he still alive?"

"He was cured of the disease with your cure and was working on that strange metal you sent me. While working on that metal, something happened. It was somehow transformed and pulled Liora and your dad into it, along with the contents of this room."

"Show me the video."

The video was heart wrenching for Brill to watch. There was his dad in the flesh. It had been so long, and Brill had buried all those emotions. Tears were welling up in his eyes as he watched. His dad was describing the process of activating the metal. Brill noticed that his hand had brushed the touch screen and started a process going that his dad didn't seem to notice until it was too late. Brill watched the events unfold as Liam had described them. Then he started the video over and slowed it down to see if he could figure out what his dad had punched on the screen. The screen was showing something called Cleon. Brill knew right away what this was. If Liam's team had missed it, then Brill was not going to share it with him. They exchanged several more unpleasantries before Brill departed and they went their separate ways.

WHERE HAD Liora and his dad gone? It was an odd sight, as some type of suction was created. This was unlike his portal system that connected the points on two platforms and used the gravity wave to push the passenger along. What Brill observed in that video was far different. Brill could not make heads or tails out of it. He and Sirum discussed many possibilities, but none sufficed, so they tried to recreate the events. Brill still had some of that strange metal and he hoped it was enough.

They set it up in in a shielded room and had every sensor they could think of monitoring the process. They ramped up the Cleon wave generator and watched. Nothing happened, not even at the quantum level. Brill was frustrated that nothing happened, but half expected this as replicating an accident is sometimes difficult to repeat. They designed a series of bursts and combinations with various quantum particles and then set it on auto. They let it go and set up alerts if anything popped.

Several weeks passed and then his phone chirped. Thinking it might be a text, Brill was in no hurry to answer it. Later in the day, he had some time to look at the text and soon realized it was the alert that the strange metal had opened up. He and Sirum were racing to the room as the light changed to a purplish haze when they noticed an odd sensation. The closer they got to the room was like running in syrup. Every step became a labor, and they were barely able to get the door to the chamber open. Brill placed is hand on the door, screaming in pain as his hand quickly withdrew from the handle. The door handle was hotter than the surface of a stove and Brill's hand showed the scars. He and Sirum made their way to the control room, looking for signs of what was going on inside that room. Brill was perplexed at what the sensors were showing. The inside of that room was pegging out at thousands of degrees, the max the sensors could detect. The initial activation of the metal happened to be captured on the surveillance system before everything in the chamber melted.

Brill slowed the images down frame by frame and there was blur of an image of a room with a platform and maybe equipment nearby. It was so blurry that Brill wasn't sure if it really was a room or just an echo of some other image. If it was a room, then the metal might have connected somewhere else on Earth. Brill noticed the gravity sensor was showing an immense pull into the center of the room before it went offline as well. With this data in hand, it took Brill several minutes before he had that duh moment realizing what he was seeing. Somehow this metal had connected to the sun and all the energy of the sun was now flooding the chamber. The calculations were flowing through Brill's head and he had Sirum double check. The room was a sealed blast chamber to protect the inhabitants inside it, but not designed for holding in an expanding pressure wave pushing outward, especially from something as hot as the sun. They calculated that the room would hold for about two more hours.

Options were limited at this point. The conversations were vetting every outlandish proposition, anything that may help.

"Sirum, is there any way you could think of to close off the X-point?"

"I don't even know what the X-points really are. How the hell would I be able to say what will shut it down."

"No need to get snippy. What are your suggestions. We just need to try something, or this thing could consume the Earth."

"Do you think we can make it jump somewhere else?"

"Maybe. You must be recalling wormhole theory from science fiction shows."

"I guess. It just made sense."

"I am not knocking the idea, just adding some levity. Let's run through what we know – this was started by bombarding that strange metal with energy in the high Cleon quantum band. We have no apparatus and don't understand why the metal connected with an X-point."

"Okay Brill, you are not providing a rosy outlook."

"Just keeping it real my friend. I do see a possibility to build on your idea of making it jump somewhere else."

"Until you fill in the blanks, there won't be much I can offer."

"Think about it. We have X-point generators. This time though, we set up the device to transport this whole room and instead of targeting another X-point generator, we make the endpoint be the X-point in the center of the Earth. How we do this is where I really need your help."

"Makes sense from a theoretical perspective. It would be a long shot to do in less than an hour, but I'll try."

"Great. At a minimum, let's just get this thing out of here."

"Can you measure the energy output?"

"I can tell you how much entered the chamber before the sensor was destroyed, but not what is there now." Looking through the data, Brill found it. "Looks like seven thousand terajoules."

"What? That is the same yield as a one megaton nuclear bomb."

"Yes, lots of energy and consistent with the energy of the core of the sun."

"So why don't we send this back to the sun."

"Love it. How?"

"I was being sarcastic."

"Maybe, but it's the idea we need to pursue. Exactly what I was looking for."

"Okay...I don't see how we can funnel enough energy into the X-point generator to move it. We're barely able to transport an automobile."

"It's right in front of us."

"I guess, but that would mean we have to wait till the chamber fails and then we don't get any second tries."

"Gets the adrenaline going, doesn't it?"

"Uh, I am not thrilled with this option at all."

"That solves one problem, but the bigger one is how to direct the portal to go where we want it, somewhere off world."

"Brill, I've heard you mention that each X-point has its own gravity wave. Do you have the sun's signature? Any way to point this one to there?"

"My thoughts exactly and I have figured out the signature of the one in the sun. Once we get the generator going, we need to tune it to the sun's gravity wave in the form of an opposing gravity wave. they should attract like opposite ends of a magnet after that. When the chamber fails, it will amplify that anti-gravity wave with its power and zoom right to the sun's X-point and hopefully shut down the problem."

The portal proved more challenging to get in place and balanced than they anticipated. Brill was hooking up the power unit when he brushed aside sweat dripping down his brow. The first few times, this action was autonomic until he realized the temperature was dramatically higher than when they started. Brill inspected the chamber, noticing that several pinholes had opened up, allowing for the release of the interior heat and energy. They picked up the pace and got the last wires in place when a plug the size of a quarter burst forth from the chamber wall, nearly taking off Brill's arm.

"Damn that was close. FIRE IT UP NOW." He yelled at Sirum.

"I'm not done."

"We will all be done for if you don't fire it up. The whole damn thing in going in a matter of minutes."

"Done. It's now active."

The unit had a thirty second ramp up phase. They watched with bated breath behind a temporary blast shield, knowing there was nowhere they could go if this failed, so they stayed put and watched. The portal hit full activation just as the chamber wall collapsed in a burst of immense white light. They were fortunate to have been behind a blast shield with some UV protection. Even through that shield, the light was nearly blinding to them. They watched as the unit hit full power and then ramped up further with the power of the sun. Then the room went dark. At this point, neither of them was sure if the darkness was due to them possibly going blind or if the portal disappeared. After a few minutes, the sun blindness faded and they picked up the dim light from the hall. Cautiously craning his neck around the blast shield, Brill felt confident enough to step out and inspect the area. Just as they had calculated, the whole chamber had disappeared. Brill was surprised that the portal had also vanished. To where was anyone's guess, but he hoped it was the core of the sun.

With disaster averted, they began to piece together the events that had led up to and through the chamber being transported. That odd metal was key to opening X-points, now that they had its signature frequency. It was able to somehow connect to an X-point without the need of the portal. Brill filed that bit away for future use. The data collected had Brill feeling low, as he was very concerned that Liora may have met a similar fate as their chamber. The footage that Liam had shared with him had also shown that brief jump to another chamber before showing oblivion. This did not bode well for Liora he thought.

With little hope of Liora's survival, Brill turned his attention to improving the X-point portal and refining and ramping the global system of portals. Sirum's love of astronomy had him constantly bugging Brill to figure out how to travel the stars with the portals. Brill resisted more out of fear of destroying the Earth, as controlling the exit point eluded him. Buried deep within his portal research, Brill grew distant from Sirum, as he was always pushing Brill to change focus. This time though, Sirum came in person, since Brill had avoided the last seven calls.

"Brill, you have to see this."

"Sirum, I am tired of you being stuck on this space portal idea."

"It's not that my friend. I found something."

"Something? Space is full of somethings."

"It's a giant asteroid. One that is headed straight for Earth."

"I've heard this before, literally every time I turn on the TV."

"I was not descriptive enough. When I say giant, I mean ginormous, like the size of the Earth itself."

"So you found a rogue planet. What makes you so certain it is headed for us?"

"A few months ago, I was looking for planets near stars when this thing crossed my view. Since then, I've been tracking it and determining how fast it's moving. The odd thing is it just appeared out of nowhere."

"What do you mean it just appeared out of nowhere?"

"Well, I had my telescope on the same line of sight towards Alpha Centauri when it just showed up. I went back and looked at the previous footage and sure enough. It was not there and then it was."

"How can you be certain it just did not cross your path?"

"Because it is headed towards the vector that the telescope is pointed. The odd part is that it appeared to pick up speed. Looks like it is moving slow enough that it won't be here for five years, and then Armageddon."

Over the course of the next few weeks, Brill grew more and more convinced of Sirum's claims. Especially since he had seen it with his own eyes. Now Brill was entirely consumed with this as a side project. Sirum's measures now showed a steady approach velocity that clearly

tracked the Earth and was on a beeline for the planet, although that
endpoint was five years in the future. At Sirum's urging, Brill was now
trying to figure out a way to use the portal to get close to the object.

The odd metal was Brill's focal point, and he needed a larger
quantity of it, so he and Sirum set out on a quest to find more. They
knew it was in Sri Lanka, but that was a long shot to get it there. The
other option was in the Kashmir region where Major Thomas had
been wounded a few years ago. A portal had been recently built in
that region with the specific intent of getting them in and out easily.
Brill didn't suspect this metal would be easy to find, as the only clue
of its whereabouts would be that it is shiny. The exact coordinates as
to where Major Thomas had been wounded were unknown, but the
battle scars on the land were still present. They started there and
systemically scoured every patch of bare earth. They hoped it would
be right there glistening in the sun, but no luck. An area of the battlefield showed clear depressions where bombs had been dropped and
detonated, three of them.

They brought shovels as a backup option, hoping to not have to
use them. Brill pushed the shovel down as far as it would go and then
stomped on it with his foot. He soon realized this was a big mistake,
as his leg resonated with the pain of all that downward energy going
right back up into his leg. Apparently his first choice was on top of
solid rock. He tried a new spot, this time a bit more gingerly in
driving down the shovel. He was glad he did not go all out on that as
it also hit solid rock. He tried several more, as did Sirum. Everywhere
was solid rock. They moved on to the next bomb drop area and same
effect. They had not selected the last area first, as it was on the side of
a steep hill and difficult to stand upright. This time the shovel hit pay
dirt, literally. Though shovel after shovel did not yield their prize.
The sun had set, and the twilight was fading when Brill though he
caught sight of a reflection.

"Sirum, hand me the flashlight."

"Did you see something?" As he handed over the light.

"Maybe...yes, there it is. Help me dig around here."

After another 20 minutes of digging, now in the moonlight, they had uncovered a very shiny plate sized rock. Brill set up the scanner and could not register anything. He thought that was a strong enough indication that this was their prize. Brill picked it up with both hands and was amazed as how light it was. Once he had it all the way out, it was about the size of a basketball, yet light as a feather.

They headed back to the portal, being careful to avoid any contact with people, since this area was not known for its hospitality. They carefully rounded the corner of building that had provided them cover when they got the attention of a group of local youths. They immediately recognized Brill and Sirum as outsiders and started moving their way. Brill sensed they might be in danger and picked up the pace to the portal. They were now in full sprint, as were their pursuers. When they were about two strides from the portal, their pursuers were within an arm's length. Brill had remotely activated the portal and was about to step through when the strange metal was yanked out of his hands and tumbled to the ground right next to the portal magnetic field generator. The youth reached down to pick it up before Brill could get to it. As he touched the surface of the metal, something like bolts of lightning reached out from the surface of the metal and struck down the man, along with all his friends. Brill approached them to offer help. He turned over the one who had touched the metal and almost threw up at the sight. The man's face had been stripped clean of skin and muscle, leaving only the blood vessels and nerves. A ghoulish sight right out of a horror movie. Brill went to aid the rest of the crew and a similar sight repeated itself.

Seeing where the danger lay, Brill wouldn't touch the metal but started scanning it to see what was happening at the molecular level. All the standard energy bands showed nothing. When he switched to the quantum level, he was surprised to see the high level of muon particles in this metal and was even more surprised to see that the portal was giving off Cleon waves. This was a new measure he had recently implemented, after spotting it on the screen when his dad and Liora disappeared. Brill shutdown the portal and waited till the Cleon waves subsided, as he wasn't sure if they were somehow causing the issue. With no more Cleon waves being emitted, Brill wanted to see if the metal still reacted with something living. One of the men that tried to ambush them had been shocked to death, but still had enough flesh that Brill thought he may be a good test subject. With the cells in that man's body still active, he thought it would behave as a living being would. He took the man's hand and threw it towards the metal. First try missed, but on the third try he landed it right on the metal. No sparks and no reaction. Brill was hesitant to touch it but figured the nanobots would protect him if need be.

Brill reached down with caution to poke the metal. His fear of being ripped up kept him in cautious repose until his confidence built up enough to pick it up. With the metal in both hands, he realized a new finding had been uncovered today, although at the expense of those men who attacked them. This created a difficulty for Brill as neither he nor Sirum saw a way to get the metal through the portal.

"Brill, what if we set the metal on the portal and then power it up? Would it transport something on the platform?"

"It might work, but I'm not sure if we could avoid something catastrophic from happening."

"As long as we don't touch it while the portal is active, we should be able to transport it home."

"My concern is being on the platform with the metal when the portal is active. Will it destroy our flesh like it did those guys?"

"Can you activate the primary portal in your house and send it there? If so, we could use the portal nearby my house and drive over there."

"Worth a try."

With the metal squarely in the middle of the portal platform, Brill brought up the power. Nothing happened, so he punched in the codes to active his personal portal and sent it to his house. They waited a few minutes to see if any anomalies occurred and were pleased to see all was calm. They transported to a portal near Sirum's house and began the fun of figuring out how to use the metal.

The metal had arrived in Brill's house without incident. Brill went to the Well trying to find a way to shield the metal from Cleon waves, as that seemed its Achilles heel. Each time Brill now entered the Well, he was careful to avoid the ancient enemy at the core, though the knowledge buried there was a temptation. He knew he had to take more care in the Well, due to his physical body now residing in that place he called the bridge between Earth and the Well. His search for the Cleon waves or the like led him to something the Nurizzi called zirge beams. The more Brill leaned the less it looked like the Nurizzi invented them and the more it looked like they learned them from somewhere else. Brill followed that trail of discovery to the earliest point in the Well where it showed up, which was a trail leading into the core. It became clear to Brill that knowledge of Cleon waves, called by many other names, had originated in the core. This was a strong temptation for Brill, as he needed to understand how to modulate them and ascertain how they were attracted to muon particles.

Now more determined than ever to venture down into the core, Brill devised a way for his body to be revived, if he got lost down there. His idea was to program the nanobots to hold on to a sliver of his consciousness and reel it back in if they sensed his body fading. Seemed like a long shot to him, but he had limited options and he really needed that knowledge. He tested the waters venturing into the outer regions of the core in search of the tie in of Cleon waves to X-points. The zirge beams or Cleon waves seemed to be an answer to the Nurizzi's quest to develop more powerful weaponry. They would direct those beams into a type ore to generate a very powerful explosive. The later uses of this technology evolved into them using the approach to generate faster than light space travel. Not once was it associated with X-points. Brill was getting frustrated in the lack of connection between the two. The path was now evident, as he would have to go deeper into the core, and he was certain those ancient beings would know he was there.

The sense of going from the outer regions of the core into the uncharted territory was like going from shallow to deep water. The immense cold and unfathomed depths presented itself to Brill. Brill thought at times he was swimming in honey and progress to the core center was near impossible, so he took a lateral vector. The X-points were now his primary quest and just as he was about to land on the answer an intense pull on him yanked him away from his prize. Down, deeper into the core, against every sense of will he had to turn back. Something had him and he pulled with all his conscious ability to break free. Whatever it was had latched onto the essence of his consciousness and Brill was losing himself. Then he felt a taught line back to reality reveal itself. He knew right then his safety line had been activated. The return trip was slow, as it was fighting against something in the core. On the way out, his consciousness was pulled right through the knowledge of the X-point. His interest was so strong in learning this knowledge that he fought against his own lifeline.

Brill caught the bit of info he risked his life to get. Those beings were using highly focused muon particles, shielded in a carbon shell, to connect to a planet via the Cleon waves. Brill watched as they were unsuccessful in connecting with any planet. Except one, the planet Nuir, the Nurizzi home world. As he watched the Nurizzi learn how to access the X-point into the Well via the zirge beam/Cleon wave, his consciousness was yanked back to the bridge and none too soon. When Brill awoke, he could see his body had been in clear distress. The recorded vitals showed that he was dead or near death many times as his lifeline pulled him back. Glad now he had devised that plan and he was so glad to be back that he didn't sense what had followed him back. Just a speck of what was holding onto him in the core had stayed with him and now knew a way out. The knowledge those beings had sought since the Well had trapped them before time began had been given to them in an act of recklessness by Brill...

13

CROSSROADS

The realization that the portals were emitting Cleon waves had Brill very concerned on the consequences, especially with the learning that muon particles created some type of negative interaction. Brill went in search of anywhere else on the planet that Cleon waves existed and was disappointed that only his portals were emitting these.

"Sirum, what do make of these portals emitting Cleon waves?"

"What exactly do Cleon waves do, other than interacting with muon particles?"

"The Well seems to indicate they are needed to create the quantum tunnel. We use that tunnel to bridge one portal to the other with the aid of a magnetic monopole."

"How far do they travel?"

"Something I need your help in determining."

They worked the better part of a month to make an orbital detector to find muon particles, one that could be attached to a satellite, but with little success. Brill had invested in a new communications satellite and had Sirum design it so that they could put their detector in it. They were running out of time when one of Sirum's students inadvertently provided them with the break they needed.

Sirum had been teaching at the University the last few years. One of his graduate students was eating up all the new physics that he was teaching. The student, one Gillian Drake, or Gill as she liked to be called, had even gone as far to put some of the theories into practice.

"Brill, you have to meet Gill, my graduate student. She figured out how to detect muon particles from a distance and we may be able to use her work to develop what we need."

"Hey, I will take any help I can get, as all I get these days are all those crackpots who think they can create a Utopia with the portals."

"She thinks if you generate small amounts of Cleon waves, any muon particles will attract to them, even from a distance."

"Great, when can you bring her over?"

"Well, she is outside in my car. We needed the solution so bad I was hoping you would want to meet her right away."

"What. Why did you leave her out there? Bring her in now."

Sirum hurried out to get Gill, eager to utilize her brain power. "Brill, I would like you to meet Gillian Drake."

With hand outstretched, "Dr. Everly, a pleasure to meet you."

"Please call me Brill. I understand you have made some progress with our challenges with muon particles?"

"Thanks Brill. Please call me Gill."

"Perfect. What do you have for us?"

"Your idea of muon particles was so advanced, it had me intrigued when Dr. Lars first presented them. I had to see how real they were, so I developed a detector, but in order to that I needed to figure out how to generate and detect the Cleon waves."

"Interesting and very impressive. We knew we could generate the Cleon waves, but have had a hard time detecting them unless right in front of the source. How sensitive is your detector?"

"Well, very sensitive. I put the Cleon wave generator on its lowest setting and was able to detect that specific Cleon wave over 1000 miles away."

"How do you know it was that specific Cleon wave and not coming from the portals?"

"Oh those. My Cleon wave generator showed me that they come

in the equivalent of different frequencies and yours are ultra-high intensity, and they generate so much energy, that I just tune them out."

"Really? I did know you could do that. I am eager to see it in action."

"Gill, don't forget to tell Brill about your clever discovery."

"Thanks Dr. Lars. I was saving the best for last. Dr. Everly, hold this." She mentioned this as she handed Brill a device that resembled a large, barreled rifle.

"You got me on this one Gill. What is it?"

"What you have there Dr. Everly is a way to direct the Cleon waves towards muon particles. It focuses the Cleon waves into a discrete tight beam."

"Wonderful, Gill, what do I do with it?"

"I made it in the hopes it could connect with a muon emitting substance across great distances. Maybe like from here to the moon."

"Genius. I see where you are going with it, but how would you get the beam to go to the portal where you want it?"

"You anticipated my problems Dr. Everly. I was having that trouble with my first prototypes and found I could modulate the Cleon wave into a unique signature. This allows for a connection to be made across great distances without interference, since the Cleon waves travel across the quantum space."

"Brill, she was able to turn this device into a detector. She put a Lithium acetate film in front of the Cleon generator to essentially take a picture when it pulls the muon particles back to it."

"Very clever Gill. Sirum, I assume you're telling me this now because you included it in the satellite?"

"I figured that was a given, but even more important is that we might be able to see all the muon particles on Earth, most likely deposits of that metal."

"How would that be possible? I don't see how the muon particles can travel unless they are bombarded with energy."

"Brill, it's the Cleon waves. Their very presence attracts muon particles so strongly that the muon particles are pulled from their source. This then hits the lithium acetate film, allowing us to essentially map the location."

"Hmm, must be some quantum level event, as I still don't see how that could happen."

"Dr. Everly, will you be able to shut down all the portals at one time? I am concerned their Cleon wave generation will pull any muon particles away from our detector."

"I think I can set a global shut down under the guise of a maintenance update. How much time will you need?"

"If you do it for ten minutes every hour for the next week, we should be able to map the entire Earth."

"That would cause too much of a travel disruption. How about I just shut it down entirely for a week?"

"If you shut it down entirely, I should be able to map it in three days."

"That would be better Gill, as people have become so dependent on them for transportation, they don't know another way. Plus they really could use an overhaul of their motors. I will put out a press release of a 3 day shut down in a month's time."

A Month Later

"Let's see what it shows from orbit. I was waiting till you had the chance to meet Gill until I activated it."

"Dr. Lars, if you set it on auto-modulate, it will run through the billions of individual Cleon frequencies."

"Good idea Gill, as I don't suspect any one frequency will capture every muon particle. What is its speed of frequency generation?"

"It should be able to run all the frequencies simultaneously, as I made modulator similar to how a prism splits a beam of light, one input and billions of outputs."

"Sirum, start with the house, as we have that metal there and we know it emits muon particles."

"Excellent thought Brill, setting those coordinates now."

The feedback from the satellite started coming through. The metal was down in the basement lab. The satellite was scanning right over that location, but nothing appeared. Gill was crestfallen, but undeterred.

"Dr. Lars, try bumping up the resonance lens to get it closer to the wave generator."

"Sure thing."

After a few minutes the image went from blank to a blurry light. Sirum made a few more adjustments to the lens. After a few more modifications, the outline of the metal appeared with distinct edges, along with density and size calculations. After three days of mapping the Earth, multiple hits on deposits of muon containing substances were obtained.

"Look at this Sirum." Brill said pointing at a location off the Eastern coast of the USA.

"What am I looking at?"

Pointing to the huge deposit, "That's Bermuda. Look at how the entire seabed around the island is a muon deposit. It looks like it has a geometric pattern."

"Brill, I've seen that pattern before."

"Yes, but where?"

"Recall that backscatter image you had done on the X-point orbiting the Earth? It was that exact image."

"Yes, yes you are right. Scan that X-point in orbit. I am curious on its muon distribution."

They rotated the satellite to image the orbiting X-point. The live image pulsed a bright light for a microsecond, indicating a muon particle distribution, then it disappeared. When the X-point next opened again, about 24 minutes later, the light of the muons appeared again and then instantly disappeared. Then scene played out over and over. Watching until they were convinced of what they were seeing, Brill finally spoke up.

"Maybe the muon particles are interacting with the Cleon waves and they cancel each other out."

"Makes sense and also makes sense why we have not detected the Cleon waves from the orbiting X-point."

"I wonder why our portals generate such powerful Cleon waves."

"Maybe it's because they don't have the muon particles around them."

"You may be right Sirum. That argument makes more sense, as that image I was pointing out is what I believe to be an X-point. One that leads somewhere other than the sun."

"I thought you said the only other X-point that existed on Earth was at the core of the Earth."

"I did say that, but I also said it was the only other one likely connected to the sun, which is why the core of the Earth is so hot."

"You need to wrap it up Sirum, as the portals go live again in 15 hours. In that time, let's try some experiments in the Bermuda Triangle."

"What did you have in mind?"

"Can you design and make some sensors surrounded by a modulating Cleon wave generator?"

"We have the sensors already, putting them together with the wave generator should be no problem."

"They need to be more than sensors, as I want to track where that X-point dumps out."

"That may be challenging, as I am not sure how to track something across that network."

"Neither do I. Gill seems very creative, let's see what ideas she has."

Gill had separately been working on her doctoral thesis, involving quantum particle tracing. When she got the call from Brill, she dropped everything to help out.

～

"Dr. Everly, I am eager for you to see my research and it may do what you want."

"Thanks Gill. We are on the clock, as the portals go live in a half day. I feel their activity may hinder us."

"Did you really want to go through the Bermuda Triangle?"

"I see you just read the coordinates of our intended target."

"Always thought that was folklore and not something real."

"It may very well be folklore, but I am hoping it's an X-point of a different kind."

"My work is all theoretical at this point."

"We are after any idea at this point. You live in this day in and day out, so your ideas will be fresher then Sirum and mine. Let's hear what you have."

"You know how neutrino's decay over time? Well, that was the start of my work. The decay pattern is unique to the neutrino generation. I think you can make a high energy neutrino, unlike anything in nature. Its high energy will mean it will travel faster than anything in the quantum space."

"I sorta follow you but need more details to fill in with my knowledge. Please continue."

"As you taught us, the quantum space is not linear, nor anything that conforms to our three-dimensional space. With every point accessible from anywhere at any time, we should be able to instantly see the unique neutrino and its energy pattern through the regular X-points. Those X-points each have unique neutrino emissions, at least the few I have been able to map. With that said, we should be able to use those X-points to 'map out' where it went. Just look for the one with the double neutrino emissions."

"Great. Let's do it."

The sensor/wave generator was built over the next few hours and dropped in the airspace in the center of the Bermuda Triangle. The first few passes through the Cleon wave cycle had a slight bump in X-point energy. Given the high level of muon particles in the seabed, they decided to ramp up the Cleon wave generation to the highest energy the device could handle. It looked like a failure until they got into the super high energy bands.

"Gill, did you see it? It looked like the teracycle energy bands were causing a bump in the energy emissions in the ground."

"I definitely saw it. Let me try something. Here, let's see what this does."

"Gill, did the sensor blow up? I don't see any transmission."

"I don't think it's destroyed. Looks like it just disappeared around 0.17 teracycles in Cleon wave generation."

"We were moving through those energy bands at a fast pace, let' try it from the other direction and see what happens."

"Here it goes." She started pushing the highest energy possible and stepping down from there. "Yes, Dr. Everly it disappeared right at 0.17 again. The video confirms it."

"Now it makes sense. The triangle disappearances were only recent reports, mostly with powered devices like boats and airplanes. If the motors on those somehow generated Cleon waves at this frequency, it would explain how they just disappeared."

"Dr. Everly, we have one sensor left. The one with the neutrino generator. Should we send it."

"Oh crap. We have 10 minutes. Can you get it in place before the portals go online?"

"It will be close, but we should be able to hit it."

With seconds to spare, the sensor/generator was activated and disappeared as expected. They turned their attention to the satellite, since they had equipped it with a quantum mapping sensor. That sensor was a longshot to pick up the neutrinos, but they were hopeful. It took some reprogramming of its core logistics and having to send up a few more lenses to attach to it.

The first pass at quantum mapping was targeted to looking for X-points and really being able to see them at the quantum level. Brill had coordinates for what he believed were X-points across the universe, so they started there. Tuning the sensor to pick up a few odd spinning leptons, bosons, and anyons. After that adjustment, the data streamed in of the types of energy bursts they see from the Earth orbiting X-point and the constant ultra-high-energy flow from the sun type of X-point. Though they started noticing a wide variety of high energy patterns. Brill suspected those to be stars that ranged from quasars to the types of suns orbiting Earth-like planets.

Aside from that interesting flood of data, they started mapping out the neutrino emissions from those X-points. Gill's idea of using a high-energy neutrino made the searching much easier, as there were very few of those. It took about an hour before they homed in on the exact neutrino signal. Though they could see it from the quantum mapping, translating where that was in normal space was still a guessing game. The sensor with the neutrino emitter was also programmed to map the stars in the sky and then to try to travel back to Earth.

All this new information, along with the coordinates from the bridge to the Well, gave Brill the idea of how to set up interstellar portals. Though that would have to wait, as the immediacy of what to do about the impending doom from an oncoming Earth-sized asteroid was the thought at the forefront of his mind.

"Brill you have to see this."

"What am I looking at?"

"I turned the satellite sensor to look at the oncoming asteroid and noticed an odd pattern."

"What do you mean an odd pattern?"

"It looks as though it's full of muon particles and that is likely what is pulling it to Earth, and not at a constant speed."

"How is that possible?"

"Once I saw the weird muon emissions, I had the sensor simultaneously map out the Cleon wave emission from your portals. They seem to match."

"Match? How so?"

"I've collected several months of data now and it is very clear that when more than 100 portals open at the exact same moment, there is a million-fold increase in muon particle emissions from the asteroid. That has the effect of increasing the asteroid speed by 0.1 meters per second."

"Doesn't sound like much of an increase."

"You are not following me. My guess is that it is the portals that are pulling the asteroid to Earth."

"Are you saying I will be to blame for this impending destruction?"

"Unfortunately, yes, as it's the portals emission of Cleon waves that is the problem, but that ultimately leads back to you."

"What if we shut down the portals?"

"Won't matter. The asteroid is already at a terminal velocity, meaning when it gets here it will plow right into the Earth."

"So there is nothing we can do."

"Well, that is not even the worst of the news."

"More! What could be worse?"

"It looks like the globalization of the portals that you completed a few months ago, has had the effect of speeding up the time with which it will hit Earth."

"Shit! How much faster?"

"Looks like those portals increased its speed so much that it shaved off almost 2 years. We now have 3 years and 7 months."

"Damn that's bad. Can we use Gill's device to shield the portals from emitting Cleon waves?"

"That was to focus them, but we might be able to adapt it to shield the emissions."

"Until you figure out how to entirely shield them, just shunt the waves into the X-point at the Earth's core. That way it won't keep attracting the asteroid and will buy us some time, maybe keep it from speeding up anymore."

"Gill and I will get right on it."

"Oh I hate what comes next. I have to get Liam's help in warning the world of the impending danger and let him know I may have a way to help out society by creating portals to other planets."

"Good luck with that."

14

END OF THE LINE

The end of the line for the Earth was fast approaching, though almost 4 years would seem to be an eternity to the general population. Brill had to swallow his pride and get his enemy's help, one Colonel Liam Rhett. Brill's blood boiled at the thought of ever talking to that bastard, and now he needed to plead for help from him.

Brill had Liam's number pulled up on his phone, but he couldn't get his finger to hit the call button. He sat there looking at his phone, reliving all the negative interactions with Liam, especially the loss of Liora. Finally he gave in and squelched his pride, hitting the call button.

After several rings, Liam's admin picked up. "Colonel Rhett's office. How may I assist you Dr. Everly?"

"Please leave a message for Liam that Brill called and has information of grave importance."

"If you could elaborate more, I am sure that may impact his response time."

"No, that is all I can say until I talk with Liam. Thanks."

"It may be some time before he can get back to you, as he is currently out of pocket."

"Understand, please let him know it is urgent."

About 3 weeks later Brill's phone showed Liam's number calling. "Dr. Everly, this is Liam returning your call."

"What took you so long? I left an urgent message."

"Dr. Everly, Brill, this was the best I could do, as I have many matters of national security I deal with daily. What is the grave importance that you could not leave it as a message?"

Tension was boiling through with Brill. "You arrogant ass. I said it was urgent and you should have taken me at my word."

"What could possibly be so urgent?"

The urgency is that there is a planet sized asteroid headed to Earth, more like on a direct beeline for Earth."

"How long before it hits? My team has not noticed any extraterrestrial threats."

"It will be here in 3 years 7 months."

"That is a very long time away. What makes you so sure it will hit Earth?"

"We have been tracking it for the last few months and it seems to be speeding up. Its path is following Earth's motion in lockstep without deviation."

"Say you are right, what do you expect me to do?"

"I am hoping you have the resources to build spaceships and take a small fraction of humanity to the stars."

A slight laugh escaped Liam. "You amuse me Dr. Everly. Do you really expect me to believe this? I suspect you are still mad about Liora and concocted this to make a mockery of me."

"Come now Liam, I know of your Mars habitat project and the multiple spaceships you have been building these last few years."

"I really don't know what you are talking about Dr. Everly. This conversation is done."

"Wait. Please at least inform the public of the coming threat."

"You really expect too much. As I said Dr. Everly, this conversation is done."

With that, Liam hung up and Brill was left staring in dismay. Brill sat there staring at the asteroid tracking data for the longest time.

Then he had an idea. He would hold a press conference and let people know of the danger.

IT TOOK MORE effort than Brill realized to get a large contingent of the press to show up. He had to promise big news to get all the major outlets to cover his announcement. Today Brill was very nervous. He had been in front of large crowds many times, but this was different and made his stomach queasy. He took the podium and began his prepared remarks to a stone-faced audience.

"Welcome. You likely know me as the guy who built the portal system." A frog crept up in his throat, clearing it before continuing. "Sorry about that. In my efforts to expand the portal system, I've been looking to the stars. A few months ago, my team found an asteroid larger than the Earth headed right for us. Our calculations show that this asteroid is on a direct collision course with the Earth in just under 4 years."

The reporters sat in silence for several minutes before the first one raised her hand. "Dr. Everly, why are you calling a press conference and not alerting the government?"

"Thanks for asking. I have already informed the government, NASA, and every agency I can think of, but none of them believes me."

She continued, "Maybe there is a reason for that."

"I am telling you so you will let the world know. If the governments have pressure on them, then they will put together a survival plan for humanity. This is real people. It is an extinction level event. The Earth will likely be destroyed. Any more questions?"

Half a dozen reporters then raised their hands and Brill pointed to the first who asked, "Aren't you the guy who invented that psychic chair?"

"What? No, that chair was to understand how minds interact. The point here is that the Earth will be destroyed in almost 4 years."

The next question really riled him up. "You were on the most wanted list for multiple murders, how did you get out of that?"

"You people just don't get it. This isn't a press conference about me. I am trying to get the world to prepare for what is to come.

This next reporter hit at the heart of what most people would feel if they were watching. "So, you are saying the world will be destroyed. What exactly can people do? Are we to just prepare to die, since you have no escape option for us?"

The back and forth continued for some time. At the end of it, the reporters were mocking him and making light of the dire warning. Brill stood there dumbfounded that they didn't take him seriously, even after showing them the video of the asteroid. The headlines the next day were all about the crackpot genius who claims the world end in 4 years and that he suggests people prepare to die.

BRILL BEGAN WORKING in earnest on way to get people to a new world. He could see from the bridge to the Well that there were worlds out there, he just needed a way to get there. They began experimenting using the directed Cleon waves to try and open up a portal in the X-point over those planets. Sirum had found a nice clearing near Brill's old lab, the one that Liam had destroyed. With Sirum being the Astrophysicist, Brill had gladly turned over this part of the effort to him. They had set up the magnetic monopole device but replaced its monopole generator with that of the Cleon wave generator. The hope was to use the focused Cleon waves to connect across the stars. With the Cleon waves, Brill had expected a monopole to be on a directed wave to the coordinates across the galaxy, though he had no idea if there would be enough muon particles there to open a portal to that X-point.

"Brill, tune the generator to the upper frequencies. We'll see if those generate a hit."

"I'm just not seeing it. Maybe we are looking at it wrong."

"Not sure I follow."

"Well, we are trying to shoot this thing through normal space, yet we know the muon effects are in quantum space."

"I still don't see it, as the Cleon waves will plow through quantum space just like they are through normal space."

"Not really. Think about how difficult it was to get the magnetic fields to line up from one entry portal monopole to the exiting portal monopole. Remember how they kept getting interference from the Earth's magnetic field?"

"Okay, I get that part. There is definitely a quantum level effect with those, since we had to overcome the quantum entanglement. The Cleon waves though, I don't see it. I trust your intellect, so what's your plan?"

"We need to somehow get all the Cleon waves to be focused on the quantum level, allowing us to avoid the interference of normal space. Are you up for a long shot?"

"You have me curious now, what do you have in mind?"

"First, we need to find a really small piece of that muon metal. Let's pull up the map of where those deposits are."

"I still don't see where you are going with this, but some of that metal exists right here in Nevada...just pulled the coordinates. When do you want to go?"

THE SATELLITE SCAN showed a deposit of the muon containing metal about a hundred miles from Brill's old lab, in the literal middle of nowhere. Sirum had the idea of using the same detector on the satellite to help zero in on the deposit. They took Nevada state highway 50 till it intersected with state highway 270. They jumped on Home Stake Road and drove on it till it about ran out, close to the coordinates. There was a dirt road the detector indicated they needed to travel, but it was blocked with a locked rusty gate. Pulling up to the gate and inspecting the access, a decision on whether to break it open and go on or find a new location was running through Brill's head. The need to get the metal here and now was more pressing than getting caught, plus the use of the portals had caused car travel to almost come to a halt. Brill proceeded to the rear of the SUV to find the bolt cutter he had packed in there so long ago, from the days when it was needed at his lab. Holding the bolt cutter, Brill paused to reminisce on the days when he used this to get into his old lab, before he renovated it. Shaking off that memory, he cut the lock, which easily broke with the heavy rust. It looked like ages since it was last opened, so they were less concerned about getting caught and proceeded at a leisurely pace.

The road went on for 80 miles, though its condition made it less of a road and more of a hazard, as there were some car-sized potholes they carefully avoided. The detector indicated they were getting close. They parked the car and set out on foot. The detector was a mocked-up metal detector where Sirum had replaced the guts of it with the Cleon wave generator and the readout to show when they picked up muon particles. It worked a lot like a compass where the needle on the detector would ping in the direction they needed to go. Distance was an unknown variable; it could be a foot away or another 50 miles. The sun had long set, so they set up camp for the night, as Sirum had tripped several times over rocks and the snakes were starting to move in the cooler evening air, seeking a warmer spot.

The fire they wanted to build required digging down in the sand to make a small fire pit, as the wind was still strong, making it difficult to hold a flame. Brill didn't realize the detector was close to where he was throwing the dirt from the fire pit, being pitch black with only his headlamp to light where his head was turned. The third shovel of soil Brill tossed partially on the detector. What followed was a loud screeching sound, much like a wounded animal. Both he and Sirum hit the ground and turned off their lights. They waited for about 30 minutes with no further sounds before they resumed their activity. The next shovel full landed right on the detector and the sound happened again. Brill froze. As he turned his head from side to side, a strange light similar to salt in a fire, was bouncing on the ground in rhythm with the weird noise. With caution Brill approached the spot and focused his headlamp there. Right away he saw the detector laying on the ground with bouncing light particles and sound coming from it. Staring for some time at this sight, it dawned on him what he was seeing.

Brill just realized that the dirt he had inadvertently thrown on the detector must have contained minute particles containing muons. Because the detector was emitting high levels of focused Cleon waves, those muon particles were causing the same reaction they saw in Kashmir. Brill grabbed the detector and started actively looking for small muon containing rocks or metals. It wasn't until he put the detector down in the hole he was digging when it pinged for a hit. Brill fished around in the hole pulling out several pea sized particles. He threw a few at the detector and only one caused the sound and sparks. He picked it off the detector and threw it again with the same result. This gave him confidence that it would continue to be detected by the device Sirum had built. Brill continued this exercise for some time until he had filled a backpack full of the muon metal. He hoped this would cover them for the foreseeable future, if they ever needed to make use of more of that muon metal.

"I think we have found our prize. Ready to head back?"

"Why don't we just make camp for the night and go back when there is daylight? My ankle hurts from the last hole I stepped in."

"We can make camp, just be ready to fend off snakes at night. Our sleeping bags are nice warm places they will see and try to enter."

"Damn, I thought you had a tent in that backpack. Well hell, let's trudge on back, just go slow."

"No, I wanted to save room to collect the muon metal. I think your hurt ankle will make us go slow, so no problem."

The trip back to the car was slow going with Sirum nearly breaking his arm on several falls. Brill was eager to get to the next phase of his plan, one he had yet to share with Sirum. To keep from falling asleep while driving, Brill opened up about what he had in mind with the muon metal.

"I need to chat or we will wind up in the middle of the desert and not know how we got there."

"Tell me, does it eat at you that Liora just disappeared? I mean they never found her body nor any body parts, so she couldn't have exploded like Colonel Rhett said."

"I don't buy one word of what that bastard says. Now that we see what the effects of the Cleon waves are with the muon metal, she may have been transported somewhere or sometime else."

"What? I understand the somewhere else, but how could she travel in time?"

"Just a theory I have batting around in my head. Recall how I proposed that memories are just temporal coordinates?"

"Vaguely."

"That idea just won't go away. For the life of me, I don't see where else she could have gone."

"If that is true, then she would have to have gone back in the past, since the future is yet to be a memory."

"I know. I have yet to figure out if that is even a possibility with the muon metal and Cleon waves, just an idea."

"If she did go somewhere else on Earth, then why hasn't she contacted us?"

"That is the troubling part that has me thinking she traveled in time, somehow. Enough of that discussion for now. I have a different idea on how to track the muon metal in quantum space."

"I won't even venture a guess."

"Yeah, this idea is out there even further than the time travel one."

"Not sure how that is possible."

"Well, I was thinking about holding one of the smallest muon metal particles we found and then having you hit me with the Cleon wave generator."

"Your shitting me."

"Nope. I would want you to use the lowest power setting you can manage and then I will transition my body to the Well bridge."

"What could that possibly accomplish?"

"My thinking is that the Cleon waves generate a tight bond to the muons and that will follow me into the quantum world."

"Okay, so you can locate where that bridge is in quantum space. What good with that do?"

"You forgot to connect the dots. Remember in that place that I can see images of X-points or more like the exit out of the X-point. My brain seems to translate those into some type of place. If I can physically push the muon metal into one of those X-points, then we should be able to track it to its endpoint."

"Ah, yes those mysterious images you keep talking about. Suppose you are right, how the hell will we make a portal there?"

"One step at a time my friend." With that comment, they arrived back at Brill's house where they promptly crashed on their beds.

BRILL WAS nervous on what would happen when he was bombarded with Cleon waves while holding the muon metal. Sirum's thumb started to press the activate button on the wave generator when Gill burst in, "Wait."

Sirum's heart skipped a beat with that yell as he rotated around to face Gill. "I hope you have a good explanation for interrupting us."

"I figured it out."

With a perplexed look, the word 'What' simultaneously left both Sirum and Brill's mouths.

"I figured out how you won't blow your hand off when Dr. Lars activates the Cleon generator."

A questioning look crossed Brill's face. "Sirum, you didn't tell me I would lose my hand."

Sirum stammered..." I didn't think you would."

Gill jumped back in, "I made these gloves for you Dr. Everly. They are made from Gillininte, which is what I call what I made from the muon metal."

They both looked at her as Brill questioned. "How? Nothing will melt that metal."

"Ah, that was before you had me around. Since it seems to react with the Cleon waves, I was mixing them with other types of radiation, when I found a combination that would melt the metal. So, I named it after myself."

"Would either of you care to explain how this will prevent my hand from blowing off? It should still contain the muons."

Sirum turned to Gill. "Gill, care to explain? I am not sure what you have either."

"Sure Dr. Lars. When I had it melted, I combined it with elemental carbon. Once I did that, it allowed me to mold it to whatever form I wanted. Interestingly, before I did that, I was trying out the Cleon waves to see if it would spark and I saw they caused the combined carbon and muon metal to dry down to form Gillinite. What you have there are gloves that are essentially indestructible."

Brill put on the gloves and mustered his courage. "Well, I guess it's better than bare skin." Brill then picked up the smallest piece of the metal he could find and said. "Hit me with Cleon waves Sirum and I will transition to the bridge. Please start with your lowest power setting across all bands and then max it out after 5 minutes."

ONCE CLEON WAVES were hitting the piece of metal in his hand, the sensation throughout Brill's body was an electrical stimulus to every nerve he had. Brill screamed in pain but transitioned to the bridge anyway. He couldn't imagine how painful it would have been had he not had the gloves that Gill made. Instead of entering the Well, Brill paused at his destination, the bridge to the Well.

The particle of muon metal that Brill was hold started to burrow into his glove. The heightened fear Brill was feeling had him heavily focused on that particle and how to get that particle to drop off his glove. Then the strangest thing happened, the particle began to spilt into thousands of smaller particles. This then happened over and over until there were so many he could no longer count them. Brill was focused on pushing them away from the glove when they burst forth right over Brill's head and hovered over the X-point images, every single image. As they did this, Brill had the idea of tagging them so that each individual super small particle would be trackable across the quantum space. The only thing at hand he could think of to tag them with was the Gillinite. He took off the gloves and held them in the palm of his hand with the same focus and intent he had on the original particle. These likewise burst in countless small particles that matched themselves up with the muon particles. He could see that each muon particle now had a unique signature, one he knew he could track. Brill noticed that only one paired particle entered an X-point image until every single one of them were gone.

His focus was now on finding a suitable planet to test out to see if they could find it and send a portal there. Thousands of images passed by until he settled in on one that could have been a duplicate image of Earth with the exception that continents were wrapped around the planet at its center and a few other wraps higher up in latitude. The spatial coordinates were an easy memory for him but finding the signature of that paired muon particle took him a while.

THE DETECTOR HAD BEEN SIGNIFICANTLY MODIFIED by Sirum to try to track the tagged muons in the quantum realm. He kept having to modify the detector to reduce the background noise, as the Gillinite was in the lowest band of the detection range. He adjusted the detector to auto scanning, as the cosmos was infinite. Fortunately Brill had some type of coordinates that he was not yet able to crack.

Gill had a keen eye and noticed that part of the signature resembled quasar signatures. Her idea was to locate the closest quasar to Earth, which was still 600 million light years away, and see what it looked like in quantum space. The process was similar to how a telescope homes in on a star and magnifies it. They knew the general stellar coordinates, so they opened an X-point generator to focus on that direction. It had no endpoint, so the detector could fire its Cleon waves into that quantum space and see if it returns a hit. Brill was surprised to see a hit on the first try. They mapped other quasars and that had the same effect. Soon, they had a quantum spatial map using the quasars as reference points to known space. Brill was highly impressed with Gill's ingenuity and asked her to keep helping locate the paired muon metal. With the quasar roadmap, they set up hundreds of the portals as detectors and began a massive effort to find the exact paired muon metal in the coordinates Brill had memorized.

Six Weeks Later

"Brill, we have a hit."

"Finally. Let's see it."

"Here you go. Look at the beautiful galaxies."

"That is cool. Where the hell is that?"

"That was recently discovered and is 1 billion light years from Earth. It's in one of the six galaxies trapped by a supermassive black hole."

"Likely why it took us so long to find it. I've been thinking about how to get a portal there."

"So have Gill and I, but let's hear your idea first, as they are usually better."

"You're too modest my friend. I was thinking we could try to lock onto the paired muon particle with the X-point magnetic monopole and hopefully create enough of a portal to push stuff through."

"I like your idea and ours was similar. Gill, why don't you say, as it was your great idea."

"Thanks Dr. Lars. We were thinking that the paired muon metal must have exited an X-point over that planet, if the assumption holds that all Earth-like planets have an orbiting X-point. We ran the experiment on our own X-point to see how much velocity an exiting paired muon particle would have and measured that over time. From that we can estimate where in space the X-point may be and then target the one-way magnetic monopole to hit that orbiting X-point. Once we have a lock, we have an outlet point and can push one of our functioning portals there."

"Love it. Your idea is way better than mine. How do we then get that portal to the surface of the planet in one piece?"

"Remember the Mars rovers and how they put it in a honeycomb of balloons so that it would roll on the surface and the balloons would absorb the force of impact. We do the same thing with our portal and send it to the surface, but we will aim for the ocean and float it to land."

"Sweet. When do we get started?"

"Already ahead of you Brill. Once we got the hit, we started scanning for the X-point and should have it located within the day. We already have the encased portal ready to go."

Five Days Later

It took another 5 days to nail down the orbiting X-point. As soon as they had a hit, they sent a test satellite through to make sure it wasn't the core of the planet.

"Brill, come on over we have the hit and just sent the satellite through."

Brill was at Sirum's lab within an hour and eager to see their new destination. His hopes were high that this could be the new Earth. If it was, he knew he would need to name it and had one particular name in mind. He had created imaginary places when he was a kid and the name Gallia was one that stuck with him, as it was his escape fantasy world, a place he always felt safe.

The satellite returned beautiful pictures of the stellar clusters around this planet. This planet had a bird's eye view of a massive nebula filled with impressive colors. As it scanned around, the planet came into view. The black hole was still hundreds of millions of light years away from this nebula, so they had time to plan for that eventuality, if he could get people evacuated there.

"Oh my, are those real time satellite images? That is beautiful. Can either of you get a measure of the size of the planet?"

"Yes. The readings are coming back now. Looks like it is about one and half times the size of Earth. Wow. Look at those continents. They go all the way around the planet, and it looks like there are 5 or 6 of those circular continents and no obvious large, isolated ones."

"That is the image I saw in the Well bridge. Let's send the portal through and on down to the surface. Try to aim for the continent around the equator."

"Okay. I'll let you have the honors, as its your discovery."

"No, you should do this Gill. It was your brilliant ideas that got us here."

The encased portal made its way through the X-point and they lost contact with it. If it were successful in landing on the surface and righting itself, it would call the waiting portal built specifically for traveling so far through quantum space.

Hours ticked by with their eyes fixed on the detector screen. Any contact would show success. Brill was confident it would work, as he had modified the nanobots to do self-assembly of the portal. Although slower than a human would be at assembling the structure, it shouldn't have taken so long, given the relativistic effects of a distance more than a billion light years away.

"Finally. I see it." Sirum yelled with delight.

"Is it able to accept the portal connection?"

"Only one way to find out." With that Sirum punched the power on the outgoing portal from Earth to Gallia and hoped for the best.

"Looks like it initialized and found the other portal. You wanna be the guinea pig Brill and step through to see if it's safe?"

"Uh no. My nanobots may revive me to a point, but if it's the middle of space, then I have no hope. Send the robot please."

"Gotcha. Gill thought you may say that, so she went to get it ready while we were waiting. I'll let her know it's ready to send."

Gill opened the door a few minutes later motoring in what looked like a miniature tank. "Ready to go doctors."

The robot was a very large version of a remote-controlled car that had its own AI to drive its decisions when it made it to the destination if it couldn't connect back with them. Sirum loved driving the thing as he considered it his toy. He worked it up onto the portal platform with ease and activated the connection path. The magnetic monopole required several million times more power than a local portal transportation. The portal finally transferred the robot to the planet.

This much power going into the portal was a new experience for them. Brill held back Sirum from shutting it down, as he was curious if the magnetic monopoles would destabilize over such a distance.

"Brill, I'm starting to get feedback in the power generator. It's like power is being feed into it the capacitor."

"Maybe it is. I was curious what the monopole would do to the quantum tunnel. It must be pulling electrons back to the source. Let it keep going."

"What? Those aren't quantum particles. Also, I just shut off the power, it's now giving us power. Not sure how that is possible, but I'll route it to the power grid."

"Sirum my friend, looks like you just created an infinite power source, at least until the power runs out of this region of quantum space."

"If I didn't see it, I wouldn't believe it. I don't have a clue as to why? I would love to hear your thoughts, as I'm sure you've already got a rationale."

"You're the physics guy, but I do have a guess based on my learning from the Well. From what I gather, electrons poison the quantum level, as you mentioned those aren't quantum particles, but they can enter the quantum realm. They apparently build up after a while and need an outlet. Could be they go out through black holes, the Well wasn't clear on that. Our quantum tunnel gave them an outlet and the capacitor was like a magnet to them."

Sirum let out a shout of joy, cutting Brill off. "Damn that's beautiful. Sorry, the robot is giving us images of the planet."

"Let me see." Brill said crowding him out of the viewer.

"Hold on...I'll put it on the flat screen."

"Sweet. Looks like the portal made it to landfall, as intended."

"It may be there now. Probably had to crawl to land by the looks of it." Sirum said pointing as he panned out the robot camera.

"That is even better as the honeycomb may not have withstood the impact. Let's have a look around. Is there air there?"

The robot ran through a series of measures on air and water quality and several other measures mostly of interests to scientists. They had also sent several satellites through the spatial X-point to remain in orbit and provide them with communication and mapping technologies. The robot launched several weather balloons to get a feel for important aerial phenomenon and temperature gradients as they rose.

~

A Few Weeks Later

The images were wildly vivid. The water had a turquoise tint with a salinity not unlike the oceans on Earth. Animals and vegetation were in abundance. Rain was collected and analyzed to be fresh water. The oxygen was several percent higher than Earth with nitrogen, argon, and the other gases very similar to Earth's atmosphere. The satellite data showed there to be many smaller islands off the coasts of the continents that ringed the globe. There were five continents that wrapped themselves entirely around the globe with salty water in between each. The oceans in between each continent were completely isolated from other oceans. Polar ice caps also existed at both poles, though in less abundance than Earth. The satellite showed this planet was closer to its sun that Earth is and its sun had a tad less radiation output.

They were eager to see if there was any intelligent life. The AI built into the robot continuously analyzed every inch of that planet using the satellite data, looking for any signs of civilization. Nothing turned up above or below ground on that front, even using thermal imaging to look deep underground. If there ever had been sentient life there, it had long since departed, as there were no visible remnants on the surface. This finding perplexed Brill, as he was certain that the Well showed him that all planets with X-points had contained life before they were thrown out across the unknown due to the invasion of that ancient enemy. He had always assumed that the life he saw was sentient. It just occurred to him that it just may have been plant and animal life.

A smile crossed Brill's face as he pondered these things, and a new thought just crossed his mind. 'What if he were to give each nation on Earth their own planet?' Brilliant by his own standards, though the next hurdle put him back in a down mood. There was just not enough time to evacuate a whole population, especially when nobody believes that the Earth was going to be destroyed.

The smile soon faded into a frown as the weight of the situation hit him hard. He was responsible for this, for the death of humanity, all because of his arrogance. Everything he had brushed aside was now bearing down on him. It was his curiosity/fault the Nurizzi discovered humanity could access the Well. It was his arrogance that populated the world with portals without fully understanding their impacts. Had he taken time to understand their Cleon wave emission, he could have figured a way to shield them. Now it was too late. The planet-sized asteroid heading full steam towards Earth was unstoppable and fully his fault.

The guilt was now more than he could bear. Tears started streaming down his face and he fell to the ground sobbing. Sirum and Gill thought something was wrong and rushed to his side. All Brill could do was raise his hands and plead to God, "Help me. It's my fault. Please help."

TO HELP ASSUAGE HIS GUILT, Brill went into the Well to try to find some answers. Before heading back home, Brill looked through many of the images that constantly flowed around the bridge. Landing on a planet that resembled Earth, Brill determined its gravity wave frequency and headed back. Brill thought this would be a good second target to get a portal into the X-point orbiting the planet.

His return home this time was different, there was a strong pull on his effort to get back to his reality. The pull increased in strength and then Brill was somewhere different. Every sense of his being was compressed. His physical body was in this place where it felt like he was being squashed, as every inch of his skin was being pushed inward. It took Brill a few minutes to get his eyelids to open and actually see what was happening. This place looked like the inside of a kaleidoscope as nothing would come into focus and the things around him looked wavy like that. Brill strained to physically turn himself around. Once his eyes were now looking in what was behind him, his heart literally skipped a beat in what he saw next. Their eyes were extremely large with multiple facets. Then he realized this was not one eye but countless numbers of individual eyes that were also being squished together so that all their faces pressed together to form one giant pair of eyes.

The sense Brill got from this thing was its familiarity. The shape of it was anyone's guess, as this place distorted everything. The familiarity then sunk in and he realized these were some of the creatures trapped in the core of the Well. It hit him that he had let them out or showed them the way and the universe must have long ago anticipated this happening, creating a trap to spring on them when it did. Now that the trap was sprung, Brill had no idea how to get out, so he willed himself to try and move. The languid pace was labored, but eventually he was able to put some distance between himself and those creatures. Brill's eyes caught sight of a long strand of light, though it looked solid and it extended well beyond the edge of this place. The end of that light was some distance away, if distance could be measured in here. His will was stronger to move than to give up, so he labored on and eventually reached the strand of light.

At the edge of the light, he was hesitant to put his hand in, as it looked like a stream of lava and fear overtook him. It was a beautiful sight the way it moved or flowed; he wasn't sure which. Mesmerized by the undulation of the light, Brill didn't realize he had already waded in until it was too late. Once his head had submerged in the light river, he saw that it was a lifeline his nanobots had created to get him back to the bridge. With the outward rush that was pulling him along, he turned back to see what had captured him and was astounded to see a black hole in all its splendor. Seeing it with his own eyes, something no human had ever witnessed, left him in awe and he could not take his gaze off of it. Once clear of the event horizon, his trip back picked up speed and was soon a blur. He was almost back to the bridge when the quantum world turned upside down.

This time the journey felt as if he were falling through quicksand, just a sinking pressing feeling. Normally the trip to the bridge and then into the Well is a smooth transition. He struggled to access the quantum tunnel, moving through many dead ends until he landed upon the right choice. The bridge was a rush of color and static shock, nearly freezing him in place. Brill thought something may have gone awry with his nanobots when they pulled him out of the black hole. Nothing was materializing when he tried to visualize the X-point tunnels, as that side of the bridge was no longer accessible. He felt as if the whole place was imploding.

Finding the Well from there presented an even greater challenge. Its access in the past was inherent, the same as breathing, done without thought. Now he pushed into where he knew it to be but failed to find access. Every entry point had vanished except one, a small fracture into that realm where he gained entry and then experienced the most intense pain he had ever encountered.

The pain came across as being in the throes of a hurricane looking like he was inside a shattered mirror. Heading towards the core, nothing would come into focus. The deeper he headed into the core, the more certain he was that this place was coming apart. Knowledge of any kind, past or present, was not reachable. All he could discern was chaos, both in sound and sight. Brill went to and fro, but nothing presented itself, no connection to any mind. Then something slammed into him and he felt as if every molecule of his being was ripped apart. A booming voice screamed at him, "YOU CAUSED THIS BY FREEING THE ENEMY. THIS PLACE IS NO MORE. YOU WILL NEVER BE ALLOWED HERE AGAIN!" He could sense the being coming for him when he was pulled out of the Well, through the bridge, into the quantum space with a force more painful and intense than that of the black hole. In that instant, Brill realized he had doomed more than humanity and would never be able to return to the Well.

THE END

PREVIEW OF BOOK 3

'*Gallia, what a beautiful name.*' This thought rattled through Brill's head as he landed on this name for his newly discovered planet. The name had long stuck with him, back from the days when day dreams were vivid adventures to far away lands and Gallia was his sacred place. Now it was a reality and the saving grace for humanity. So lost in his thoughts that he didn't notice Sirum sitting beside him.

"Brill, did you hear what I said?"

"...What?"

"Time dilation. That is what we are dealing with."

"I must of missed part of the conversation. Please repeat it."

"The reason the portal is giving us energy back. It is time dilation."

"You are going to have to fill in a few more of the details for me."

"Well, just a theory at this point, but I suspect we will see a massive time lag once the portal shuts down. I am guessing the power feedback we are seeing is the bleed through of 'time energy' and we are the lagging time, so the energy flows back to us."

"Okay you have really lost me now. What the hell is 'time energy'?"

"You have heard of entropy right?"

"Of course. It is the progression from order to disorder and the decay of the universe."

"In the formal sense yes, but it is also the loss of energy from decaying photons. So, if we are behind in time from the exit point in the portal, the energy from those decay photons has to go somewhere and the universal law of physics must hold. That is, energy flows from a stronger source to a weaker source."

"Still sounds sketchy, but I will give it to you for now."

"Not sure you heard me Brill. Once the portal shuts off, the massive time delay could be hundreds or even thousands of years."

"We could use that to our advantage, if it's a real thing."

"How so?"

"We could send workers ahead, shut off the portal, and then turn it back on when years have passed. That would allow for the building of all the perks of modern civilization. You know, roads, sewers, water plants, and the like."

"Interesting idea. Do you really think those early arrivers are going to give up the products of their work if hundreds of years have passed?"

"We will have to first see if it's real and then figure out how to make it only be a short interval, such as a few years."

A laugh escaped Sirum, "You have high hopes, but I don't think we will ever have that level of control."

"I have the utmost confidence in your abilities, especially now that Gill is working with you."

Coming your way soon